They would have found the body sooner, if it hadn't been two-for-one Mai Tai Night

Six months ago, if anyone would have told Em Johnson she'd end up divorced, broke, and running the dilapidated Tiki Goddess Bar on the magical North Shore of Kauai, she would have told them to shove a swizzle stick up their *okole*.

As if all that isn't bad enough, when an obnoxious neighbor with a grudge is found dead in the Goddess luau pit, suspicion falls on Em and the rest of the Goddess staff. With the help of a quirky dance troupe of over-the-hill Hula Maidens, Em and the cast of characters must band together to find the killer and solve the mystery before the next *pupu* party.

"I want to be a Hula Maiden, too! Reading this fresh, funny mystery made me yearn to hang out at the Tiki Goddess, sip one of Uncle Louie's drinks and watch a certain super sexy-fire-dancing detective entertain the crowd. This is a story for anyone who's ever been to Hawaii, dreamed of going to Hawaii, or wondered what it would be like to live in our 50th State. I loved this book!"
—*Susan Elizabeth Phillips*

"MAI TAI ONE ON is that rarest of novels—one that is both emotionally satisfying and laugh-out-loud funny. As a part-time Hawaiian resident, I absolutely fell in love with Jill Marie Landis's spot-on glimpse into a Hawaii that most tourists never see. Smart and sassy, fun and endearing, MAI TAI ONE ON will sweep you away. Once you meet the quirky, real-as-your-best-friend Hula Maidens, you'll wish the book would never end."
—*Kristin Hannah*

"Jasmine-scented jungle, jewel seas, white beaches; an irresistible glimpse at real life on the North Shore of Kauai. MAI TAI ONE ON is a fun and fabulous book."
—*Stella Cameron*

D0009561

To all of my hula sisters, past, present and future:
You are a constant source of inspiration,
laughs and aloha.
Mahalo!

1

Drinks on the House

They would have found the body sooner if it hadn't been two-for-one Mai Tai Night.

Before all hell broke loose at the Tiki Goddess Bar, Emily Johnson was hustling back and forth trying to wait tables and bartend, wondering if her uncle, Louie Marshall, had slipped out for a little hanky-panky. She couldn't care less that the seventy-two year old was romantically involved, but why did he have to disappear when the bar was the busiest?

Drenched in the perpetual twilight that exists in bars and confessionals, she sloshed an endless stream of sticky, pre-made mai tai mixer into hurricane glasses. Then, just the way Louie taught her, she added double jiggers of white rum and topped off the concoctions with a generous float of dark Myers's.

Six months ago, if anyone would have told her she'd be living on the North Shore of Kauai divorced, broke, and managing a shabby—albeit legendary—tiki bar, she would have told them to start spinning on a swizzle stick.

Em checked her watch. It was 7:45. Not only was her uncle MIA, but her bartender, Sophie Chin, was an hour and a half late. With no time to worry, Em convinced herself that sooner or later, Sophie would show. The twenty-two year old desperately needed the job. In the three months that Sophie had been working at the Goddess, she'd never been late, so Em didn't mind cutting her a little slack.

When Em's cell phone vibrated, she pulled it out of the back pocket of her cargo shorts and flipped it open expecting to hear Sophie's voice.

It wasn't Sophie. It was her ex.

"Em, we need to talk." His voice was muffled by the noise in the crowded bar.

"We've done all the talking we're going to do, Phillip." Em tucked the phone between her shoulder and ear hoping it wouldn't slip and fall into the ice bin beneath the bar.

She thought she heard him say, "I want the Porsche." Em laughed.

If he hadn't screwed half the women in Orange County they would still be married and he would still have his precious Porsche. Now they were divorced and she had sold the only asset she'd been awarded in the split.

She glanced over at the small stage in the back corner of the room, where the musicians were about to start the evening's entertainment.

"I'm busy, Phillip. Don't call again." She snapped her phone shut, shoved it back into her pocket, and wished it was that easy to forget how he'd humiliated her.

A tourist walked up to the bar asking how long it would take to get his order. There was no time to dwell on Phillip. She had to focus on making drinks until Uncle Louie or Sophie appeared.

On stage, Danny Cook, singer and guitar player, began to warm up the crowd with his rendition of *Tiny Bubbles*. He reassured the audience he was not in any way related to the infamous voyager, Captain Cook, who discovered the islands and started the first real estate boom. Behind him, his cousin, Brendon, tried to keep time on a drum set that had seen better days.

Back in the ladies room, the Hula Maidens were fluffing and primping, adding final touches to their "adornments" before they took the stage. An enthusiastic group of mostly seniors, the Maidens relied on dramatic costuming to distract from their not-so-great dancing.

Em topped off the tray of tall, shapely hurricane glasses with pineapple slices, cherries and lime wedges carefully skewered onto miniature plastic swords. For a final touch she added brightly colored paper umbrellas—warning flags that the drinks were packing a memorable headache.

She was about to heft the tray to her shoulder and step out from behind the bar when a ruddy cheeked, overweight female tourist with a sunburn and a bad perm burst through the front door screaming for help.

Em rushed around the bar. "What's wrong?"

The woman kept screaming. Patrons set down their drinks and stared.

Em grabbed a glass of water off a nearby table and tossed the contents in the woman's face.

The screaming abruptly stopped. The tourist gasped. "There's . . . there's . . . there's a man roasting . . . in the barbeque pit . . . outside!"

"That's Kimo, our luau chef," Em said. "In fact, we have plenty of tickets left so if you'd like to—"

"No!" The woman yelled. "He's not cooking. He's . . . burning up! You have to do something! It's horrible. It's . . . " The woman's eyes rolled up and she collapsed.

All over the packed room, chair legs scraped against the scarred wooden floor. Dozens of rubber-soled thongs slapped skin as locals and tourists grabbed cameras and ran for the door.

There *was* a strange odor in the air. Em glanced around the nearly empty room. Danny Cook was still singing. Only Buzzy, the aging hippie who lived down the road, continued to gnaw on some barbequed ribs. Nothing had fazed Buzzy since he had some bad mushrooms back in the 70's.

Em propped the unconscious tourist against the carved tiki base of a bar stool and followed the crowd around the corner of the building to the back parking lot. Two and three deep, folks ringed the *imu*. Em hoped to God, Kimo, the cook, hadn't tripped and fallen into the luau pit where he roasted pig.

Em gagged and covered her mouth as she got closer. The air smelled like a mix of singed hair and burning rubber.

"Call 911!" Someone hollered.

"Did already!" At least five people yelled back.

Though the last thing she wanted was to see Kimo roasting, Em forced her way through the throng to get to the edge of the pit. Her pulse was hammering even before she saw a man's body lying face down atop the coals. Fully clothed in a pair of baggy navy blue shorts and a stained white T shirt, he was short and stocky with thick calves that showed above the tops of his black rubber work boots.

The melting boots gave him away.

"*Ohmygosh*, that's Harold," Em whispered. Afraid she'd pass out, she took a deep breath and immediately wished she hadn't. She gagged again and tried to concentrate on the crowd.

Kimo suddenly materialized at her side.

"Poor buggah," he mumbled. "Uh oh. Here comes Uncle Louie."

Em spotted her six-foot-three-inch uncle's thatch of white hair above the crowd. She shoved her way back out of the circle and ran to his side.

Louie was still spry, attractive, and the picture of health. He had been an impressionable eight-year-old when Victor Bergeron's Trader Vic's Restaurants were all the rage in his home town of San Francisco. At twenty, dreaming of exotic jungle haunts, tiki drums, and cocktails named after WWII bombers and airmen, he set off to explore Polynesia. Against his family's advice, he married an island native, settled down and established the Tiki Goddess Bar on the North Shore of the northernmost inhabited Hawaiian island. Then Louie Marshall sat back and waited for the world to come to him.

Every day he donned one of over fifty loud Aloha shirts, a kukui nut necklace, baggy white linen shorts and flip flops. Most days he worked from sunup to well into the next morning. He was tan as a coconut and physically in great shape. He still surfed. Only his mind was failing, or so Em had been told.

"What's going on?" He tried to see over the crowd. When Louie looked down at Em, his expression went blank for a second, as if he had no idea who she was or what she was doing there.

Em glanced over his shoulder, half expecting to see Marilyn Lockhart trailing behind Louie. The Hula Maidens were convinced the woman they nicknamed "the defector" was after him. Marilyn wasn't a young gold digger. She was sixty-five if she was a day. She had danced with the Maidens until she became fed up with their antics—she wasn't the first—and went on to join another troupe.

"Someone fell into the luau pit, Uncle Louie," Em could barely get the words out.

Louie's face may have paled. He was too tan for Em to be sure.

"Who?" he asked.

"Harold Otanami."

"Is he all right?"

"He's dead." Em figured there was no way Harold wasn't dead by now. "At least I hope so," she mumbled.

Roasting alive was too horrific to imagine.

"Dead! After all these years." Louie shook his head. "I can't imagine that old bastard gone."

The sound of sirens echoed along the coastline. The Kauai

Police Department's substation and the Hanalei fire station were side by side, a good twenty minutes away.

Em's gaze drifted to the luau hut, a lean-to shelter built not far from the pit. Beneath the thatched roof, the remains of tonight's traditional smoked kalua pig lay spread out on a huge wooden table that served as a carving board. Seeing the roasted pig carcass complete with its head so soon after viewing poor smoldering Harold nearly did her in.

She noticed some folks were actually taking photos of Harold's remains. Others, pale and shaken, huddled together in small groups. Neighbors were starting to gather, swelling the crowd.

"We've got to get these people back inside," she whispered.

"Are the Hula Maidens ready?" Louie glanced over at the dark-green, wooden building that housed the Tiki Goddess Bar and restaurant.

Em noticed most of the aging dancers had left their makeshift dressing area in the bathroom to join the crowd around the pit. The huge sprays of variegated leaves pinned atop their heads stuck out like spear tips. They looked like a squadron of tropical Statues of Liberty.

"When *aren't* they ready to dance?"

Without warning, Louie cupped his hands around his mouth and shouted, "Drinks on the house!"

2

Sophie Shows Up Late

The minute Sophie Chin saw six cop cars in the Goddess parking lot she was tempted to drive straight back to the 'Jungalow,' a small studio she rented from one of the Hula Maidens. Instead, she forced herself to take a deep breath and keep going.

Not everything is about you, Sophie. Get over it.

It was one thing to talk about starting over. It was another to convince other people that you'd changed. Every time she saw a cop car, she flinched. Every time she saw a cop, she was certain he was looking for her. On Oahu, she was one of the first people to get questioned whenever anything happened in her neighborhood. Typical when you had an arrest record and lived on an island.

At least that's the way things had been in Honolulu. She was hoping her prior arrest wouldn't come to light on Kauai. At least not for a while.

Instinct told her to run for it, but she couldn't have negotiated a U turn anyway. The highway was jammed with rental cars, rusted-out local beaters and pick-up trucks. The bumper to bumper crawl down the winding two-lane road had added to her already late arrival and mounting frustration.

Trying to stay calm, she reminded herself how just a month ago three cop cars had been dispatched to the Goddess when a Karaoke crowd went sour. A visiting flight attendant and a bank teller had a lover's spat and both men ended up with black eyes. Everyone quickly joined in. Tables and beer bottles flew. Not unusual with the late night crowd.

But tonight in the parking lot, a uniformed cop was busy rolling out yellow plastic crime scene tape, cordoning off the luau pit. There was a definite stench in the air as Sophie edged her beater Honda into the only available space in the side lot and grabbed her purse.

She glanced in the rear-view mirror. Her dark island eyes stared back. Long ago she'd given up wishing she didn't look so much like the Chinese half of her family. She'd grown accustomed to the cocoa colored skin she'd inherited from a *hapa*—half-Hawaiian—great, great somebody in the family tree. In the islands, looking "local" helped more than hindered.

She raked her fingers through her black hair. She wore it two inches long and right now, the tips were tinted day glow orange. A line of metal rings pierced her right eyebrow.

Too late to think about a makeover.

She slid out of the car and headed for the front door.

Inside, the bar was a madhouse. Locals were lined up shoulder to shoulder. Every seat at every table held a tourist. Tabletops were littered with empty paper luau trays and dirty glasses.

Through the dim light, she saw Danny Cook valiantly strumming away on stage as the Hula Maidens struggled to execute a dance number. All over the island, ancient Hawaiians had to be spinning in their graves.

Sophie nudged her way through the throng. Once behind the bar, she tossed her purse in a safe spot and edged toward Em Johnson, who was busy filling red plastic Solo cups with ice.

"Did the pork go bad? It smells gross out there."

Years ago, her Chinese grandfather had owned a plate lunch restaurant in Honolulu. An outbreak of botulism shut him down for weeks. Grandpa loved to joke and say, "Hard to get fresh monkey." But everyone inside the Goddess looked perfectly healthy.

"Harold Otanami fell into the *imu*."

Sophie gasped. "What? No way."

"A tourist ran in screaming that someone was roasting in the pit. Sure enough, it was Harold. He must have fallen in."

"Is he badly injured?"

Em shook her head. "He's dead. It was horrible."

"You saw him?"

"Everyone saw. People were taking photos. Uncle Louie yelled 'Drinks on the house' just to get them all back inside while the police investigate."

Em looked as if she'd been dragged through the parking lot by her hair. She was thirty-four-ish. The blue eyed *haole* beach girl that Sophie always wanted to be until she was thirteen and found out in junior high that you were supposed to hate *haoles* or at least act like it if you were going to avoid trouble.

Em's blond ponytail was slipping. Her white tank top was covered with a rainbow of fruit juice spatters and *kalua* pork grease. From the little Sophie knew of Em's past, the woman's life on Kauai was completely opposite from the one she left behind in Orange County.

"Sorry I'm late," Sophie said. She couldn't afford to lose this job. There wasn't another person on Kauai willing to hire her without references. If Em Johnson hadn't been so desperate the day Sophie appeared, she would have never landed the job.

"No worries. Take these out to the lanai." Em handed over a tray full of longneck beer bottles with lime wedges partially stuffed into them. "This is for the table on the right side of the door. Then start bussing. We're already out of glasses."

Sophie expertly navigated the crowd and made it out to the lanai. She delivered the beers and noticed the coroner's wagon had arrived. An EMT ambulance was standing by, though it was obviously too late to help Harold Otanami. A second bank of giant spotlights was being assembled. Half the parking lot was already as bright as day.

Cars were parked along the side of the road, wedged into every available space as locals and tourists alike stood around gawking. In a place where nothing changed from day to day except the weather, any diversion was always welcome. There was nothing like a good death or disaster.

Sophie caught sight of a fine, looking police officer walking toward the building. He was tall and like her, a local of mixed heritage. Mostly Hawaiian. She quickly turned away without making eye contact and began bussing the tables, piling paper plates, crumpled napkins and dirty glasses on the serving tray. The cop walked past her without pause and headed straight for the bar.

She knew the kinds of questions he'd be asking.

She also knew he'd be hard pressed to find anyone who had anything good to say about the victim, Harold Otanami.

3

Em Gets Interviewed

Em looked up, hoping Sophie was back and coming around the corner of the bar, but it was Uncle Louie.

"Flora fell off the stage." He shook his head and poured himself a liberal shot of Malibu rum over ice and added a lime wedge.

Flora Carillo, a sixty-year-old Hula Maiden, was the group's token, almost 100% Hawaiian who owned a tourist trinket shop in the Hanalei Center. Among other items, Flora sold poorly made knock-off rayon muumuus from China, overpriced plastic tikis, junk jewelry and fold-up rain ponchos. The other Maidens constantly griped that Flora danced to the beat of a different drum. After watching her dance, Em was pretty sure the woman heard no beat at all. Her lack of rhythm continually caused confusion among the ranks and was one of the reasons Marlene Lockhart had defected. Flora had become a Hula Maiden by default when none of the serious hula *halau* would take her.

Tonight wasn't the first time Flora had taken a dive over the edge of the stage, either. She fell off a lot of things. It was no secret among the Maidens that the Gatorade bottle she always carried was filled with gin, not water.

Em tried to reassure Louie. "Flora usually bounces right back. Look, she's already climbing back onto the stage."

Flora's floral rayon covered rear end, not exactly her best side, was facing the audience. Luckily, the crowd was still too shaken about Harold's death to pay much attention to the show.

"What if she sues?" Louie's latest obsession was law suits.

"And risk not performing here anymore?"

"Nobody's watching the show tonight anyway," he noted.

Em noticed the noise decibel was higher than usual as people hollered to one another over the amplified guitar and drums.

"They're too busy swilling free liquor. That was generous of you, Uncle Louie, but it's time we cut them off."

"Get enough drinks in them and maybe they'll forget about seeing poor old Harold like that." His brow crumpled as he gazed around the room. "I'd hate to have anyone sue me for post dramatic stress."

"Post traumatic," she corrected.

"That too."

"If we keep this up, somebody might suffer death by mai tai," Em said. "Then where would we be?" Worried about the night's loss just when they were starting to make financial headway, Em closed her eyes and shook her head. "After this dance number, you've got to get up there and announce that we've served all the free drinks we're going to."

Louie's shoulders drooped as he walked toward the stage where the Maidens were in the middle of executing a series of mismatched hip rotations. Lined up like oversized dashboard bobble dolls, the women's ample hips bumped and ground in so many different directions they made Em dizzy.

After ripping open another package of plastic cups, she glanced up and recognized a man watching her intently from across the bar. Roland Sharpe was the kind of guy women couldn't help but notice. The Maidens all sang his praises, and he was well known all over the North Shore. He was over six feet, dark and exotically handsome. Like Sophie Chin and so many islanders of mixed ancestry, Hawaii's history was written in his DNA.

She'd seen Roland running on the beach a few times, mostly in the late afternoons. He sprinted by the house looking like a well-honed bronzed god. A police detective by day, he moonlighted as a fire knife dancer. The image of Roland Sharpe half naked, twirling long, flaming knives on a dark beach was hard to shake.

It was a definite boost to her ego to discover him checking her out—until she noticed he had a small notebook in one hand and badge in the other.

"Miss Johnson? I'm Detective Roland Sharpe of the KPD. Is there any way you can spare me a moment alone?"

"It's *Ms.* Johnson, just for the record." Em spotted Sophie across the room and waved her over before she caught a glimpse of her own bedraggled ponytail and dirty tank top in the mirror behind the bar. The detective was after information, she reminded herself, not a date.

Sophie hurried to the bar. Em and the bartender exchanged a silent glance and Sophie took over. Em led the detective toward Uncle Louie's office, a small room in back. As they passed the stage, the Hula Maidens stopped dancing long enough to turn their heads and ogle Roland—one of the only times they moved in unison.

"Hey, Roland," Kiki Godwin the self-appointed head of the Hula Maidens shouted. "I need you on Saturday night. Call me."

Kiki, in her early sixties, was a long-time North Shore resident and colorful fixture in the community. Married to Kimo, the bar's chef and jack-of-all trades, Kiki was a notorious flirt. She was also a wedding coordinator and party planner. She was a good twenty years older than the detective, and Em hoped all Kiki needed Roland Sharpe for was his Samoan fire knife expertise.

Em ushered him into the back office and closed the door. Muted guitar music, the offbeat thump of the drum and the din of high-pitched conversation reverberated through the wall. Once she had taken over as manager, Em had put the Goddess on a tight budget. They couldn't afford to hire a professional hula troop, let alone an entertainer as renowned as Roland. Not only did the Maidens perform for free, but they brought in friends and visitors to fill the place, even in the off season.

"It's not very quiet in here, but it's the best I can do," she said. "I really can't be away from the bar long." At least Sophie was back. Whenever Louie worked the bar alone, they somehow lost money.

Em watched Roland study the photos lining Louie's office walls; black and white and color images of her uncle standing beside smiling heads of state, former presidents, countless celebrities, local patrons, neighbors and friends. The building that housed the Tiki Goddess was a hundred years old. It was weathered and sorely in need of a face lift, but the bar was always listed in tourist guides as the number one stop on Kauai for food, fun and old-time local-style entertainment.

Finally the detective turned around. "If you'd rather, I could interview your uncle first."

"I'd rather you didn't interview him at all, but I suppose that's inevitable."

"Why not?"

"Let's just say my uncle's memory isn't what it used to be." Louie's mental deterioration was the reason she'd moved to Kauai.

The plea for help from the Hula Maidens had come when she was most vulnerable and in need of a change.

Em asked, "Any idea how Harold ended up in the *imu*?"

"Nothing conclusive. Do you know of anyone around who had a grudge against Mr. Otanami?"

"Who didn't?"

Detective Sharpe's left eyebrow shot up. The rest of his face remained completely placid. "Go on."

She shrugged. "Harold rubbed a lot of people the wrong way."

"Somebody mentioned that he had an argument with your uncle over the parking lot easement."

Em nodded. "That's been going on for years. That and the smoke problem." It suddenly dawned on her that she had no idea where Louie had been earlier. He hadn't showed up with Marlene.

"You mentioned your uncle's mental capacity."

"Wait a minute." Em shook her head. "My uncle is forgetful, but he's not crazy enough to kill Harold."

Roland sat on the corner of the desk. "It's my job to ask questions, Ms. Johnson."

She took a deep breath, reminded herself to calm down. Back in California, her therapist had tried to bring her around to accepting that not all handsome men were jerks like her ex. The concept hadn't quite jelled.

He glanced down at his notes. "Tell me about the smoke thing."

"We called Harold the smoke monster. When rubbish piled up in his yard he was too lazy to recycle, so he'd burn it. He was continually burning rubbish, even when it wasn't a burn day. Tires, plastic bottles, whatever. The trades pushed the smoke directly at the bar and the stench was horrible. The air would fill with sickening noxious fumes, and we'd get greasy black residue all over the lanai railings and tabletops. We were forced to shut all the windows to keep the smoke out. People would drive by and think we were closed. One or the other of us was always asking him—politely—to knock it off. Ask anybody. It was disgusting. We're pretty sure he did it on purpose."

She thought her explanation would satisfy him. He made a couple of notes and then asked, "Were you over there earlier?"

"Not today. I've been here in the bar since noon. On the day of a luau I do food prep, take reservations, return calls and sell tickets over the phone. I had no time to go over and hassle Harold."

"How long have you been on Kauai?"

"Six months. Almost six months."

"What prompted your move?"

"How is this relative to the case?"

He shrugged and did the eyebrow lift again. "You never know."

"Kiki Godwin and the Hula Maidens got together and sent me a letter and a one-way ticket. They're concerned that my uncle is showing signs of early dementia and since I'm his only living relative, they asked me to come help out for a while."

"So you just up and moved to Kauai?" He was staring at his little notebook. "No ties on the mainland?"

"Not anymore." Her parents were gone. She had no siblings. Phillip was out of her life. She was a thirty-four year old divorced orphan. Broke, too. She figured that was way more than Sharpe needed to know.

Roland stood in stoic silence, staring.

Em sighed. "The letter from the Maidens arrived right on the heels of my divorce being finalized." As far as she was concerned, the letter couldn't have come at a better time. She had no idea what she was going to do after a much-publicized messy divorce and finding out her husband had burned through all of their resources.

She'd flown over to Kauai expecting to check in on her uncle, stay a couple of weeks, then head back to Orange County to pick up the pieces and find work, but she'd been lured by the magic of the island as well as the challenge of helping Louie turn his declining business around. It wasn't long before she found herself agreeing to manage the Goddess and stay on indefinitely.

The breathtaking beauty of Kauai had as much to do with the decision as Uncle Louie's mental health—which for the most part wasn't as bad as the Maidens led her to believe.

"I'll be talking to Kimo, as well as the dancers. Your waitress's name is—?"

"Sophie Chin. She's actually a bartender."

"She local?"

"Yes. She's local. From Oahu. Sophie was late, so she couldn't have seen anything."

He looked up. "Has she ever had a run in with Harold?"

Em wished she hadn't brought it up. "As I said before, who hasn't? None of us would kill Harold and be dumb enough to toss him into our own luau pit, would we? Besides, a murder like that could ruin business." She thought she was making a joke, but apparently, Roland Sharpe wasn't fond of smiling.

Detective Sharpe opened the office door. Just beyond, customers were lined up cheek to jowl at the bar. The dining room and the front lanai were packed, or as the locals would say, the place was *choke*. Outside on the highway, a conga line of cars snaked slowly by. There wasn't a parking space left in the lot.

Roland nodded. "Yeah. Real bad for business. Thanks for your time, *Ms.* Johnson."

4

Kiki Talks Too Much

Kiki Godwin didn't care about how Harold Otanami had ended up in the luau pit any more than she cared how the over-capacity crowd came to be at the Goddess. She was thrilled any time the place was packed. It was an opportunity to work the crowd handing out business cards.

Kiki was an event planner on the North Shore. For years, she was the one and only event planner on island, but lately wedding coordinators and party planners were popping up as fast as weeds on a golf course. Thanks to women like Marlene Lockhart, a wealthy upstart who was trying to get her hooks into Louie, Kiki found herself working harder and harder to book events.

Thankfully, her own business had picked up since Louie's niece took over managing the Goddess. Kiki made it a point to be here almost every night not only to hula but to work the crowd.

At first, the idea of Em Johnson, a young *haole* woman from the mainland, running the beloved yet derelict local hang-out was simply too much for some of the bar's old cronies to bear. But once word got out that the Maidens had orchestrated Em's sudden appearance by sending her a convincing letter claiming Louie appeared to be suffering a touch of dementia—Kiki had taken quite a bit of license inventing that one detail—the locals had started showing up again. With elbows splayed and butts riding carved tiki bar stools, the regulars known as the Chairmen of the Board watched Em's progress in silence.

After going through the paper bags full of receipts and bits of papers that constituted Louie's account books, Johnson had come up with ways to fill the place. Karaoke was expanded to three nights a week. Happy hour was a hit with the tourists. Danny was hired to play two more nights a week, and different original tropical concoctions by Louie were featured as the Drink of the Day at half price. As often as possible, the Maidens worked themselves into the show, and Em couldn't complain if they were a little off now and then. After all, they danced for free.

Kiki didn't mind taking full credit for single handedly coming up with the brilliant idea of sending for Em to keep the Goddess from going under. Six months ago, Louie Marshall was barely able to pay his bills, and the writing had been on the wall. If business hadn't picked up, Louie would have had to sell out, and Kiki's worst fear was that he'd sell to Marlene Lockhart.

The always fashionable resident of Princeville—a well-manicured planned golf community up the hill across the Hanalei River—had been trying to get her hooks into Louie for almost a year now. Kiki couldn't tell if Louie knew that Marlene was really after the Goddess and he was just stringing the woman along to get into her white Bermudas, or if the poor man thought Marlene actually cared about him. Fat chance.

The Goddess was one of only two commercially zoned pieces of real estate on the entire north end of Kauai, and it was right on the beach. It was no secret Marlene wanted Louie to tear down the ramshackle wooden structure and build a trendy upscale restaurant with a fancy banquet facility for wedding receptions, luaus, and other events. She wanted an establishment that was nothing like what the Goddess had become over the years—a tacky tiki bar that was the "Cheers" of Kauai.

If Louie went belly up and Marlene bought the bar, or worse, Louie married the woman and she took over the Goddess, then Kiki's own business would be in jeopardy. Not to mention the Maidens would be without a place to rehearse and perform.

Except for the occasional mercy invitation to dance at business openings or fundraisers, without the Goddess they would have next to nowhere to dance in public. There would be no joy, no costumes, no reason to go on. To Kiki and her hula sisters, hula was life.

Six months ago Kiki had held a meeting and the gals came up with their scheme to improve business. They sold *lau lau*—pork wrapped and steamed in taro and ti leaves—and held car washes for fund raisers. They bought a one-way ticket for Em and wrote asking her to help. Now, thanks to Harold's unfortunate demise, things were going better than Kiki ever hoped.

Tossing her head back and pretending to laugh with abandon at a joke she hadn't quite heard over the din, Kiki batted her false eyelashes at a twenty-something tourist and his fiancé. She was just about to hand him one of her "Kiki's Kreative Events" cards when Roland Sharpe walked up to her with a notebook dwarfed in his left hand.

"And *this*," she explained to the tourists as she grabbed hold of Roland's right bicep, "is our local *fire dancer*." She looked Roland up and down and then winked at the fair-skinned bride-to-be from Iowa. "You haven't lived until you've seen our Roland with his hips wrapped in his short *malo* while he tosses flaming Samoan fire knives in the air to the sensuous beat of a Tahitian drum. I can book him for your wedding, honey. Just give me a call."

The fire dancing detective didn't crack a smile. "I need to ask you a few questions, Kiki."

No one could hear but everyone was watching. Kiki loved nothing more than an audience, so she decided to milk the moment.

"Why, sure, Roland. You know that I'm always the first to hear anything around here. Ask away." She tossed her head and smiled at those sitting nearby.

He took the wind out of her sails when he said, "Let's talk in private. Come with me."

She followed him off the front lanai and around the corner of the building. The parking lot was bathed in artificial light. Harold's remains had been carted away and a crew from the fire department was hosing down the parking lot and the *imu*.

"Howzit going, Kiki?"

"Fine, Roland. What would you like to know?"

"Let's start with how long you've been here today."

"Let's see. I had a wedding this morning. At Lumahai. It couldn't have been more perfect. Just as the bride and groom arrived, the clouds parted and there was enough of a mist to produce a stunning rainbow—"

Roland interrupted. "So when did you get *here*?"

"Around three-thirty or four. I had to help Kimo set up for the luau. I make the *lomilomi* salmon. It's tradition that I help him, because Kimo squeezes the salmon too hard. He doesn't know his own strength." Her right eyelash felt a bit loose as she blinked up at Roland and hoped the harsh light didn't magnify her wrinkles.

"Did you happen to see Harold next door today?"

"Not really."

"Is that a yes or a no?"

"It's a 'not really'. I didn't see him, but I know he was there because he had a damn fire going. Kicks up my asthma, actually, and it's almost impossible to see through the smoke. Louie and Kimo tried to talk him into burning any day but luau day."

"Anyone go over and talk to him about it today? Did Louie? Or Kimo?"

"Not me. Not Kimo. Sophie went over this morning and Harold pissed her off as usual."

"Sophie's the bartender."

"That's right. She's a great gal. You just gotta look past the piercings and tattoos." Kiki rolled her eyes. "I guess it's the style nowadays, but it's certainly not glamorous."

Roland made a notation.

Kiki wanted to sing Sophie's praises, make sure Roland got the message that the girl was okay.

"Sophie's a real addition to the staff. Louie's charming and can talk the pants off of anybody, but it's always good to have some young blood in the mix, especially someone who can relate to the late night crowd that shows up after we all leave at nine. She doesn't let anyone push her around, that's for sure. Not even Harold."

"Go on."

"Like today. After she got back from chewing him out, Harold actually doused his rubbish fire. I asked how she managed that and she said she knew how to get to him."

"How upset was she when she went over there?"

Kiki blinked again. Her damn eyelash *was* loose. She tried to press it back into place with her pinkie. "She wasn't mad enough to kill him, if that's what you're thinking Roland."

"Thanks, Kiki. I think I've got enough for now."

"Hold on a second," she said. Kiki tugged her girdle down and yanked her strapless bra up beneath the fabric of her colorful wrap-around *pareau* before she went on. "You know, I wouldn't put it past Marlene Lockhart to pull something like this."

"Marlene Lockhart," Roland jotted a note. "The event planner?"

"Honey, I'm *the* event planner. She's just an upstart whose been cozying up to Louie. Everyone knows what she really wants is the Goddess. She'd like to tear the place down and start over."

"How do you know?"

"She contacted a friend of mine who's a contractor and wanted to know if the building was worth remodeling or if it should just be torn down."

"Was she here earlier?"

"She's always hanging around where she's not wanted."

"Did you see her?"

"No, but—"

"Why would she kill Harold Otanami?"

"To ruin business here. To force Louie to sell to her. I'd say hearing that someone landed in the luau pit will keep quite a few customers away."

He closed his notebook, shoved it into his back pocket. "From the size of the crowd that's still here, I doubt it."

"Any more questions?" She'd talk as long as he wanted, hopefully clear up any misconceptions she might have given him about Sophie. They started to walk back to the lanai together.

"Nope. None for now. Thanks."

Kiki sighed. "About the gig Saturday night. I need you for a reception for a couple from Toledo. The bride's mom really, really wants a fire dancer. Can you make it?"

"Sure. Consider me booked. I'll be in touch."

Kiki was admiring the twinkling icicle lights that had been strung up across the front of the building two Christmases ago—it didn't matter that it was now July—when she noticed Leilani Cabral, Harold Otanami's niece, pulling into the parking lot in her black Mercedes. In the spotlights, the expensive car was as shiny as Leilani's ebony hair.

Everything Leilani did, everything she owned, everything she had become, mirrored perfection. Rumor had it she was born and raised in a run-down plantation worker's shack tucked in Hanapepe Valley. She'd scrapped and clawed and climbed her way to the top of the heap. Recently named Island of Kauai Properties national number one broker/agent, she hadn't sold anything listed for under two million dollars in the last three years.

The fact that she'd married the Honorable Judge Warren Cabral was a testament to just how far she'd come—but Kiki had a feeling that Leilani didn't think she'd gone far enough.

Concern was etched on her otherwise perfect features as Leilani stepped out of her car. Kiki couldn't help but notice the way the woman's eyes widened when she recognized Roland. She tucked a strand of her dark hair behind her ear and started toward them.

Kiki only knew the woman by reputation, but she wasn't about to miss anything. The girls would want all the gossip, so Kiki lingered beside Roland as Leilani approached.

"Roland. What a surprise." Leilani had to tip her head back to look up at the detective, who towered over her. "Why is my uncle's driveway blocked off with crime tape? Whatever's going on over here, he still needs access to his driveway."

"How about we find a quiet place to sit?" He flipped open his spiral bound notebook again.

Kiki kept silent—definitely a challenge—hoping to hear what Roland told Harold's niece about the murder.

"What's going on?" Leilani glanced toward Harold's house and back up at Roland.

Roland cleared his throat. "Your uncle is dead."

"Dead?" Leilani gasped. "Harold is dead?"

"Dead as a doorknob." Kiki couldn't help herself.

"Kiki, do you mind?" Roland nodded toward the front of the Goddess. "Don't you have to hula or something?"

"Not really," Kiki's strapless bra was listing south so she reached into her sarong, gave the bra a yank and held her ground.

Leilani clasped her hands. "What happened? Did my uncle have a heart attack? I warned him about smoking. I tried to get him to have regular checkups."

"Oh, he was smoking," Kiki chuckled.

Roland shot her a dark glance and then looked up at the crowded lanai. "Maybe you should sit down, Leilani."

"I'm fine. Go on."

"Your uncle was murdered," he said.

Even Kiki gasped. So much for the theory that Harold somehow stumbled into the open *imu*.

Roland turned to her again. "Really, Kiki. Go. Please."

She huffed and made a big deal of walking away but quickly found a spot up on the lanai near the railing where she could still overhear the conversation. Sophie walked over to take her drink order. Kiki mouthed "white wine" and waved her off. When she looked around she noticed Roland and Leilani Cabral were still right below her but standing closer together.

"My uncle was *murdered?*" Leilani's voice drifted clearly on the trades. The woman's hands were shaking. "Who in the world would want to murder Harold? Why?"

"That's what we're trying to find out."

"But," she squeezed her eyes shut. A lone tear escaped. Leilani brushed it away. "How did he die?"

"It wasn't pretty."

"Go on."

"Someone split his skull open with a machete, then dumped him in the luau pit around back. We haven't anything to go on yet."

"A machete?" Leilani took a deep breath. "Did anyone see anything? Hear anything?"

"Initially a lot of folks were standing around the *imu* when Kimo opened it, but unfortunately, they'd all gone inside to the buffet line right before Harold's body was thrown in. The cars in the lot blocked the view from the road."

Kiki was amazed when Leilani took hold of Roland's hand and pressed it between both of hers. The woman gazed into his eyes. Leilani's were filled with tears.

"I hope you'll find the bastard who did this," she said. "My uncle was a such a hardworking, simple man."

"Not to worry," Roland assured her. "We'll get 'em. Will you be all right?"

She nodded. "I'll be fine. Is . . . is there someone . . . who should I call?"

He dug in his pocket, pulled out a card and wrote a phone number on the back.

"This is where your uncle will be taken after the coroner releases the body. They'll help you."

"Thank you, Roland. I'm so glad you're here."

"We'll get the murderer," he promised again before he paused. Then he asked, "Where were you tonight, Lei?"

Lei? Kiki thought. *There's more to them than meets the eye.*

"I was up the mountain at Kokee, out of cell range, until late. I was attending a real estate seminar. Is there a problem?" Her hand fluttered to her throat. "Am I in any danger? Could some criminal out for revenge be after Warren? Or both of us?"

Though Roland hadn't answered yet, Kiki doubted the killing was some kind of revenge against Warren Cabral. Leilani's husband was known for letting more criminals walk than he jailed.

"Not that we know of," Roland said. "Where is your husband?"

"On Oahu. He'll be back tomorrow."

Roland made a few more quick notes. When the music grew

louder, Kiki was forced to lean further over the railing to hear.

"What made you stop by Harold's tonight?" Roland asked Leilani.

She wiped the corner of her eye. "My uncle doesn't . . . didn't . . . have anyone but me. I haven't talked to him in a while, so when I couldn't reach him tonight, I decided to stop by."

When Roland took Leilani's arm to walk her to her car, Kiki finally stepped away from the rail. She checked her watch and realized she had a little time left before the last hula performance. She looked around, spotted a table for six filled with upscale young tourists in expensive Tommy Bahama resort-wear, and hoped she'd brought enough business cards to go around.

5

About Sophie's Chat with Harold

It was time for the Maidens' final number and not a minute too soon as far as Sophie was concerned. The dishwasher couldn't keep up with the need for glasses, and they were nearly out of red plastic Solo cups. On a normal night the older set usually cleared out in time to be home by nine. The North Shore was considered "country" and nine p.m. was like midnight for most folks, but tonight the place was still packed at ten.

Once Louie put an end to the free booze, drink orders dribbled down to next to nothing. Adrenaline and shock had worn off and the crowd had quieted as the realization and horror of what they'd seen finally set in.

Sophie began to wipe down the bar with a wet towel. There was no hope for the floor. It was flip-flop deep in sticky fruit juice.

As customary, Uncle Louie took the stage and gripped the microphone.

"And now, for all you *kama'aina* and *malihini* alike, it's time for our traditional finale. The Hula Maidens are going to sing along with me as they dance to The Tiki Goddess Song. This is a number I wrote back in 1965. It's dedicated to my late wife, my very own hula gal, Irene Kau'alanikaulana Hickam Marshall."

As if on cue, Louie's eyes filled with unshed tears. Old timers elbowed tourists and told them to stand, watch and listen. A hush fell over the room as Louie slowly made a half turn. With a dramatic bow and a sweep of his arm, he indicated the life-sized oil painting of his wife, Irene, hanging above the stage.

Louie whispered into the microphone loud enough for all to hear, "To you, Sweetheart, aloha."

Danny started strumming. Brendon searched for the beat.

Then Louie began to sing and the Hula Maidens began to dance.

All the regulars and return visitors held hands and began to sway back and forth in time to the music. If they didn't exactly know the words, they tried to mouth them anyway.

> *Brown skinned girl of my dreams*
> *Standing there by the shore*
> *Dancing 'neath the moon beams*
> *I'll never love anyone more.*

When Louie began the chorus, everyone sang at the tops of their lungs.

> *My Goddess. My Tiki Goddess.*
> *I'll never love anyone more.*
> *My Goddess. My Tiki Goooodess.*
> *I'll never never, never, never, never*
> *Love anyone moooooore.*

After a couple more verses, the crowd stretched out the last goddess until it became an off-key howl.

"Mind if I ask you a few questions, Miss Chin?"

Sophie jumped, turned around and discovered the fire-dancing detective at her elbow.

"It's Ms. Chin."

"I shoulda known." He introduced himself.

She couldn't tell if Roland Sharpe was trying to be funny. As far as she was concerned, cops didn't have a sense of humor. She scanned the room, made eye contact with Em who was chatting with a table full of guests by the front door. Em nodded, encouraging.

Sophie took a deep breath. She was nervous, too much to hope it didn't show.

"I heard you spoke to Mr. Otanami this morning."

"Yeah. I did."

"About?"

She wanted to say, if you heard about it you already know what it was about. She made nice and said, "Burning his rubbish pile. I went over to tell him to put out the fire because smoke was so thick in here we were gagging on it."

By the time she got to Harold's sagging screen door that morning, her eyes and throat were burning. She was ready to hit him in the head with one of the two by fours on his rubbish pile.

"Miss Chin?"

The detective was waiting for an answer.

"I'm sorry. What did you say?" she asked.

"How did he respond to your asking him to put out the fire?"

"He ignored me and added more rubbish."

"Was that the end of the conversation?"

"Not exactly." She watched him scribble something in his notebook. "He threatened to put up a sign at the parking lot entrance."

"What kind of sign?"

"No tourist. *Haole* go home."

"Your response?"

To lie or not to lie?

"I said, 'Try it, old man.'"

"Kiki said you threatened him."

"Really."

"Yeah."

She paused. *Mahalo, Kiki, for that.*

"I told him he'd be sorry. Then I said no more Karaoke for you. That's what Em said to tell him."

Sharpe scribbled faster.

"He'd be sorry how? What did you mean by that?"

"I told him if that fire wasn't put out, he'd never be allowed to sing Karaoke here again."

"No Karaoke? That's it?"

"Yeah, but Harold lived for Karaoke. Twice a week he was in here. He'd smoke a joint, shuffle across the parking lot and down three of Louie's famous *Huli Huli* Boolies. Then he'd sing Shania Twain's *Feel Like a Woman* and Dean Martin's *That's Amore!* before he stumbled back home."

"So the threat to cut off the Karaoke was the end of it?"

She tapped the silver stud pierced through the middle of her tongue against her front teeth. "Not exactly," she admitted with a shrug.

Telling the truth just might prove to be dangerous.

"What happened next?"

"He threatened to kill me. He said, 'Mebbe I kill you!' Then he shook his fist at me."

"How did you respond?"

Sophie took a deep breath and sighed. She could very well lie, but someone could have been walking by on the road or the beach. Anyone could have overheard.

"I said, 'Watch who you threaten, old man.' I told him, 'Mebbe I kill you, too.'"

His pen was moving at warp speed across the miniscule notebook pages. His handwriting was as neat and even as if rolling out of a printer.

"Ms. Johnson said you were late to work tonight."

"I left to go to town around one."

"This is luau night. They didn't need you here earlier?"

She shook her head no. "With Kimo and Kiki helping out, that cleared me to run into town."

"Shopping?"

"Renewing my license."

"The Motor Vehicles Department closes at five. The luau starts at six. When exactly did you get here?"

"Maybe around eight. It was almost dark. I had a couple other errands to run. I stopped by Walmart for some makeup and stuff. Then I sat in bumper-to-bumper traffic through Kapa'a. Even the by-pass was backed up. The air conditioning is out in my car. I was hot and frazzled and so I stopped at my place to shower."

"Your address?"

She gave him Trish Oakley's address. "I live in a small studio under her house."

"Was she there? Did she see you?"

"No. She was here. She's our luau photographer and sometimes she dances hula with the Maidens."

Sophie and the detective were both island born and bred. She could tell by his expression he knew as well as she did that calling any of the Maidens a hula dancer was stretching it, but she also knew their hearts were in the right place.

"So, you stopped by your place and showered, then came straight here. You arrived about what time again?"

"Just before eight."

He rifled through his notes. "After the body was found."

She had had plenty of time to get back to the North Shore, hassle Harold again, somehow lure him into the parking lot and shove him into the *imu*.

"I didn't kill him," she said.

Detective Sharpe met her gaze and held it. "Somebody did." He suddenly reached into his pocket and pulled out his cell phone.

"Excuse me a sec." He communicated to someone on the other end in a series of yeah-yeahs and grunts before he hung up and shoved the phone back in his pocket.

Again, he searched her eyes. No way would she look away first.

"As I was saying, someone killed Otanami. We found the blade of a machete in the *imu* pit under the body. The handle burned up. His skull was split open."

6

Hurricane Harold Moves On

It was one-forty-five a.m. before the place was empty and Em, Kiki, and Sophie could finally sit. At a table close to the stage, Em sipped at a mug of herbal tea. Kiki was halfway through yet another glass of house white. Sophie's choice was diet soda. Kimo had left two hours ago.

Louie insisted the women relax while he mopped the floor behind the bar.

"Gee," Kiki said, looking around, "it feels like a hurricane just hit this place and moved on."

"Hurricane Harold," Sophie mumbled.

"Who could have done it?" Em traced her finger around the edge of her mug.

"Why did they do it?" Kiki wondered. "He was a bastard, but there are a lot of those running around. Not exactly a reason to kill the poor guy."

Sophie was unusually quiet.

"You okay?" Em asked.

"Just tired."

"Town day," Kiki said.

Town day explained it all. It was a good hour's drive into Lihue on a two-lane highway with traffic that brought to mind songs about paving paradise to make parking lots. Most folks saved up their list of errand stops and groceries and took along coolers to keep frozen food from thawing on the way home. Town days were definitely exhausting.

"Did Harold have any family?" Em couldn't wipe the image of Harold's body out of her mind.

"Shark Lady was out front earlier," Kiki volunteered.

"Shark Lady?" Em asked.

"Leilani Cabral. Harold's niece." Kiki replied.

"Why Shark Lady?" Sophie massaged her temples.

"She's a realtor. Local. Has her face on all those bumper stickers that say Keep Kauai Kauai. She caters to the Malibu-Aspen-Hollyweird crowd."

"Ah. That one. I've seen a lot of her For Sale signs around here."

"Yeah, she's all talk about Keep Kauai Kauai when she's really selling it off like crazy. She only deals in high end stuff—"

"Those two big estates on the beach near Limahuli are her listings. I saw her picture on the For Sale signs," Em said. "It looks like a photo from Glamour Shots."

"That's her. She flies to Honolulu for monthly haircuts and Botox injections. Years ago she was on the County Council but she lost her seat over rumors that she was taking bribes from developers. Nothing was ever proven, of course. Since then, she married a judge." Kiki smiled. She loved gossip almost as much as hula.

"Convenient," Em said.

"Very."

Even though the place was empty, Kiki leaned closer and lowered her voice.

"I think she's tight with Roland."

"Who?" Em asked.

"Shark Lady. I could see it. Something's going on."

"You think?" Sophie leaned in.

"I'll find out if anything's up when Suzi gets back in town. She went to high school with both of them." Suzi Matamoto was one of the Maidens. A realtor herself, Suzi was born and raised in Kapa'a.

"Everyone knows Roland, right?" Em's brow puckered.

"Not intimately," Kiki chuckled. "You interested?"

Em shook her head. "I've sworn off men."

"Leilani and Roland looked pretty chummy when he told her about Harold earlier," Kiki said. "Pretty chummy."

"How'd she take the news?" Sophie's dark eyes mirrored concern.

"She actually shed a tear. One. More than that would have ruined her make up."

"Pretty awful," Em said. By now everyone knew Harold's death was no accident.

"Pretty scary," Kiki added. "Who'd do such a thing?"

"Question is, why murder him?" Em wondered aloud.

"Roland was pushing me hard about the smoke thing and the argument I had with Harold today," Sophie volunteered.

"Ridiculous," Em said.

"That's what I told him," Kiki nodded in agreement. She polished off her wine and picked up her purse. "So, what time tomorrow, Sophie?"

"It's already tomorrow," Em reminded them.

"What time for what?" Sophie asked Kiki.

"You were going to teach us a new hula."

Sophie shrugged. "I haven't danced since I was kid. I'm not sure I can remember the whole thing."

"Make it up where you need to. We have to have a new number for the Slug Festival."

"Slug Festival?" Em hoped she'd heard wrong.

"Actually, it's the ASEF, the Apple Snail Eradication Festival, but I like Slug Festival better. They started it in 1989 to commemorate the introduction of the apple snail to the island. Somebody had the bright idea to farm escargot in the taro patches alongside the taro."

"Let me guess . . . " Sophie started.

"You got it," Kiki finished. "The snails started eating the taro."

Water-flushed muddy taro fields spread out across the Hanalei Valley like a huge checkerboard of rice paddies. Glistening in the sunlight, against the backdrop of lush green mountains with their trailing waterfalls, the taro fields were a photographer's delight.

"Is there anything you don't celebrate here?" Em still couldn't wrap her mind around a festival dedicated to slug eradication.

"Hey, Kauai is trying to overcome its Newly-Wed-Nearly-Dead image. We need to attract tourists that aren't on a honeymoon, celebrating retirement, or checking it off their bucket list." Kiki slid out from the banquet along the wall.

"And you think a *slug* festival will bring them in?" Em wanted to know.

"So how about it Sophie?" Kiki asked, ignoring Em. "What time?"

"Ten. I'm going to sleep in."

"Perfect. I'll email the Maidens and let them know." Before Kiki headed for the door, she paused and turned to Sophie. "How come you didn't tell us you knew how to hula sooner?"

"She *didn't* tell you, remember?." Em reminded Kiki. "You saw her on an old Merrie Monarch Festival DVD."

"I'm really not that good," Sophie said.

Kiki walked back to the table. "*Not that good?* Your *halau* danced at the Merrie Monarch!"

"What's the Merrie Monarch Festival?" Em wanted to know.

Kiki shook her head and rolled her eyes as if it should be common knowledge. "Only the Olympics of hula. Three days of competition on the Big Island. Only some of the best of the best hula *halau*—schools—directed by the top *kumu*—their teachers."

"I was only seventeen." Sophie tried to shrug off the praise.

"Oh, and now you're over the hill. What are you? Twenty?"

"Twenty-two."

Em noticed how Sophie shied away from talking about her dancing. In fact, she never said much about her past at all.

"I've got to get home." Kiki headed for the door again. "Kimo will be wondering what happened to me."

"You okay to drive?" Em asked.

"Ha! I'm good. Besides, the entire KPD is probably following the coroners' van back to Lihue. They aren't going to miss all that action." The twinkle lights were off. The parking lot was no longer lit up like a movie set. The front lanai cast a dark backdrop behind Kiki as she stood in the doorway. She blew a kiss to Louie across the room.

Sophie stood up. "Anything else you need done tonight?"

Em glanced over to the bar where Louie was carefully stacking clean glasses.

"We're done. I've got to get Louie to stop. He's got more energy than the rest of us put together."

"Remind him it's time to feed David Letterman. That'll get him going."

"Good idea. 'Night Sophie."

"'Night, Em." Sophie paused. The glow from a rainbow of tinted glass globes overhead gilded her eyebrow piercings. "Hey," she added, "I'm sorry I was late tonight."

"No worries," Em said.

Sophie told Louie good night and left. As Em stared out into the dark night, she heard Sophie's old Honda engine kick in. With a clink and a clunk, the rusted beater slowly rattled away.

While Louie puttered behind the bar, Em thought about the day she hired Sophie. She'd had seen the bruises not quite hidden by the tattoos on Sophie's arms. She had also noticed how young and vulnerable Sophie looked. How desperate.

Em looked past Sophie's pierced eyebrows, her spiked and tinted hair and into her troubled eyes. Em offered her a sandwich during a casual conversation that passed for a job interview.

The longer they had chatted, the more comfortable she felt with Sophie. Instead of trying to pass herself off as something she wasn't, the girl confessed she'd been on island less than two weeks, having just moved over from Oahu. She was living in the beach parks, sleeping in her battered heap of a car like so many of the island's homeless.

When Em asked why she'd left Honolulu, Sophie had shrugged. "I needed a change."

Em decided to hire her on the spot. She knew all about needing a change and having to start over.

Now, exhausted, Em finally slid out from behind the table and picked up her empty mug.

"Come on, Uncle Louie. We'd better get home."

Home was a rambling beachfront bungalow next door. Em had fallen in love with the place the first time she saw it years ago. When she arrived six months ago she had moved into one of Louie's large, airy spare bedrooms without a qualm. Tropic breezes blew through the wide open rooms with their high-vaulted ceilings and woven-mat floor coverings. Em loved falling asleep to the sound of rain thrumming against the metal roof.

"One second," he called. "I'm almost through putting a little something together for Letterman. "

Em walked behind the bar and watched as Louie carefully measured white rum into a jigger. He poured it into a cocktail shaker filled with ice, added some simple syrup, a touch of powdered ginger, some lime juice and then a couple drops of Tabasco sauce.

Louie's red macaw, David Letterman, was touchy when it came to spices. Touting himself as a professional mixologist right up there with the likes of the legendary Donn Beach of Don the Beachcomber and Victor Bergeron of Trader Vic's, Louie prided himself on his extensive Goddess drink menu. He made up an equally well-concocted legend for every drink. But David Letterman, the taste-testing parrot, definitely had the last word on whether a libation was a keeper or not.

"Are you sure David likes ginger?"

"Depends. I think this is going to be a hit." Louie turned off the lights over the bar as Em locked the front door.

Together they headed through the office and exited out the back. Louie carried the cocktail shaker. The parrot only needed a thimble-full. The rest was Louie's nightcap.

Em tipped her face up to receive the kiss of the light misty rain sifting down from a passing cloud. Even the seductive scent of jasmine carried by the balmy night air couldn't erase the horrific memory of what happened to Harold Otanami.

She tried to erase the image from of her mind.

"What are you going to name the new drink?"

"In honor of Harold, I'm calling it Great Balls of Fire."

7

The Right to Remain

By 10:45 a.m. the next day, hula practice was in full swing. Recorded Hawaiian music was playing loud enough to vibrate the liquor in bottles lined up behind the Goddess bar.

Sophie tried to help the Maidens perfect the *ami*, a basic hula move. Unfortunately, the pre-and-post menopausal bag of middle aged mixed nuts she was trying to teach had more enthusiasm than co-ordination.

The women were all crowded onto the small stage. Instead of paying attention, a couple of them were forearming each other, struggling for space in the front line. The width of the Goddess stage could handle only four or five in a row—not counting Flora—whose talent for dancing wouldn't fill a jigger, but seven Maidens now vied for the front row. No one wanted to be left out of the limelight.

The only one not wrestling for a spot was Little Estelle Huntington—and that was only because she was confined to a motorized Gad-About parked on the floor below the stage. Little Estelle, a former Rockette, was ninety-five and the mother of Big Estelle Paulson. Big Estelle wasn't much bigger than her mother but the women needed a way to distinguish between the two of them in conversation. Big Estelle was already in her early seventies.

Little Estelle never let her daughter or the rest of them forget that she was the only professional dancer among them. She was also an escapee from an upscale retirement home on the mainland where her son had insisted she'd be much happier than living at home alone. She wasn't. Ever since Little Estelle had moved in with her daughter on Kauai and joined the group, she had been campaigning to have the girls vote Flora out of the *hui*. Little Estelle and her daughter spent most of their time bickering with each other.

"Ladies, let's try a right *ami* one more time," Sophie began.

"Ready? One, two, three and four." Flora and Kiki rotated their hips in opposite directions and immediately caused a pile-up down the line.

"You're always out of step, Flora!" Little Estelle snapped from her Gad-About on the floor.

"Not! I'm on beat. Everybody else is always ahead." Flora, outfitted in another ankle length floral muumuu, looked like a float in the Rose Parade.

"If you know so much, how come you don't get up here and show me, eh?" Flora held both hands up to her cheeks and feigned surprise. "Oh! I forget. You can't even stan' up."

"Kiki's hogging the middle of the line again and I can't see around her." Lillian Smith wore her hair in a perm that resembled cotton candy, complete with a pink rinse, and was a serial whiner. The others no longer paid much attention to Lil.

"So? *I'm* the one who arranges all the practices," Kiki reminded her. "I'm the one who finds teachers. I deserve to be center stage." Kiki had been basking in one spotlight or another—ever since she reigned as co-Queen at the St. Perpetua High School Homecoming nearly a half-century ago.

Lillian adjusted her black-framed, rhinestone-encrusted glasses and patted her pink hair. "Well, *I* brought that expensive sushi *pupu* platter to the last practice."

Kiki obviously didn't care how many *pupu* platters Lil hauled in. "You missed three classes last month *and* our bowling alley appearance. If you'd been at practice, you might not have gotten tangled up in the curtains during our grand exit at the *Kapuna* Competition."

"Yeah," Flora adjusted her muumuu. "Good t'ing you landed on my Reggie when you was blinded and fell off the stage."

"Good thing Reggie weighs three hundred fifty pounds," Trish Oakley, the photographer, chimed in. Reggie was Flora's son. "Like falling on a mattress."

Kiki laughed and slipped into a pidgin accent like Flora's. "Good t'ing he like sit up front."

"Hey, can I help it if I missed the last minute changes because my daughter lives in Colorado?" Lil whined. "She had a *baby*, for heaven sake. I *had* to be there."

"Pretty rude of her to pick July to drop her load," Kiki mumbled.

Usually the Maidens' bickering amused Sophie, but not now. Not today.

"Knock it off!" She clapped her hands. When that didn't shut them up she said, "You all need a break. I'm buying *one* round. What'll it be?"

Miraculously moving as one, the Maidens quickly filed off the stage. Since it wasn't noon yet, most of them opted for Tiger Shark Attacks, Louie's version of a Bloody Mary. He'd mixed his first Tiger Shark in '73 to commemorate a close call he'd had while surfing off Hideaways. A huge tiger shark had taken a two-foot-wide bite out of the side of his surfboard.

The board was on display over the front door.

Sophie was behind the bar filling glasses when Detective Roland Sharpe suddenly appeared in the doorway.

The Hula Maidens, scattered about at various tables near the stage, fell silent. The only sound in the room was the rhythmic creak of the dusty overhead fan.

"Aloha, Roland," Kiki waved.

The detective nodded in her direction but didn't smile. He was all business as he headed straight to the bar where Sophie had paused with her hand around the neck of a vodka bottle.

"Miss Chin," he began. "I'd like you to come into town for more questioning."

She let go of the bottle. "More questioning?"

"You were one of the last people to see Mr. Otanami yesterday."

"I already told you everything—"

He gave her a knowing look and lowered his voice. "I think you know why I'd like to talk to you again. There might be more that you recall now that you've had some time to think about it."

"Are you arresting me?" Her heart was racing so fast she was afraid she'd faint.

"No."

"Then why can't I answer you here?"

"I'd prefer the station." He looked at the women across the room. Sophie did too. They were all listening.

"Fine." She shrugged. No doubt he'd dug around, found her arrest record. She could make this hard or she could make it easy. She picked up her purse and started around the bar.

Without warning, the Maidens all jumped up and rushed to her side. Chairs left in their wakes careened off Little Estelle's Gad-

About as she pushed the pedal to the metal and rolled across the room at high speed. Sophie had expected the women to shy away as the detective led her across the room. Instead, they surrounded her like a phalanx of exotic birds.

"Roland, come on. You can't arrest Sophie," Flora protested.

"What's she done?" Lillian demanded.

"We *need* her, Roland." Kiki pleaded. "This is a very important practice."

Sophie watched as the dark-eyed detective silenced them all with a look.

"I'm not arresting her. I'm just taking her into town for further questioning."

"Take us all then," Big Estelle piped up. She was used to bossing her mother around.

"Yeah. Take us all!" Flora yelled.

They began to chant. "Take us all! Take us all!"

Kiki leaned close and whispered to Sophie, "Choose to remain silent." Then she turned to the pink-haired woman beside her and ordered, "Hurry, Lillian, go get Em."

The Iowa transplant was the lowest Maiden in the pecking order, so Lil shoved her glasses up the bridge of her nose and sprinted out the door.

As the detective walked on one side of Sophie, Kiki was on the other. She wrapped her arm around the girl's shoulders. "No one goes to jail for murder on Kauai," she whispered. "At least not for long."

"I didn't murder anyone," Sophie protested.

They reached the patrol car and Detective Sharpe opened the back door. A bead of sweat slipped down Sophie's temple. She wiped it away.

Trish Oakely's freckles stood out in the bright sunlight outside the Goddess. Roland placed his hand atop Sophie's head as she bent down to lower herself into the back seat. Trish had grabbed her camera on the way out. Now she snapped off a couple of quick photos.

"Don't worry. We'll get you out on bail," Trish promised.

"Bail?" Sophie's eyes smarted. "I'm only going in for questioning."

She didn't have two dimes to rub together, let alone bail. Her car was repaired with duct tape and not worth squat. A public defender was the best she could do if she had to lawyer up.

"No worries. We'll get you out. You're our hula sistah now." Flora opened her water bottle and took a long swig. She palmed the top of the bottle and offered it to Sophie. Sophie shook her head no. Last thing she needed was gin on her breath.

Trish stepped aside and Em suddenly appeared in the open car door. Sophie's cheeks flamed as she stared up at the woman who had taken a chance on hiring her and even found her a place to live.

"I didn't do anything." Sophie whispered. There was no reason in hell that Em Johnson or anyone else should believe her. She half expected Em to fire her on the spot.

"We'll be right behind you." Em reached in to the car and gave her shoulder a squeeze.

"Listen, Em . . . " Sophie wanted to tell her about Oahu, about her past, but it was too late. Roland had already started the engine. Em closed the door.

As the KPD cruiser pulled out of the parking lot, Sophie let the tears come. She was as scared as she was pissed, but most of all, she was in shock that the Maidens were lending their support.

No one had ever been there for her. Not even during small-kid time when she was a *keiki*. No one had stood up for Sophie Chin. Not ever.

8

Two Sides to Every Story

Em sat alone in the waiting area at KPD's booking station. The Maidens had insisted on being there, but their bickering was drawing attention so she sent them off to the café at the Tip Top Motel for ox tail soup and told them to stay put until she called.

Forty-five minutes later, Roland Sharpe walked into the waiting area without Sophie. Em's heart jumped into her throat. As he headed toward her, she got to her feet and met him halfway across the lobby.

He glanced around the room. "Where is the entourage?"

"The Tip Top," she said

He nodded toward a couple of chairs off by themselves. "Let's sit down a minute."

Bad news, Em thought. *He's separating me from the herd.* She followed in his wake. He waited until she was settled, then sat beside her.

"Are you arresting her?" She couldn't believe she was asking that about Sophie.

"No."

Em's relief was short lived.

Roland added, "Did you know she has a record?"

Em took a deep breath and closed her eyes. She'd hired Sophie without a single recommendation. Hired her on a gut feeling that Sophie was a nice gal who needed a break. Now she wondered if maybe her judgment was in a shambles after Phillip. She hoped she wasn't crazy to still have faith in people.

She thought about telling Roland that yes, she knew and that she wasn't dumb enough to hire someone without references, but she was too shook up to pull it off.

"No, I didn't know. How . . . what was she arrested for?"

"Accessory to robbery. Possession of narcotics." He glanced down at her hands. She followed his gaze and hadn't realized she was holding her fingers in a clench in her lap. She let go and smoothed her palms down her shorts.

"If she was guilty of all that, why isn't she locked up?"

"She was underage and was an accessory—she was driving a get-away car. The possession charge was eventually dropped."

"So if the charges were dropped . . . "

"She's still guilty of making poor choices."

"How old was she then?"

"The holdup took place when she was seventeen." He let a beat go by before he added, "If I were you, I'd think about firing Ms. Chin."

"Are you arresting her for Harold's murder?"

"I've nothing to hold her on. No evidence. No witnesses."

"It could have been anyone."

"She got into it with him that day."

Em shook her head. "She couldn't have killed him."

Em knew there were times she herself had fantasized various ways of getting rid of her ex. Separating him from his dick and letting him bleed to death for instance, but she would have never actually done it.

Roland sat back and propped his left foot on his right knee. He jiggled his foot and stared at Em for a few seconds, then shook his head as if giving up on her.

"I wish you'd take my advice."

"I'm here to drive Sophie home. Is she free to leave yet?"

"Don't say I didn't warn you." He stood up.

"No need. You'll see." Em rose, too, clutching her purse. She prayed she was right.

"I'll send her out," he said.

Em watched Roland Sharpe walk away. It was one thing to defend Sophie to the detective. It was another knowing Sophie hadn't been up front about her record. Then again, Em had only herself to blame. She hadn't asked for references. She hadn't asked much of anything.

Five minutes later, Sophie walked through the door and into the waiting area. She saw Em and hesitated a beat before she continued across the room.

When she reached Em, Sophie didn't shy away from meeting her eyes. "I didn't expect to see you here."

"Didn't Roland tell you I was waiting?"

"No. He just said I could leave." She lowered her voice. "I'm so sorry, Em."

"I trusted you, Sophie. You should have told me about your past."

"Would you have hired me?"

"You never gave me the chance to decide for myself."

"You're right. I should have been up front about my arrest record. I could have told you earlier, before Sharpe picked me up, but then it was too late." Her gaze never faltered.

Em looked around the lobby. "Let's head out to the car."

The minute they stepped outside the air conditioned building, sultry heat enfolded them. Em stopped walking. She hitched her purse under her arm and turned to Sophie.

"Roland told me you were charged with some very serious offenses—"

"But I never even served time."

"What happened? I want all of it."

Sophie took a deep breath. "I was seventeen when I started dating the boyfriend from hell. It was his big idea to rob the ABC Store near Lewers Street. He said no big deal if I drove the car. Said I wouldn't do time because I was underage and he was right, I didn't go to jail, but it went on my record. Aiding and abetting. I got off on probation because it was a first offense."

"But not your last."

"A year later, he asked me to pick up a duffle bag he forgot at the gym. The cops had been watching the place, suspecting drug deals were going down. I had no idea. I walked out carrying a duffle full of dirty gym clothes and enough *pakalolo* to be charged with transporting."

"You got off again."

"I had no idea I was carrying pot. The only thing I was guilty of was being stupid."

"Your boyfriend was arrested."

"No, he wasn't, but one of the other guys was. He owed Jimmy a favor so he testified that I had no knowledge of what was in the bag. I got off. Afterward, I tried to break things off with Jimmy."

"But . . . " Em could guess what was coming.

"I filed a restraining order. He'd moved on already. New

girlfriend. A sixteen year old. Unfortunately, there are plenty of guys just like him in Honolulu. Once you get caught up in that kind of crowd, it's hard to get out. When I finally got enough money together to ship my car, I moved over here to start over."

Em knew all about loving the wrong man and being deceived. She knew what it was to barely have a dime to her name, too. Eight years into her marriage an old girlfriend of Em's called from the airport in Costa Rica to report that Phillip was there with another woman. Em wouldn't have believed a word except for the fact that Phillip was in Costa Rica—supposedly on a fishing trip with his buddies.

Em's friend backed up the revelation by emailing cell phone photos. Sure enough, Phillip was all over another woman, touching her, kissing her in public. Once Em began to unravel the truth, she found out her big shot Newport Beach public accountant had been a player for years. She hired the best divorce lawyer money could buy and thanks to her friend's photos and Phillip's own admission of guilt—he tried to play the sex addiction card—she definitely had the upper hand. But his infidelity wasn't the only shock. She discovered their bank accounts were close to empty and the house was mortgaged for three times what it was worth.

What hurt the most was that many of their so called friends had known about Phillip and his affairs all along, but nobody had bothered to tell her. No longer able to afford the Newport Beach social scene or lifestyle, Em cut herself off. Alone and adrift, she was floundering when Kiki's letter and the airline ticket from the Maidens arrived.

She had only met her uncle once before and that was back when she and Phillip had honeymooned on Kauai. Phillip thought Louie was certifiable even then. Em preferred to think of her uncle as eccentric. Louie thought of himself as a castaway and kept the Tiki Goddess Bar open as a shrine to his late wife. But once Em had really gotten to know Louie, she found him to be an endearing, hardworking, sincere man. Which is what she had believed about Sophie—at least the Sophie she thought she knew.

She hated to think she was a complete idiot when it came to judging people.

"I swear to God I didn't kill Harold." Sophie's voice brought Em back.

"I know that," Em said. *But do I really?* She wondered.

"I wouldn't blame you if you fired me."

Em stared at Sophie for a moment, hoping she'd made the right decision. She needed to trust her own judgment as well as Sophie.

She smiled. "I'm not firing you. I need a bartender." She shook her head and sighed. "Besides, the Maidens would riot."

9

A Late Night Development

"Someday, huh, kid?"

Em glanced over at Uncle Louie, wondering if he'd forgotten her name.

"You can say that again." Somehow it was already 10:30 p.m. She and the Maidens had driven Sophie back to the North Shore late that afternoon. Em could tell the girl was still shaken, but she had insisted on working her shift at the bar that evening.

"Glad you told Sophie to close up early. She should be over here within the hour with the cash box." Louie glanced out toward the dark lanai. Just beyond, waves crashed against the beach with rhythmic enthusiasm. Rain ran off the roof in beaded rivulets.

Em shrugged. "I figured why not close early? The place was all but deserted except for Buzzy, and he can drink at home." She silently assured herself the cash box would soon arrive, safely tucked under Sophie's arm.

Louie attributed the slow turn out to all the commotion after the murder last night. Not only was it raining steadily now, but too much unexpected excitement tended to wear everyone out.

The door of David Letterman's cage rattled as Louie reached in to pour his latest version of Great Balls of Fire into the macaw's drinking cup. So far, so bad.

"What number try is this?" Em asked.

"This is only my fourth." Louie smiled at her from across the room.

Em watched David Letterman dip his deadly beak into his cup. He drank, swallowed, and then let out an ear piercing scream and cries of "Yuck! Yuck! Patooie!"

The bird nervously began pacing back and forth across his perch, shaking his head and muttering, "Yuck! Yuck! Patooie!" over and over. He punctuated his outrage with exaggerated spitting sounds.

"Okay, okay. I'm sorry," Louie apologized.

"I told you he hates ginger," Em said.

Louie refused to listen. "Too much Tabasco, maybe." He downed what was left in the shaker and started over. At this rate Louie would end up on the floor next to the cage.

"Maybe you should just make some adjustments to the mix in the shaker instead of polishing off all the rejects."

"Gotta start fresh." The word came out *freesh*.

Just then Trish Oakely appeared on the back lanai with a hoodie sweatshirt tossed over her head and clutching a gallon-sized Ziplock bag full of photos. Her camera dangled beneath the sweatshirt.

"I saw your light on. Sophie said she was closing up and that I should come on over."

"Come in," Em called out. Louie greeted Trish with a hug and an aloha. He offered her a drink from the small tiki bar set up in the corner of the room.

Trish declined and made her way to the coffee table, a low, bamboo-and-glass affair that had been around since the 40s. The redhead shrugged off her hoodie and draped it over a bar stool and then handed the Ziplock to Em.

"Photos from the luau," Trish said.

Em opened the bag and started shuffling through the photos. There were shots taken of tourists standing around the *imu* listening to Kimo's spiel about how local hunters had delivered the pig cleaned and already salted and wrapped in banana and ti leaves. Then it was buried and roasted on hot coals for hours. There were posed photos of couples and family groupings in front of the luau hut or beside the huge, carved tiki Louie had shipped from Tahiti back in the '60's. Some of the guests were posed in front of the Tiki Goddess sign.

None of them looked like they had Harold's blood on their hands.

"How in the world would we know if any one of these people killed Harold?" Em wondered.

"I thought about that," Trish said. "I figure there might have been someone outside when the pig was uncovered, someone loitering out there who didn't attend the luau." She took the pile of photos from Em and shuffled them until she found one that she had taken inside the Goddess. "I went from table to table taking photos and placing orders for copies. This afternoon I matched the outdoor shots with the indoor shots and there are only two people who were outside at the time the pig was dug up who weren't around later for the luau. Two people who went missing."

Em sat up straighter and patted the cushion beside her. "Show me."

Trish sat down, held out a photo and pointed to a couple wearing hiking boots and back packs. "These two."

"Great. Serial killer hikers?"

"I met them. They seemed like a real nice couple. He is a professor of some kind from back east. They're hiking out to camp in the Kalalau Valley for a week. Longer if they can make their provisions last, which should be easy since they only eat raw."

"Raw what?"

"Raw everything. It's like being a vegan or something. Only raw fruits and veggies, eggs, even raw meat. That's why they didn't stay for the luau. The sight of the whole pig coming out of the *imu* about did them in. Can't imagine what they'd have done if they saw poor Harold."

"Enough said." Em held up her hand.

"They said they'd pick up the photos when they came back through town," Trish added. "We need to find them."

"Why would they want to kill Harold?"

"Obviously they aren't into cooking anything, let alone Harold. I don't think they wanted to kill Harold any more than you do, but what if they were hanging around out there after we all came in? Maybe they saw something that might be a clue."

"Maybe," Em agreed.

"So someone needs to go talk to them."

"Hike into Kalalau?"

"They planned to stop at Hanakapi'ai Beach for a couple of nights first," Trish said. "I'd hike in and look for them tomorrow morning, but I have a wedding to shoot at two."

"One of Kiki's events?"

"Yeah. A real blowout. The bride and groom are getting married underwater." Trish rolled her eyes.

When David Letterman started shrieking again, Trish levitated a foot off the sofa and shoved her fingers in her ears. Photos scattered all over.

"Poison! Poison!" The macaw screamed. "Take it away!"

"Sorry. Sorry, Dave." Louie was frantically trying to unclip the water cup from the side of the cage. David Letterman started to go for his hand.

"He's nuts," Trish whispered.

"Louie or the parrot?" Em whispered back.

"Both."

"That's why I'm here, remember?" Em said.

"So can you hike in there tomorrow? Try and find these two?" Trish handed her the photo of the hikers. The young woman was smiling. She had long, red-gold hair that hung in rippling waves past her shoulders. She would have been beautiful if her skin wasn't the color of a carrot. The man was older. Tall and lanky with round John Lennon style wire framed glasses. His long gray hair was pulled back into a ponytail.

"I could use an outing, that's for sure." Em had hiked to Hanakapi'ai only once before, shortly after she'd arrived on island. She'd been looking forward to doing so again but hadn't made time.

Just then, Sophie walked in carrying the cash box. She waved at Louie and headed for Em and Trish. Em felt a wave of relief and smiled.

"You can set that on the desk." Em waved toward the old battered wicker desk on the far side of the living room. "Want anything to drink?" she offered.

Sophie watched Louie putter behind the bar. David was still spitting patooies. Sophie shook her head. "No, thanks. I don't think so."

Em could see the girl was uncomfortable. "Have a seat," she said.

She thought Sophie was going to decline but then she sank into the rattan chair across from the couch Em and Trish occupied.

Em filled her in. "Trish may have found a couple of witnesses."

"If they'd seen someone kill Harold, don't you think they would have told somebody?" Sophie frowned and locked her fingers between her knees.

Trish nodded. "One would hope. They may not have seen the actual murder, but they might have seen something that, on hindsight, might have been a little suspicious. It's worth asking them."

"Did you tell Roland yet?" Sophie looked concerned.

"Not yet."

"I don't know." Sophie shook her head. "It's pretty far to go just on a hunch that they saw something. Why not wait until they hike out?"

"It could be weeks before they come back and it's only two miles." Trish said.

"I'm looking forward to it," Em said. "I'll leave as soon as it's light in the morning."

Sophie looked even more uncomfortable. "You shouldn't have to go up there. Let me go. I really don't mind."

Trish shook her head. "You shouldn't be seen on the trail to Kalalau. Somebody gets word of it and pretty soon everyone will think you're on the run and that you're going to hide out in the valley like Ko'olau the Leper."

"Who?" Em asked.

"Ancient history. Forget it." Trish waved her off.

"At least let me go with you, Em," Sophie suggested.

Em leaned forward and lowered her voice. "I don't want Louie working the bar alone all day. Every time he's there by himself, we lose money. I need you here. I'll be in and out of there in a few hours. If I leave early, I can be back by noon, one at the latest."

Trish stood up. "Speaking of going, I hate to break up the party, but I've got to get home."

Em helped Trish gather the photos, keeping the one of the professor and his carrot-colored companion. She promised to call Trish as soon as she returned.

With a glance at Uncle Louie, who was frantically making notes in his Booze Bible, Em went back to the couch and slouched down again.

Sophie sighed, leaned forward and dropped her voice. "Thank you for trusting me."

"I do trust you. That's why I'm going to do everything I can to find out who really killed Harold so we can clear your name."

For the first time since last night, Em saw Sophie smile.

10

The Raw Eaters

Em left at dawn, drove to the end of the road and parked. When she got out of Louie's black Toyota pick-up, she made sure to leave the doors unlocked so the bums who broke into rental cars parked at the trail head wouldn't have to break her windows.

The truck looked pretty local, so she wasn't all that worried. She signed into the log book at the bottom of the trail and started up the steep, rock-lined path that canted up the mountainside.

She picked her way along a packed-red-dirt trail that was as slick as marble in some places. Roots formed two-and-a-half foot steps on steep slopes. Natural booby traps of woody vines thick as her wrists protruded from the ground here and there. The trail was only three feet wide at the most. In some places there wasn't a bush or a blade of grass to break a fall over the cliffs to the wave-battered rocks below.

A wide expanse of golden sand was edged by a strong shore break. A sign on the beach posted the latest drowning-body count but rarely kept swimmers out of the water. A cliff with a wide-mouth cave was cut into the far end of the beach.

By the time she reached Hanakapi'ai, muscles Em didn't remember having were screaming. She'd polished off all her water. Sweating and parched, she still had to cross a clear-running stream to reach the sand. Though dying for a sip of water, she didn't dare take a drink. She'd heard enough horror stories about the dreaded leptospirosis bacteria and flesh eating disease that lurked in some of Kauai's streams and rivers.

Scanning the beach, she saw a handful of tents set up here and there. Nude men and women basked on the sand like sleeping monk seals.

There were plenty of drop outs on the North Shore and a few

were the real deal. Others were wanna-be-hippies who were actually retired dot-comers, former day traders, or merely spoiled brats the locals had nicknamed trustafarians—kids living off of trust funds. They "survived" on overpriced organic food and bottled designer juices and water from the local health food store.

At least her folks' generation boasted real hippies who fought for causes like world peace, ending the draft, or at the very least, burning bras to liberate breasts.

She easily found her hikers sitting under a huge plum tree near the cave on Hanakapi'ai Beach. They'd put up a tent and stripped down to their birthday suits. The man was tall and even thinner than he appeared in Trish's photo. Behind his round granny glasses, his eyes were unusually bright and glassy. A benign smile curved his lips.

Em would have recognized the young woman anywhere. She was the color of a papaya, a lovely pale orange all over. A pile of fruit was stacked on the ground before her. Nude, she looked like Eve contemplating not just an apple but a whole fruit salad. Em smiled back.

"I'm Em Johnson and I run the Tiki Goddess Bar in Haena. Our photographer said that you stopped by our luau two nights ago."

The man offered his hand.

"I'm Professor Nelg Nelson, Chairman of the Anthropology and Archeology Department at the University of North Carolina." He turned to the young woman beside him. She was half the professor's age. Probably a student, Em guessed.

"This is Namaste," the professor added. "Have a seat." He indicated one of the large flat rocks near the front of their tent.

Em sat and tried to keep her gaze from drifting south toward the professor's flaccid penis. It looked a lot like a baby turtle's head peeking out of a thatch of kelp.

"Nelg is an interesting name." Em had no idea how to segue into a conversation about Harold's murder. "Is it Swedish?"

"Actually, it's 'Glen' backward, but I think it adds a certain flair." He smiled over his glasses, reached for his backpack and pulled out a joint. "You don't mind if I smoke?"

"Not at all." Em figured she'd better start asking questions before the professor got any higher. Before she could begin he said, "I find the custom of the luau quite interesting and a bit sad in its current format."

She took a deep breath and quickly cut him off before he could go on.

"Actually, Professor, I'm here because someone was murdered on luau night. His body was found in our *imu*. Since you were there . . . "

Namaste spoke for the first time. "Surely you don't think we killed someone."

Em shook her head. "Of course not. I was just wondering if you may have seen anything out of the ordinary, anything that, in hindsight, might seem suspicious. Since you didn't actually come inside, it's possible you might have crossed paths with the murderer."

Namaste shivered. The professor took a hit off the joint and offered it to Em. She shook her head no and he passed it on to Namaste. Em decided pot smoke evidently qualified as raw enough.

Nelg Nelson held his breath for what seemed an impossible amount of time. Finally he coughed, blinked and stared at Em.

"The victim lived in a small green house to the right of the parking lot," she prodded.

"Ah." He nodded and smiled over at Namaste. "The place with the sculptures in the yard."

"If you want to call them that, yes," Em said. Harold had a penchant for collecting junk and turning it into what he liked to call yard art.

Nelg shook his head. "I can't recall anything out of the ordinary. Lots of people. Tourists. Cars."

Namaste finally spoke up. "The smell of smoked pork was making me nauseous. I had to leave." She started nibbling on a papaya as if it were an apple. Em had never seen anyone eat the skin before.

A Boy Scout troop appeared on the trail, crossed the stream and fanned out along the beach. Four of them broke from the main group and soon became more interested in staring at Namaste's exposed female anatomy than exploring the cave or beachcombing. Em figured a fresh Brazilian wax trumped flora and fauna every time.

"Doesn't it bother you to have them staring like that?" Em whispered to Namaste.

"Body parts are natural. I have nothing to hide."

"You can say that again," Em mumbled.

"The professor and I believe in the purification of the body through Tantric yoga, the consumption of raw foods, and plenty of water." The young woman reached over, grabbed the professor's hand and gave it a squeeze. "Don't we, Nelg?"

Em was fairly certain the professor would agree to anything Namaste wanted him to if it gave him access to her orange tinted portal.

"Would you like a drink?" Nelg handed Em a bottle of Fiji water. He obviously didn't notice the contradiction in the fact that their water of choice flowed from plastic.

"You're certain you can't recall anything out of the ordinary Friday night?" Em hoped something might break through the professor's ganja haze. The joint had disappeared. The Boy Scouts were motionless, mesmerized and barely breathing by now. Nothing like a good fantasy and a contact high.

Em glanced at her watch. She reached into her pocket for a Tiki Goddess business card. "If you think of anything, anything at all that might help, don't hesitate to call." She thought for a moment. "You do have a cell phone?"

"And a computer. Though neither works back here," Nelg told her.

"How long do you plan to stay in Kalalau?" Em asked.

"As long as we can sustain ourselves on the wild fruit that grows in the valley. I'm here doing research on a Lost Tribe that legend says lived in the far reaches of the Kalalau Valley, trying to connect them to the tales of the Menehune, the little people who supposedly lived here before the first wave of Polynesians arrived. Most people discount the tales as mere legend, but recently skeletons of miniature people have been excavated from the floor of a cave on Flores, an island near Bali. This new species, *homo floresiensis,* is a fantastic find. They were hunters who used stone tools and so I'm searching for evidence of their existence here—hoping to prove they were the reality behind the mythical Menehune."

As he spoke, the professor opened his back pack again, and this time he rolled a joint the size of a hefty cigar. He urged Em to take a hit. She stared at the joint, recalled she'd been smoking pot the night she met Phillip. She'd wound up dancing on a table in a club in Newport, riding around naked on the back of a flatbed truck and woke up the next day engaged and remembering none of it.

She stared at the joint in the professor's hand and thought, why the hell not? Em took a drag. She held her breath, her eyes bugged out and eventually she fell into a coughing fit, but the euphoria that eventually followed was worth it.

A few tokes later, when Nelg suggested they go all soak in the huge tide pool trapped in a low spot on the beach, she pulled off her tank top and shorts and stripped down to her designer thong and bra—leftovers from her former life. She followed Nelg and Namaste down to the pool and slipped out of her undies.

She savored the caress of a gentle passing shower on body parts that hadn't been bared in public since the time she and Phillip checked into an exclusive adult beach club outside of Puerto Vallarta.

Lolling in the warm salt water was as good as a massage. The sun was warm, the air velvet. The Boy Scouts earning Voyeur badges had doubled in number. When Namaste invited Em to partake of their raw feast of papaya, squash, mountain apple and peanuts, Em said yes.

She'd been working nonstop since she arrived on Kauai and now, and despite that fact that she was on a mission, she realized she hadn't been this carefree in months. It didn't take much to convince herself that it would be good for her spirit, good for her soul, and definitely good for her aching muscles to hang out a while longer.

So what if she wasn't back by afternoon? Sophie was safely out of jail and tending bar with Louie. And Harold wasn't getting any deader.

11

Meanwhile Back at the Goddess

The next morning, the inside of Em's mouth tasted like the bottom of a bait tank by the time she finally got home. She'd stayed in Hanakapi'ai far longer than she'd intended. The day got away from her and since it was too dangerous to hike back down the trail in the dark, she'd spent the night.

Her eyes were dry, her head felt stuffed with coconut husks. Now and then she experienced flashes of a weird dream she had while sleeping in Nelg and Namaste's tent.

She'd been standing at the podium during one of the O.C. fundraisers she used to chair for the Women's League—stark naked. Harold Otanami suddenly appeared and arm wrestled her for the microphone. He won and started to belt out "Great Balls of Fire."

As Em ran from the banquet hall nude, she grabbed a table cloth off a nearby table, whipped it off and sent place settings and food flying. Phillip and his latest love toy were fortunately at that very table. They ended up dripping raw fruit compote. Just as she reached the door, a ten foot high pile of miniature skulls and bones appeared and blocked the exit.

"And that, Emily Johnson, is why you quit smoking pot years ago." She admonished herself aloud as she skirted the Goddess parking lot. It was only 9:30 a.m. and already the Hula Maidens' cars were there.

She pulled around the back to avoid being sighted and slipped into her uncle's house. Em expected David Letterman to start shrieking—as a watch parrot he was better than a Rottweiler—but this morning he was silent. She found him lying on the floor of the cage, belly up, sleeping one off.

Louie had finally perfected his Balls of Fire concoction.

She quickly showered, changed, brushed her teeth three times, and headed for the bar.

Before her eyes adjusted to the dim light, the Maidens who were present accosted her.

"Where have you been?" Lil whined, her hair looking exceptionally pink. "We thought you were dead. Or worse."

"I was—"

"There's a murderer running around loose, you know?" Kiki was furious. "Nice of you to call and tell someone you were all right."

"Cell phones don't work in Hanakapi'ai."

"We just called the police," Flora confessed.

"You didn't." Em had enough of the police already. From behind the bar, Sophie's pained expression said she felt the same.

"We didn't call 911. We only called Roland," Kiki clarified. "We thought you were dead, but he wasn't convinced."

Sophie came out from behind the bar and handed Kiki a fresh glass of chardonnay.

"Did the hikers see anything?" Sophie asked.

Em pictured Professor Nelg and Namaste naked as Adam and Eve beneath the plum tree.

"Nothing out of the ordinary. At least nothing they can recall. With as much *pakalolo* as they smoke, I don't know how they remember their own names." Then again, the professor did pronounce his backward.

"I know one thing," Kiki said, "Roland and the KPD boys aren't any closer to solving this thing than they were before. I say we all pitch in and find the real killer. Take the heat off of Sophie."

Kiki had no idea how much heat really was on Sophie. Em feared Roland may have stopped looking for the killer to focus on the girl. All he needed was enough proof to haul her in.

"I agree," Em said. "It won't hurt to try."

The Maidens in attendance ambled back to the stage. Trish and the Estelles were not there but Suzi Matamura, the realtor, was back from a week on Maui. A perfect size six and just five feet tall in her bare feet, Suzi was the most diminutive of the Maidens. And the most coordinated. At the moment she was apparently spearheading an overthrow if Kiki didn't design a different costume for the Slug Festival.

"I just don't think we should wear ti leaf skirts," Suzi told Flora, Kiki and Lil.

Kiki turned on her, arms folded, and jutted out her chin. "And why not?"

"For one thing, to make skirts big enough to fit everyone," Suzi glanced at Flora's girth and then away, "we'll have to deforest half the island. And besides, I hate crafts. I'm not stringing ti leaves."

"*Wili.* The word is *wili.*" Kiki pronounced it 'vili.' *To twist.* We're twisting them onto a waistband. It's simple. I've made millions of them. All we have to do is hike up the mountain, pick enough ti leaves for everyone—I'm thinking close to eight hundred total—then we tie the skirts together." She punched the play button on the CD player and the music started. End of discussion.

Suzi pouted but fell into line with the rest.

"Where's Louie?" Em asked Sophie as she reached the bar.

"Out surfing. Said he mastered Great Balls. It'll be the featured drink at the next luau."

"I guessed as much when I saw Letterman sleeping it off." She glanced around the bar. Everything appeared to be under control. "While it's relatively quiet, I'm going into the office to pay some bills."

Sophie said she had things covered and added, "Some guy called and left his number. It's on the desk. He wanted you to call back asap."

Em shut the door to the office, barely muffling the strains of the recorded hula music. She recognized the mainland area code from the LA area and was relieved it wasn't Phillip. She sat behind the desk and placed the call.

A male voice answered. "Wally Williams."

"Aloha, Mr. Williams. This is Em Johnson of the Tiki Goddess. You left a message for me to call?"

"Em Johnson?"

"From Kauai. The Tiki Goddess Bar on Kauai."

"Oh! The Goddess. Yes." He sounded way too impressed to have ever been here. Em leaned her elbow on her desk and rubbed her forehead as he went on. "I'm *Fernando's* assistant. He'd like to talk to you about catering his housewarming party week after next."

"Fernando?" Em drew a blank.

"Yes. The *Fernando.* Singer. Pianist. Las Vegas's latest legend. *That* Fernando."

Suddenly the lights went on.

"Oh, *that* Fernando. I'm sorry. I had a tough night."

"Oh honey, didn't we all?" Wally laughed.

That Fernando had stepped into the vacuum left by the passing of Liberace. He was young, handsome—in a swarthy-man-in-rhinestones-and-floor-length-feather-boa sort of way—and he played one hell of a piano. *That* Fernando, *the* Fernando, wanted the Goddess to cater his party.

"Next week, you say?"

"If it's not a problem."

"No. It's no problem." She hoped. Kimo would definitely need Kiki and some of the other Maidens to pitch in, depending on the menu.

"Hold please and I'll put Fernando on the line," Wally said.

Em held. She doodled on the back of an unpaid liquor distributor's invoice. Finally a breathless voice with a thick Spanish accent came over the line.

"Fernando here. Fernando was rehearsing. Fernando is so *thrilled* that you can help us."

"We'd be happy to try. Your assistant mentioned this was a housewarming. Are you thinking of *pupus* or a full meal? A Hawaiian luau? Asian fusion? I can also line up entertainment," she said, hoping to throw some business Kiki's way. "And I can suggest a great photographer." Might as well keep Trish working, too.

Fernando sighed. "So many choices. How about if Fernando comes to your establishment next week to meet you? Perhaps you will make some suggestions? Perhaps have sample platters for us to taste?"

"I'll come up with something fabulous as well as a list of contacts." She wrote down the date he planned to be on island. "Exactly where is the housewarming going to be held?" If it was on the other side of the island, it would have to be worth their while to haul food and servers all the way around Kauai to Po'ipu.

"Fernando has just purchased a compound near Limahuli. Do you know this place?"

"I do. It's right up the road." She knew where Limahuli was. Compound? She pictured razor wire and iron gates. "We'll look forward to meeting you, Fernando."

"Please keep our meeting secret. I do not want to have to deal with paparazzi. So tedious."

"This is Kauai, Fernando. We don't have paparazzi."

"Perhaps," he said before he hung up, "you should get some."

Em paid a few bills and tried to organize the mess on Louie's desk before she went back into the bar where the Maidens were taking a break. Big and Little Estelle had finally arrived. Little Estelle was snoozing on her Gad-About with her chin on her chest. She was drooling on the yoke of her purple muumuu. Em waved Suzi the realtor over.

"Do you know anything about the recent sale of a compound at Limahuli?"

Suzi climbed up onto one of the tiki totem bar stools and shook her head no when Sophie asked if she wanted a drink.

"All I know is that the escrow is about to close. It might have already. It was all very hush hush. There are two big properties for sale side by side out there. Shark Lady has both listings."

As Em digested the information, Suzi added, "Harold worked out there, you know. I remember seeing him riding that chrome-plated lawn mower of his, the one that's the size of a Humvee."

"Really?"

"A few years back he was nothing but a mow, blow and go gardener with a sit-down mower. Then every time Leilani sold a piece of property, she got him jobs with the new owners. He went from being a gardener to Landscape Architect overnight. Instead of making ten dollars and hour he was making a hundred and twenty five."

"You ever hear of the entertainer Fernando?" Em asked her.

"The guy with platform shoes? Feathers and rhinestones?" Suzi rolled her eyes. "What about him?"

"He bought one of those properties."

"No kidding."

Em nodded. "It's not widely known, but it will be soon. He wants us to cater a housewarming." Em was beginning to see dollar signs herself. Tiki Goddess Bar, *the* Caterer to the Stars.

"Maybe Fernando did away with Harold," Suzi chuckled. "That shiny lawnmower was stealing the spotlight."

"Fernando isn't on island yet," Em told her.

Suzi shrugged. "It would be pretty hard for him to hide."

Apparently over her ti leaf costume tiff for now, Kiki walked over to join them.

"Do you know anything about Roland Sharpe being involved with Shark Lady?" she asked Suzi.

Suzi thought a minute and then shook her head. "Not since high school, but they were an item back then, for sure. He was the most handsome guy in the class and the most popular. Leilani was head cheerleader, class president and homecoming queen. Her ambition didn't just appear, she's always had it. She dumped Roland when he decided to go to the police academy and she figured out he wasn't going to be pulling down big bucks."

"Did he ever get married?"

"Roland? Never. He likes women too much to settle for just one."

"You think they might be having an affair?" Em tried to sound as if she was only making a casual query but if Roland was playing around with a married woman, then he wasn't worth admiring, even from across the room.

"I seriously doubt it," Suzi shook her head. "Roland always did the right thing."

Bored already, Kiki wandered over to call the Maidens back on stage, and Suzi hurried to join them. Sophie set down a dishrag and walked over to Em.

"Maybe this guy Fernando hired a hit man." It was the first time in two days that Sophie had mentioned the murder.

"What's the motive?" Em wondered.

"You sound like a crime show." Sophie leaned on the bar, thought for a minute. "Maybe one of Harold's other clients had a beef with him. We should get a hold of his list of accounts. Talk to them. Check them out."

"How?" Em figured she was only considering it because yesterday's *pakalolo* binge still clouded her mind.

"He probably kept a list in his house."

"What are you suggesting? A break in?"

"It's not breaking and entering if the door is open," Sophie said. "Oh, and speaking of detectives . . . "

Em followed Sophie's gaze. Roland Sharpe had just walked through the door and all six-foot-plus inches of perfection was headed straight for Em. He gave Sophie a nod that said leave us. Sophie picked up a broom and hurried out to the lanai.

"I thought you were missing," Roland said to Em. "Glad I didn't call Search and Rescue right away."

She shrugged. "I knew where I was all the time."

"Funny. So what's up? Where were you?"

"Trish Oakely, our luau photographer, and I went through all the photos taken the night of the murder. Shots taken both inside and out. We came up with a couple of hikers who were here early but didn't stay to eat. Your officers questioned everyone else. I hiked into Hanakapi'ai to ask them if they remembered seeing anything out of the ordinary."

"Above and beyond. Why didn't you call me? Let us handle."

"I figured you were too busy to spend the day hiking just to chase down a lead that might go nowhere. Which it did."

"Did it? You sure?"

"Pretty much. They didn't see or remember anything odd."

He pulled out his little notebook again. "You want to give me their names?"

"Professor Nelg Nelson and a young woman. Namaste."

"She have another name?"

Em thought of Fernando. "One name seems to be enough these days."

"You so sure of your bartender that you gave up a whole day to track down useless information?"

"I am," Em nodded. "Sophie had no motive for killing Harold."

"Maybe she just went off. Went nuts." He paused for a second. "Harold was into a lot of things. Maybe they were doing a drug deal and it went sour."

"What do you mean?" Em asked.

"Apparently almost everybody around here knew the old man was growing *pakalolo* on quite a few of the properties he took care of. A couple of plants here and there hidden in the gardens and the outdoor showers."

"You're kidding."

"I don't kid about stuff like that." He glanced over at Sophie. "Maybe she was somehow connected."

"Look." She lowered her voice. "I know Sophie looks hard core with all the tats and the piercings, but she's just a kid who's had some real rough times. Like you said, she made some bad choices. In the three months I've known her, she's never shown me anything but respect. She's conscientious. She's never been late for work."

"Except for the night of the murder," he reminded her.

"She doesn't do drugs. She doesn't even drink."

"In front of you."

Exasperated, Em sighed. "You can't tell a book by its cover. I thought you were a detective—as in somebody who wants to solve crimes."

"Maybe I already have," Roland told her. "You think you and the dancing Nancy Drews can do better?"

"At least we're trying."

"Stay out if this, Nancy. And keep those nuts in line."

"Then hurry up and find the real killer," she shot back.

The hot, fire-dancing detective did his smooth eyebrow lift and walked out.

12

Big Plans Afoot

Since no one wanted to eat anything that came out of the old *imu*, as soon as KPD gave the okay, Uncle Louie came up with a plan to move the entire luau staging area. That meant a week without ticket sales, but Kiki suggested making a big deal out of dedicating and blessing the new pit when it was finished. They'd make it a memorial of sorts for Harold and a celebration of a new beginning. The occasion was sure to bring in locals as well as tourists.

Kimo and the husband Lillian constantly referred to as "MyBob", volunteered to dig up the posts and move the old luau hut across the parking lot. They hired some strapping young men to dig the new *imu*.

The hard bodies worked bare-chested and glistened with sweat. The Hula Maidens were more than happy to make sure the beefy guys had plenty of water and sodas to drink. In between, the women practiced dancing on the shady side of the building. Car loads of tourists on their way to snorkel at the end of the road noticed the dancers and, unable to tell good hula from bad, they stopped to watch and ended up ordering drinks and lunch.

In the middle of the commotion, as Em carried an order of fish and chips out to the front lanai, she noticed Leilani Cabral pulling into Harold's driveway in her black Mercedes. Leilani got out and made a beeline for the Goddess.

Em waited for her near the steps, happy just to be outside on such a lovely day. Music from the Maidens' boom box filled the air with strains of the *Hukilau Hula*. Leilani joined Em on the lanai. Though they'd never met, Leilani filled Em's expectation of a realtor worthy of the name Shark Lady. No doubt Ms. Cabral would be every bit as successful in the O.C.

Leilani was more beautiful than the photos on her For Sale signs.

Her raven hair was cut in a stylish retro wedge worthy of Posh. Dressed in upscale designer resort wear, she accessorized with plenty of gold and jade bling. Her toenails were painted Mandarin red.

"I'm sorry about your uncle," Em said after she introduced herself.

"*Mahalo.*" Leilani shook her head. "It's still such a shock." She looked around. "I'm surprised your business hasn't suffered."

Em shrugged. "You know how people are. The tourists have no idea what happened and the locals have a dark sense of humor. We've filled in the old *imu* and moved the luau hut across the parking lot. We're having a dedication and a memorial to your uncle next Wednesday. I hope you'll come."

"I'll try. I suppose I should sit down with your uncle soon and discuss the parking lot easement—since I'm inheriting the property."

Em hoped there wouldn't be a hassle. A corner of the two properties contained Harold's driveway. The easement had always been a bone of contention between Louie and Harold.

"That shouldn't be a problem," Em said, though she figured Leilani wasn't dubbed Shark Lady for nothing. "Just let us know when it'll be convenient to meet."

She wondered what Leilani planned to do with the place. More than likely the old plantation cottage would be torn down and replaced by another MacMansion on the beach. Even after just a few months living here, Em could understand why the locals were so discouraged by what was happening on Kauai.

Just then a KPD cruiser pulled into a parking stall closest to the lanai, and Detective Sharpe stepped out.

"I'd better be going," Leilani said. "I'll call to set up a meeting."

Em's attention was drawn to the tall, mocha-skinned detective heading for the steps. "Great," she told Leilani. "Whenever."

The smile Roland and Leilani exchanged was telling. Apparently Kiki's suspicions were right—Shark Lady and the Fire Dancer definitely had a history. Was it really over? Em wondered.

"Nice to see you again so soon, Roland." Leilani smiled as she passed him on the steps. "Are you getting anywhere with the investigation?"

Roland glanced at Em and then away. "Sure. But these things take time. I'll be in touch when we come up with something concrete."

Em watched Roland's gaze trail Leilani as she walked across the lot toward Harold's.

"She inherited the place," Em informed him. "Maybe that's motive."

"There you go again playing detective. I've already looked into that angle. Leilani's got more money than she can count."

"I'll be sad to see the old house go."

"Inevitable. What's all the commotion out back?"

"New luau hut going up. Would you like something to eat? Lunch? A soda?" she offered.

"Most owners think cops are bad for business."

She noticed a few of the tourists watching them. "Around here it just gives people something to talk about."

He stepped up onto the lanai. "I'll take a burger, if you throw in fries."

"You got it."

He followed her into the dim interior. Kimo had been called in off construction duty to fill lunch orders in the kitchen. Sophie was behind the bar, laughing with a local surfer. She lost her smile the minute she spotted Roland. Em walked Sharpe to a small table in back.

"So business is still good, I see?" he said.

"Definitely. We've moved the luau hut and the *imu*, which means we had to skip the luau this week but there'll be a big dedication next week with a blessing and all. A memorial for Harold."

"Making lemonade out of lemons?"

"I guess you could say that."

His dark eyes scanned the crowded room. "Looks like things are still going great."

"They are." She refused to be embarrassed about the fact that Harold's murder had spiked business. It was what it was.

"Did you know your uncle was turned down for a second mortgage on this place a short time before you moved here?" He asked.

"No. I didn't. What does that have to do with anything?"

"The business was sinking fast until you arrived with a boat load of fresh ideas."

"If you're accusing me of killing Harold I'll take back the burger and fries."

Roland left as soon as he polished off his lunch but things didn't settle down until 4:00. Most of the Maidens had drifted off to their homes as soon as the hunks were gone, and the luau hut was secure in its new spot in back.

Em was in the office putting the finishing touches on the menu she'd worked up for Fernando when Marlene Lockhart, aka The Defector, breezed in. Em was tempted to throw herself across her notes so the woman wouldn't find out about Fernando's party. Kiki was convinced Marlene was always trying to steal her event bookings. If Marlene knew they were catering Fernando's affair she'd probably want all the details. Em wouldn't put it past her to call Fernando and try to persuade him to use her services instead.

"Hello, darling. Is that handsome uncle of yours around?" Marlene paused in the doorway and peered around the small room as if expecting Louie might be under the desk or hidden in the lateral file cabinet.

Em had to hand it to her. Marlene was always well put-together, not an easy task on an island where the trade winds wreaked havoc with everybody's hair. Kiki warned Em early on that it was a bad hair island and that she shouldn't try too hard. Somehow Marlene managed to keep her blond hair coiffed in a pageboy that rarely moved. Her outfits were all name designer-sportswear and every day she sported a different color theme. Today it was hot pink. Her plumeria earrings, her blouse, her shorts, her manicured nails and even her sandals, adorned with big fluffy silk flowers, were all various shades of hot pink.

"Hi Marlene," Em said. "Louie's over at the house."

"Great. I'll just run over and see what he's up to." Marlene smiled.

Fernando was due to arrive shortly. Em could only hope Louie would entertain Marlene until the sit-down with Fernando was over. She definitely didn't want the woman running into the celebrity.

When Marlene started to head back through the bar, Em stopped her.

"Here," she said, jumping up out of the chair behind the desk. "Go through the back door. It's shorter that way."

Em had barely closed the door behind Marlene when Sophie walked into the office.

"Head's up. Limo out front," she said.

"So much for keeping his arrival quiet." Em shook her head. She grabbed the menu and headed for the bar. On the way past the kitchen she called out to Kimo.

"Fernando's here! Got that *pupu* platter and the luau sampler ready?"

"Yep. Get 'em."

Kimo Godwin was a knight in shining armor. Born and raised in an old island family, Kimo could cook, build, repair anything, play the uke and sing. Kiki was a lucky woman when she married her *hapa-haole* husband. Em didn't know what the Goddess would do without him.

When Fernando came waltzing in, he was everything Em expected. According to his website, he'd been born and raised in Spain, a child prodigy who began performing piano concerts when he was five. He was virtually unknown until he stepped into Liberace's barely cold spotlight at Caesar's Palace.

The gold sequins adorning the huge orange hibiscus flowers on Fernando's custom Aloha shirt caught the dim light that filtered down from dusty blue-glass ball floats and puffer fish lamps overhead. A pair of knee length satin shorts and rhinestone encrusted flip flops completed the outfit.

Once inside, Fernando lowered his Gucci sunglasses and peered over the frames at Em.

"Fernando has arrived," he said.

Em offered her hand in greeting. "I see that. I'm so happy to meet you. I'm Emily Johnson. My uncle, Louie Marshall, owns the Tiki Goddess."

Fernando glanced over his shoulder. "My assistant Wally will join us soon."

"Let's go back to the office, where it's private." She indicated the bar. "Sophie will show him in. What can we get you to drink?"

"Dom Perignon?"

At a loss, Em glanced at Sophie.

"Oh, so sorry. We ran out last night," Sophie said smoothly. "Shipment's not in yet."

"Sorry," Em apologized. "How about one of my uncle's specialties? He's a renowned mixologist."

Fernando appeared uncertain for a moment, then he waved his hand. "Whatever you think Fernando would like. We leave it up to you."

"*Huli Huli* Boolie?" Sophie suggested.

"How about a Mango Tango?" Em shot back. A Mango Tango didn't pack as much punch. She didn't want Fernando out cold until he had reviewed the menu and signed a contract.

"Ah," Fernando nodded. "It is so good that you two keep the native language alive."

Em smiled as she led the way back to the office.

Forty minutes later, with the help of his assistant, Fernando had polished off three Mango Tangos and a generous *pupu* platter. He was draped across the arm of Wally Williams, the man seated beside him.

Wally was Fernando's height, though his bouffant hairstyle made him appear taller and resembled a bleached-blond football helmet. Em wondered if Wally consulted Donald Trump's stylist. It reminded her of something else, but at the moment she couldn't quite place it.

Wally was obviously more than Fernando's assistant. He doted on the man, running back and forth to the bar for drink refills and agreeing with all of Fernando's menu choices—Kimo's famous chicken thighs, egg rolls, crab leg salad and ginger fried chicken.

It was decided that Kimo would attend the party to cook and serve the barbequed chicken satay fresh off the grill. Em would be there to supervise and serve and Uncle Louie would bartend. Louie was the only unknown in the equation, but Em figured she could keep an eye on him.

After the meeting Fernando had Wally check out the bar so that he could make an exit without being seen. When Wally returned and assured him the coast was clear, Fernando looked more disappointed than relieved.

They had nearly made it outside when Leilani Cabral breezed in.

"Fernando!" she rushed up to the star, took both his hands in hers. "You naughty boy! I didn't know you were on island until I heard from someone at the Post Office. Luckily I saw your limo parked outside. What are you doing here? I thought you weren't coming in until next week."

"Fernando is *so* happy to have closed the deal and have a home on Kauai that we are hosting a gala in three days. Of course, you will be invited. In fact, Fernando was going to contact you in regards to a guest list."

"I'll be happy to help, but don't you think it's a little soon? You don't even have keys to the place yet."

"Ah, but we cannot wait to move in. After the party, we will start to break the ground and build the new guest house, pool, and screening room." He leaned closer to Leilani, as if to share a secret. He didn't bother to lower his voice.

"Fernando has signed a film contract. Soon we will be appearing in a major motion picture from the Warner Brothers!" He flexed his fingers as if there were a piano in the middle of the Goddess and he was about to play.

Obviously taken off guard, Leilani said, "That's wonderful, but—"

"Right now, Fernando will go and visit with your Uncle Harold. We find him such a colorful character. He lives nearby, yes?"

Leilani's face fell. "I'm so sorry. I haven't had time to contact you yet about him. My uncle . . . " She paused and heaved a heavy sigh. "My uncle died last week. I've been interviewing new landscape architects for you."

"No!" Fernando covered his mouth with both hands. "Harold is *muerto?*"

"Worse than dead. He was murdered," Leilani whispered. Her gaze touched on Sophie for a split second.

"But why?" Fernando cried. He reached for Wally's arm and leaned on the other man for support.

"We don't know who killed Harold or why yet," Leilani said. "The police are still investigating."

"This is terrible. Horrible. We spoke to him just the week before last. We liked him so much. He was a . . . how do you say it? He was a colorful character."

"You spoke to him? Before he died?" Leilani hiked the strap of her designer bag a bit higher on her shoulder. "What about?"

Fernando nodded. "About our plans for the property, the gardens. He said he had something very, *very* important to tell us."

"He did?" Leilani hung on Fernando's every word.

"He said he could not speak of it over the phone."

"Why don't I walk you out to your car? I'll call my office and have someone send out your keys. You can tell me more about your plans and what Uncle Harold had to say," Leilani suggested.

Em was searching for an excuse to walk out to the car with them when Uncle Louie and Marlene came strolling in through the back. His silver hair was sticking out all over his head and his *kukui* nut necklace was askew. Em sighed when she noticed his tapa print shirt was buttoned off kilter. Marlene was wearing a fresh coat of hot pink lipstick and a Cheshire cat smile.

"Aloha!" Louie greeted Fernando warmly. "This is quite an honor, Mr. Fernando. I have a couple of your CD's at the house."

If Louie did own one of Fernando's CD's, Em had never seen or heard Louie play it. She introduced her uncle and Marlene to the celebrity, then to Wally and Leilani.

"I've known Leilani for years. Seen her around Harold's." Louie grabbed her hand and held tight. "I'm so sorry about what happened to that old coot. He was a real bastard but we were neighbors for nearly forty years."

"*Mahalo.*" Leilani, obviously uncomfortable, tugged on Fernando's arm. "We were just leaving—"

Louie stared at her for a second too long, as if he'd already forgotten who she was. Then his vision cleared. He gazed toward the window facing Harold's house.

"Saw the police tramping around over there. Guess you'll be moving Harold's things out soon."

Leilani sighed. "I'm not sure. This is all very hard for me. I'm not sure when I'll get around to clearing the place out."

"Care to try a Great Ball of Fire? It's a brand new drink I concocted in honor of . . . "

Em quickly interrupted. "They've got to go, Uncle Louie. Leilani was just walking Fernando out to the limo." The last thing she needed was for Louie to launch into a conversation about Harold's commemorative drink.

"I can't tell you how much I admire your music, Mr. Fernando." Marlene left Louie's side and stepped closer to the entertainer. "To what do we owe this visit of yours? "

"We are holding a housewarming at the property Ms. Cabral sold us."

"Ah. And have you an event planner all lined up?"

"Ms. Johnson here is going to . . . to . . . " Fernando weaved a bit and leaned heavily on Wally.

"Cater the party," Wally finished for him.

"I really think we should be going," Leilani stepped up to protect her client's privacy.

"Great idea," Em agreed.

Leilani, Fernando and Wally quickly bid them a hasty aloha.

"I'll walk you out to your car, honey," Louie offered Marlene.

She paused, assessing Em for a moment. "Are you sure you can handle an upscale event like this, darling?" Before Em could answer she added, "I'd be happy to take over. I've worked with high end clients before."

Em forced a smile as wide as Marlene's. "You're too kind, but we've got it covered. Thanks. "

"Well, if you find yourself in over your head, give me a call."

Louie slipped his arm around Marlene's shoulder and winked at Em. "Isn't Marlene just the sweetest, kindest thing?"

"Just." Em followed them out to the lanai and spotted Lil Smith in the parking lot. Lil was the first of the Maidens to arrive before the evening crowd trickled in. The minute she laid eyes on Fernando, Lil's jaw dropped and her hand fluttered to her heart. She hurried over to the limo where Wally and Leilani were trying to pour the pianist inside.

Em heard Lil scream, "Ohmygosh! It's really you!"

A second later Lil was clinging to Fernando's right arm while Wally clung to his left and tried to tug him into the limo. Em raced down the stairs and headed across the lot. When she saw Lil next to Wally, Em realized why Wally's hair looked so familiar; Lillian's was styled the same way, only it was pink.

Lil was obviously beside herself. Her mouth was going a mile a minute and she kept taking her glasses off and on.

"I have all your albums. I have a scrapbook with every photo, every clipping I could find. MyBob and I have seen you perform in Las Vegas four times! When I left Iowa I never in a million years thought that I'd ever see you in person again. Imagine! Right here at the Goddess." That said Lil must have run out of breath. Her eyes rolled up into her head and she fainted dead away.

Sophie came running out of the bar to join Em.

Fernando looked down and shrugged. "What Fernando does to women is amazing, no?"

Wally finally succeeded in pulling him into the limo. Leilani jumped in after him and Em sighed in frustration. Now she might never know what Harold had said to Fernando.

Em knelt beside Lil, whose eyes were fluttering, but the woman wasn't coherent. Em looked up at Sophie.

"Grab her other arm. We've got to get her inside before someone drives by and puts out the word that we've got another body lying around."

13

Caught in the Act

By Wednesday the Goddess luau was in full swing again. The late afternoon sun was shining low in the sky. The *imu* was ready for re-dedication.

As Kiki predicted, ticket sales soared. Locals never missed an event where they could eat and pick up a little gossip. Mainland schools were out for the summer and tourist season was building. A huge pig was roasting in the new *imu* out back.

The Maidens gathered in front of the thatched roofed Luau Hut. Flora adjusted her girdle. Lil fanned her face with her hands. Big Estelle was smiling from ear to ear, completely ignoring her mother, who had accidentally jammed the Gad-About hand control and was spinning in circles. Kiki was front and center. For the evening's show she had designed new floral hair adornments interspersed with the tips of peacock feathers.

Puana Kimokane, a local kahuna, was ready to begin a *pule*, a prayer, to bless the new *imu*. The bar emptied of all but the regulars, who were permanently glued to their barstools. Everyone made their way back to the pit area to watch the opening ceremony.

Puana blew a conch shell to the four directions and then began a chant in Hawaiian. Afterward he translated. "I call upon *Akua* to bless this *imu*, to bless everyone in attendance and those who wanted to be here but could not. I call upon *Akua* to bless Harold Otanami, to keep him safe on his journey to the other side and his memory alive in our hearts and minds."

Puana posed, looking quite regal. Tourists snapped photos. *Kiawe*-scented smoke escaped the hot coals. Trish Oakley moved silently through the crowd taking photos of those gathered around. She had told Em earlier that she was convinced Harold's killer would be in attendance. On crime shows the killer always hung around at the victim's funeral—usually wearing a trench coat and shades, so Trish was on the lookout.

Em doubted anyone would show up in a trench coat, but everyone was in shades. She noticed Roland Sharpe behind a nice pair of Ray-Bans himself. He was dressed in a casual Aloha shirt and linen pants and though he tried to blend in, his stoic expression gave him away. Em knew that behind his dark sunglasses, he was carefully scanning the crowd.

After Puana finished, Kimo introduced the Maidens. Earlier, Em asked them to limit the performance to four songs, knowing they'd go on forever if she didn't. Better to get folks back inside, where they could order drinks.

The Maidens were wedged between the Luau Hut and the new pit. Em wished she'd asked Puana to mention to *Akua* to make the Maidens surefooted and keep them from falling into the *imu*.

Afraid to watch, she headed inside.

"I sent Buzzy into Hanalei to get more Tabasco," Sophie informed her when she reached the bar.

"Looks like Great Balls of Fire is a hit." Em thought folks looked glassy eyed sooner than usual.

"Your uncle is acting very weird tonight."

"What do you mean?"

"You know. Foggy."

Em knew. Sometimes Louie acted as if he'd just fallen off a taro truck. "Where is he?"

"He wandered outside."

Em sighed. She'd been on her feet since dawn. The last thing she wanted to do was chase after Louie. "Would you mind tracking him down and bringing him back? I'll take over here."

"Not a problem. I'd love to get outside for a couple minutes."

"That's what I figured."

"How was the blessing?" Sophie showed Em which order was up.

"Great. The Maidens have started dancing. Kimo should be bringing the *kalua* pig inside and then we can start the buffet line. I'll need all hands on deck."

"I'll find Louie and come right back," Sophie promised.

Sophie scanned the crowd. Louie was nowhere in sight, but she saw the back of the detective who just so happened to keep "dropping by" to see how things were going. She couldn't tell if he was dogging her, just doing his job, or if he had a thing for Em. She figured most likely all of the above.

Sophie hoped she wouldn't catch Louie and Marlene in the act as she headed for his house. But just then she caught sight of him slipping through the hedge that separated the Goddess parking lot from Harold's yard.

She waited long enough to be sure Detective Sharpe was looking the other way before she ducked behind an overweight family of visitors in matching Aloha wear and then crept through the hedge after Louie.

Harold had bragged that he'd been born in the house he lived in and had never left the island. He'd never been to Oahu. Never even seen Honolulu and didn't care to. He'd been perfectly content singing Karaoke two nights a week, adding upscale accounts to his client list, and driving everyone who worked at the Goddess crazy.

His yard showcased some of the crap he had salvaged. Rubber tires filled with dirt and planted with yellow and orange day lilies were scattered around. A four-foot-tall plush Bugs Bunny was strapped to the trunk of an African tulip tree. A bald Cabbage Patch Doll in a frilly pink pinafore was impaled upon a metal fence stake at the entrance to the driveway.

A collection of mildewed plastic chairs of all shapes, sizes and colors were lined up in a semi-circle in front of the house, as if someone might actually stop and sit down. Harold rarely had anyone over except for Leilani and a few of his septuagenarian, beer-swilling fishing buddies.

The rusted screen door was ajar and the interior door wide open. There was no sign of Louie anywhere.

Sophie glanced over her shoulder. Guitar and ukulele music drifted over from the Goddess as the Maidens danced to a North Shore favorite, *Hanalei Moon*.

"Louie?" She called his name as loud as she dared. She ran around the corner of the house, where she had a view of the yard all the way to the beach. He wasn't there or in the open garage. There was only one place he could be.

Sophie crept up the stairs to the porch. She paused just outside and hoarsely whispered, "Louie!"

Hearing no response, she opened the screen all the way and

stepped inside the front room. There were piles of papers, empty pizza boxes, and a hefty bag full of recyclable aluminum cans beside the sagging sofa. The only thing of value in the entire room was the five foot wide flat screen television which looked completely out of place in the ancient shack. The wooden floor creaked beneath her feet.

"Louie?" She whispered. The place gave her the creeps. She expected Harold to come stomping in any minute and start hollering at her in pidgin.

She headed for the kitchen. No sign of Louie, but there was a drawer partially opened near the sink. She walked over, pulled the drawer all the way open and found herself staring at a hand gun. She picked it up with her thumb and forefinger. It was so small the handle fit into the palm of her hand. *Python 357* was printed on the barrel. She checked the cylinder. The chambers were empty.

A thump from the back of the house made her jump. She dropped the gun into the drawer and slid it back the way she found it.

"Louie?" She whispered. "Where are you?" She paused to listen and heard nothing but the breeze wafting through the palms outside.

As she walked through the small living room, she nearly lost an acrylic nail trying to open a rusty cookie tin sitting on the coffee table. It was filled with old photos. She started shuffling through them and found one in faded sepia tones dated 1898. It pictured a Japanese woman in a lovely kimono. Others had been taken in Lihue during WWII. Then she came across a photo of Harold with Louie's wife, his tiki goddess, Irene Hickam.

They appeared to be in their teens, probably during high school. It was the only time Sophie had ever seen Harold's smile. The old guy had been shockingly handsome. His black hair was slicked back Elvis style, his Levi's were cuffed a la James Dean, and the sleeves of his white T shirt were rolled up above his biceps.

It had to have been a blow when Louie Marshall came along and stole his high school sweetheart, but not as much as the continuous torture of living next door and watching Irene and Louie share their lives, grow their business, and celebrate anniversary after anniversary, until Irene's sudden illness and death.

No wonder Harold had hated Louie.

Sophie put the photos back and pressed the lid onto the tin. Then she crept toward the dark hallway that led to the back room. She stopped in her tracks at a small console table shoved up against the wall. It held a lamp and a phone, a stack of papers, bills and store receipts. Right there beneath the phone was a list of names and phone numbers. When she saw Fernando's name near the bottom of the page, she figured it had to be Harold's client list.

She glanced toward the door, slipped the page out from beneath the phone, folded it into quarters and slipped it into her back pocket. Then she stepped into the short hallway.

"Damn it, Louie," she whispered. "Are you in here?"

The walls of the narrow hall intensified the sound of something large rustling around in the next room. It was either very big rat or the absentminded mixologist. She walked into the bedroom and found Louie on the floor beside the bed, sweeping his arm back and forth beneath it.

"Louie, get out of there." She stood over him as he gathered himself up and brushed dust balls off his Aloha shirt. "What are you doing here?"

"Looking for something," he said.

"What?"

He shrugged.

"We have to get out of here. Em needs you," she said.

"Em who?"

"Knock it off." It upset her to see him confused. Kiki had let her in on how the Maidens had exaggerated Louie's forgetfulness to lure Em to Kauai to save the Goddess. Louie wasn't as bad off as Em thought. "Come on, now. This place gives me the creeps."

She took his hand and led him out of the bedroom and back through the house. Just as they stepped out of the front door, the sound of tires on gravel set Sophie's nerves on edge.

Sure enough, Leilani's Mercedes was pulling into the drive. Shark Lady was sure to spot them if they didn't move fast. The car stopped beside the house.

Sophie grabbed Louie's hand. "Run!"

They darted off the far side of the lanai opposite the driveway. Looping behind the house, she paused long enough to peek around the corner of the garage. Sure enough, Leilani was out of the car, headed up the stairs.

"Is the coast clear?" Louie asked.

"Shh. She's staring at the lanai," Sophie whispered.

"Then let's make a run for it." Louie darted toward the hedge and disappeared between branches of foliage. Sophie ran after him, broke through to the other side and smacked right into Detective Roland Sharpe, KPD.

Louie was standing beside Roland, his expression that of a naughty five year old. Sophie broke out in a cold sweat and started clicking the stud in her tongue against her teeth.

"You two out for a little jog or what?" As usual, Detective Sharpe's was devoid of expression.

Louie smiled vacantly.

Sophie took a deep breath. "Louie wandered off. Em sent me to find him."

The detective scanned the parking lot and then looked toward the Otanami house. "So what were you two doing over there?"

Louie smiled benignly. "Went to pick limes. We ran out."

"So where are they? The limes."

Louie shrugged. "Not the right kind."

Just then Leilani Cabral appeared around the end of the driveway, walking at a fast clip.

"Oh, Roland. Lucky you're here. I was just about to call 911. I stopped by to pick up some paperwork and found the front door standing wide open. Then I saw *her* dart through the hedge." She pointed at Sophie and added, "She broke into my uncle's house."

Sophie couldn't see Sharpe's eyes behind his shades but she could feel the stink-eye he was giving her.

"I know how this looks, but Louie disappeared and Em sent me to find him." Sophie didn't know if she should throw Louie under the bus and admit that he'd gone inside first or not. Louie could always play the dementia card.

The officer turned to Louie. "Were you in the house?"

"What house?"

"Otanami's house."

"I guess so." Louie turned to Sophie. "Was I?"

She nodded.

"I knew it." Leilani yelled. "At the very least that's breaking and entering."

"The door was already open," Louie said. "I didn't break anything. Harold had something of mine and I want it back."

At this point, Sophie saw Em hurrying across the Goddess parking lot toward them. The sun was sinking lower in the late afternoon sky. The scent of succulent roast pig filled the air. Those gathered for the luau were on their third round of Great Balls of Fire already and feeling no pain. A small knot of guests drifted along in Em's wake, curious to hear the exchange.

"What's going on?" Em struggled to jam her stray blond hair back into a ponytail. She looked at Louie first, then Sophie.

"These two broke into my uncle's house," Leilani said.

"The door was open," Louie shrugged. "I went inside to get something of mine."

"I went in looking for Louie." Sophie added. "Like you told me to."

Em shoved her hands into her back pockets looking like she was at the end of her rope. It had been a long two weeks since the murder.

"What were you looking for, Uncle Louie? What did Harold have of yours?"

Louie thought for a second and shrugged, "Hell, I don't remember."

14

The Fire Dancing Detective

Em waited until Louie and Sophie walked away before she turned to Roland Sharpe, who towered over her. She couldn't help but notice what an effect Roland had on Leilani.

"Thanks for calming Leilani down and for letting Louie and Sophie off with a warning." Em had thanked him three times already. Relief didn't come close to what she was feeling. "I really did send Sophie after Louie. I have no idea what he was looking for in there. He might not know either."

"Just because I let them off easy this time doesn't mean I don't think they're up to no good. There's something going on and when I've got enough proof, I won't hesitate to start locking folks up—no matter who they are."

"Book 'em, Dano." The minute it was out, she wished she hadn't said it.

He pointed to the side of her head. "Your pony thing is on the loose."

She grabbed a lock of her ponytail that was dangling beside her cheek and tucked it behind her ear.

He watched intently. "You're the type who still believes in people, eh?"

"You don't?"

"No."

"Guilty until proven innocent? I don't think it's supposed to work that way."

"Something's up with your bartender."

"If I didn't trust her, I wouldn't have hired her," Em assured him.

"I've sent her description and ID to the airport officials. She can't get off the island. Unless she goes by boat."

"Oh, for heaven's sake."

"What nice little world are you from, lady?"

Nice little world? Her life had been anything *but* nice.

"In Southern California the body count usually reaches a solid ten before the first commercial airs on the nightly news, but I'm not about to give up on people yet."

"Yeah? Well just don't let all the flowers and rainbows around here fool you."

"It was pretty hard to miss the dead guy in our barbeque pit." She wasn't smiling. Harold's death was no laughing matter. They both knew it.

"*Imu.* If you're gonna live here, learn the lingo." He cracked the smallest of smiles.

"*Imu.* Schmeemu. Are you any closer to finding out who really killed Harold?"

"I can't divulge any information."

"That sounds like a no. So that's why you're hanging around here trying to blend into the luau crowd; you have no suspects other than Sophie." She rose up on tip toe, crooked her finger, indicating he should come closer. He lowered his head.

Em whispered, "Your disguise isn't working. You look like a detective in an Aloha shirt."

She took a step back. "How about I hire you for the show? You could fire dance and keep an eye on things at the same time instead of just showing up unannounced and spooking everyone."

"I'm not spooking anyone but the bad guys. Besides, you can't afford me."

"So I've been told."

He drew back. "By who?"

"Kiki. But she said you're worth it."

"Kiki talks too much."

"That's our Kiki. Besides, the Maidens would insist on sharing the spot light with you and with their luck, you'd end up torching one of them."

"One hell of a finale, though."

It was Em's turn to smile. "We've had enough catastrophes for a while. Thanks anyway."

Roland tried to appear casual as he checked out the gathering. There was a sizeable crowd lined up at the buffet table on the lanai. It was a shock when Em found herself wishing he was still looking at her. She glanced away for a second and, when she caught him watching her again, she blushed.

"Before you moved here I used to drive by this place and there'd be hardly anybody inside," he said.

"Is that a compliment? I thought you attributed our crowd to Harold's murder."

"That, too. For real, though. If this keeps up, pretty soon you'll be able to hire some quality luau entertainment."

"And cut the Hula Maidens? They're the reason I'm here."

"You really got this business turned around for your uncle."

"It hasn't been easy." She thought about the legal pad full of ideas that were still on hold.

"How do you mean?"

"Once Louie and the Maidens convinced me to stay, I came up with a list improvements for the bar. The building needs a facelift inside and out but there is not enough money to cover that. So I went with things that didn't cost much, like tablecloths and repainting instead of replacing the plywood floor with hardwood. I also thought about adding additional lanai space but . . . "

"But folks like the Goddess the way it is."

"So I found out." She shrugged. "Not only that, but all the money and determination in the world can't work miracles if popular opinion and the county planning department conspire against you. So, I made a few small changes instead of big ones. Booked nightly entertainers who work cheap and let the Maidens dance almost nightly. I've learned there really is such a thing as Hawaiian time and that you can't buck the system around here."

"Yeah, and right now Hawaiian time is ticking." He glanced at his watch. "I'd better get going."

She needed to get back inside, too.

"There's always a place for you in our show—when you lower your rates," she added.

"Yeah? Well, you get what you pay for." Sharpe walked away without looking back.

15

Fernando's Hideaway

From the rising pitch of conversation throughout Fernando's glass and concrete home, Em could tell that her idea of a Retro Polynesian theme for the housewarming was a hit.

Though Shark Lady made no secret of the fact she wished Fernando had chosen more upscale catering, even she appeared to be in a good mood. Thankfully, as Fernando had told Em, he had his mind set on helping out his new North Shore neighbors by throwing his business their way.

Undeterred, Leilani arrived and positioned herself in the entry of the luxurious home and assumed the role of self-appointed hostess, greeting guests who were arriving in vintage Aloha attire. The women showed up in everything from sleek strapless dresses from the 40s that were worthy of Dorothy Lamour, to paisley print kaftans from the 70s. The men wore silkies, Aloha shirts worth a small fortune at antique and collectables shops.

Em was busy circulating through the luxuriously appointed rooms. The house was like nothing she'd ever seen. It even had a manmade stream that ran through the great room and meandered out into the gardens where it flowed down a faux waterfall into a pond full of exotic koi.

She walked out to the front lanai to see if Leilani needed another drink. In black pants and a black Tiki Goddess tank top, Em was no competition beside the realtor in her sleek, crimson, Mandarin-style gown.

"Would you like one of Uncle Louie's special cocktails, Leilani? He's come up with a new recipe named Fernando's Hideaway." The drink was aqua, to match Fernando's eyes and boa, and served in a hurricane glass.

Leilani ignored her for a moment as she smiled and nodded to someone across the room.

"See that man?" She nodded in his direction. "That's Marley Martin, lead guitarist for the Mad Green Zombies. I sold him a home not far up the road last year."

"That's nice. Would you like a Hideaway? *Pupu?*"

Shark Lady rolled her eyes. "I make it a habit never to drink anything blue, and I rarely eat. I'll stick with champagne."

Em was about to go refill a tray with drinks when Fernando joined them.

"It's going well, yes?" He tossed one end of the aqua boa over his shoulder and indicated his white jumpsuit with a wave of his hand. "This is a copy of the very jumpsuit worn by Elvis in Blue Hawaii. The wedding scene. We look fierce, no?"

"Definitely," Em said.

Leilani merely smiled. Fernando made a habit of focusing on himself. Em wondered how she was ever going to find out what he had told Leilani the day he mentioned his conversation with Harold, which had to have been one of the last talks that anyone had had with poor Mr. Otanami. Em had no idea how to bring up the subject without sounding as if she were prying.

Then again, Fernando was already so inebriated he might not think a thing of it. He probably wouldn't even remember this conversation later.

Things had slowed down a bit. Everyone seemed to be happily chatting and filling up on *pupus* while they waited for the entertainment to start. Em decided to take a chance while Leilani was busy chatting up a late arrival about the sale of the property next door.

Em said, "Fernando, if you have a moment, I'd love to finally introduce you to our chef, Kimo."

"We would love to meet Mr. Kimo."

"Actually, it's Mr. Godwin. Kimo Godwin."

"We will meet him, too."

Fernando followed her out to the back lanai overlooking the expansive grounds. The lawn and gardens extended to the beach, where low waves rolled onto a pristine shoreline. She paused a few feet from the barbeque where Kimo was basting skewers threaded with chicken satay. So far there had been no indication that Roland or the KPD was any closer to solving Harold's murder and though Detective Sharpe hadn't come right out and admitted it, everyone knew he was focusing on Sophie. Whatever Fernando said might help.

Em took a deep breath and said, "Fernando, you were one of the last people to speak to Harold Otanami. Do you know anything that might help with the murder investigation?"

He shrugged and took another sip of his Hideaway. "He was worried about our building permit. It was impossible for him to believe the plan was already approved." Fernando smiled, showing blinding white teeth. "But of course, Fernando's name moves mountains."

Em nodded. Escrow had just closed and yet he was about to build. She figured Fernando or his "people" had bribed someone in the planning department.

"I am, after all, a big star." He polished off the drink in the hurricane glass.

"I doubt anyone can forget that." She wondered if there was any connection between Harold and the planning department. Did Harold know someone was on the take? If so, maybe he'd been blackmailing them.

"I am beloved by many." Fernando sighed. "We begin construction in the morning. We will start by grading the land." He pointed across the property, showing Em where he planned to build a huge pool, a pool house and additional guest residences. The structures would be situated away from the main house as close to the lot line of the adjoining property as allowed.

"That's quite a project. Are you worried about all the noise?" Em wondered if any of the neighbors had tried to stop the permit process.

Fernando waved his hand as if brushing away a pesky fly.

"Of course not. We have friends who bought the estate next door. They will stay in their Malibu home until we are finished building everything. The noise, pooh, no problem for them."

Just then Kimo walked over with a tray full of satay and mini crab cakes. Em introduced Kimo to the pianist and Fernando selected a crab cake and popped it in his mouth. He swallowed and took another before Kimo walked off.

"We are naturally slim and we eat what we want," Fernando told Em.

She sighed and tried to sound as if she were making an offhanded comment.

"I wonder why poor Harold was so worried?" she said.

"He was worried about our fish. He said the *koi punda* were very disturbed. This is a fish, no? *Koi punda?* We were afraid something was wrong with our fabulous *koi*. But now that we are here, we see nothing wrong with them. They are one of the reasons Fernando wanted this place so badly."

"There's something wrong with the koi?" Em fought to put the pieces together.

"Harold spoke of the bones of the *koi punda*. He was very upset about them." Fernando heaved a sigh and stared into the bottom of his empty glass. "But now we will never know about the fish bones, eh? Poor Harold is *muerto.*"

Wally Williams joined them outfitted in a vintage terrycloth pool jacket and matching swim trunks trimmed with tapa cloth fabric details on the pockets. He smiled and handed Fernando another Hideaway, took his partner's empty glass and deftly set it on Kimo's tray as he passed by.

"So, what are we talking about?" Wally wanted to know.

"The last words of Harold to me." Fernando sipped the fresh Hideaway through a green florescent straw with a pink paper umbrella attached.

"Ah. The fish bones." Wally reached up and patted his hair. Tonight it looked as if his hair spray had been applied with an air gun.

Fernando plucked a toothpick with two honeydew melon balls skewered on it out of his drink and waved them in the air.

"This is why we break the ground tomorrow."

Em was completely lost. "Why?"

"Because Harold said the fish are upset. And so Fernando's mind is made up. Tomorrow we begin. I have a special nail belt I will wear with my sequined Levis. I will be an inspiration to the crew." Fernando ate the melon balls.

Wally hooked his arm through Fernando's. "Marley Martin wants to talk to you about Las Vegas."

With a nod to Em, they wove their way across the lanai.

Em was headed over to the serving table to fill up a tray and pass *pupus* around until she saw party planner Marlene Lockhart breeze through the living room in a vintage muumuu the color of merlot. A row of koa wood bangles wreathed her right arm. Her fingernails were the same wine red as her muumuu.

Leilani had given Em given a copy of Fernando's guest list before the event. Marlene definitely wasn't on it.

"Hello, darling," Marlene gave Em air kisses. "I asked Louie if he thought I should drop by once things got rolling just in case you found yourself in over your head. Of course, he said yes."

"Actually, everything's going great."

"It's such a large affair, I thought—"

"You're very kind, but we've got it covered." Em quickly turned the topic. "That's a very nice muumuu."

Marlene ran her hands down the front of the gown and then shook her head.

"It's a little long but Louie loves it on me. The hem is soaked from the wet grass, but I'm sure it'll dry without staining." She scanned the room. "Oh. There's Louie. I'll just flit over and see if I can give him a hand."

"I'm sure he's counting on it."

Marlene looked around. "This is so much nicer than that dump you're all usually stuck in."

"My uncle loves that dump."

"Yes, well. Thank you, dear. I hate to keep him waiting. I'll see you later."

"Later." Em watched Marlene walk away before she hustled back to the outdoor kitchen. On the way Em overheard one of the guests say that he planned to hire the Goddess caterers next time he threw a party. Smiling, she moved on, anxious to get back to the main room.

Ice rattled in the martini shaker as Louie hustled up more Hideaways and regaled guests with the stories that inspired the Tiger Shark Attack and an equally popular drink dubbed Blood on the Beach. His recitals of the legends never failed to gather a crowd. With Marlene cooing beside him, he really turned on the charm.

Trish moved unobtrusively around the house taking photos. She'd come early to shoot the setup, food, and decorations. Tall cocktail tables covered in retro fabric were scattered around the lanai. The buffet table was spread out beneath a huge white tent on the rolling lawn. Kimo had borrowed someone's outrigger canoe, filled it with ice, bottles of water and soft drinks. Flaming tiki torches rimmed the perimeter of the lanai. The flames flickered in the night breeze and the scent of citronella lighter almost discouraged the mosquitoes.

Trish had suggested putting together an album Em could present to future catering clients. Em was just thinking about an expanded menu when Kimo walked up. He looked like a slow-moving ice floe in the white chef's coat she had insisted he wear. Now she was sorry, for the portly man was dripping sweat like a damp brown Pillsbury Doughboy.

"The Hula Maidens are ready to start the entertainment," he told Em. "But Big Estelle can't find her mother."

There was plenty of room for all the dancers to fit comfortably on Fernando's huge cement lanai that extended over the garden. Kiki had wanted to set up spotlights for the show, but Em thought they'd be a mood killer, so she had Kimo set up tiki torches all around. Kiki refused to be responsible if any of the maidens' adornments caught fire—which conjured the image of Roland Sharpe fire dancing. Kiki had wanted the detective to perform with them since Fernando could well afford it, but Roland was on duty tonight.

"So should they start the ceremony?" Kimo was waiting for an answer.

Em was about to say yes when Lil ran up. "We can't find Little Estelle anywhere," she whispered. "Big Estelle won't dance until she knows where her mother is."

Em set down the tray. "It's pretty hard to misplace someone on a motorized scooter. She's got to be here somewhere. Have you checked the whole house?"

When Lil nodded, the floral wreath encircling her head slid down to her nose. Momentarily blinded, she shoved the lei back into place.

"Trish said she saw her earlier riding around the house polishing off people's leftover drinks."

Em groaned.

Lil nodded, her pink hair neatly sprayed down. "Suzi saw her drive the Gad-About down the ramp beside the back lanai, but no one has actually seen her for forty minutes."

Big Estelle ran up. "My mother's missing!"

"I know," Em said. Big Estelle was unusually pale. "Are you all right?"

"Of course I'm not all right," the other woman snapped. "I'm seventy-five, for heaven's sake, and my ninety-five year old mother just drove off on a motorized scooter. Do you know this place is fifteen acres? With streams and ponds? And beachfront? She could be anywhere. She could be dead by now."

"Calm down." Lillian put her hand on Big Estelle's shoulder. "Take a deep breath. Go to that happy, happy place inside you."

"I'm going to shove something up your happy-happy place if you don't help me find my mother." Big Estelle took a threatening step toward Lil, who immediately burst into tears.

"You'll find her," Em said, stepping between them. "Round up Kiki and Suzi and Flora. Start looking. I have to work the room. Just give me the high sign when you find her and then start the dancing."

Em wished Sophie was there. They could have used another pair of hands, but someone had to stay behind and run the Goddess. To prove she was right about Sophie—to herself as much as anyone else—Em left the girl working the Goddess alone.

Louie was no help, even if he didn't have Marlene at his side. No doubt she was charming the guests and touting her own business between breaths. They were just lucky Kiki hadn't run into Marlene yet. Kiki would definitely have it out with the woman for party crashing.

Em asked Kimo to fix her another tray. Before he finished, Wally Williams hurried over to her.

"I can't find Fernando." His brow and upper lip were damp with beads of sweat. "I've looked all over the house." His voice broke.

"We have a missing Hula Maiden, too."

"Fernando is not interested in Hula Maidens. If you get my drift."

Em shrugged. "I know that. I just meant he's not the only one missing. Maybe he's out looking for Little Estelle. I'm sure he's fine."

Wally quickly became more and agitated. Em was afraid he might start tearing at his hair—if his fingers could crack the lacquer.

"What should we do?" His voice went up an octave.

Kimo finished piling bacon-wrapped water chestnuts on the tray. Em motioned for him to walk it around the room.

"Where was Fernando the last time you saw him?" Em asked Wally.

"On the front drive. He walked out to tell Leilani goodbye. I came in to get him another drink. Leilani forgot her keys and came back to get them. She said Fernando had run off to tell that old woman on the little sit-down thing to stop tearing up the grass. Then she left."

Kiki ran past the window waving the mini flashlight on her key ring.

Em hoped to God Little Estelle hadn't run over Fernando.

"Let's go look for him," she suggested.

"Oh, thank you so much." Wally stared out toward the darkened lawn. "It's such a jungle out there. I think we should enlist all the guests." Before she could say anything, he jumped up on a chair and clapped his hands.

"Please! Everyone listen up. Fernando is missing. I'd like you to help us find him."

"Is there a prize?" Marley Martin called from across the room.

"I'll create a new cocktail," Louie shouted. "Name it after the winner."

Guests began to wander onto the lanai with drinks in hand. The grass was still damp from quickly passing trade showers. Not many people cared to venture far from the bar. Just as Em and Wally headed for the front exit, Suzi came running in.

"We finally found Little Estelle." She rolled her eyes.

"Was Fernando with her? Is she all right?"

Suzi shook her head. "No Fernando yet. Little Estelle's out cold. Smells like a rum distillery. Looks like she got going downhill too fast and the Gad-About tipped over. Thank God she's not hurt. Big Estelle and the gals just loaded her into their van so she can sleep it off while we perform."

"You're not going on just yet. Fernando is missing. We were on our way out to find him." She turned to Wally. "If you want, go ahead without me."

"Oh, no. I can't go out there alone. Too many geckoes. Rats. Frogs. Who knows what else?" His hands were shaking. All the color had drained from his face except for two bright blotches of cranberry blush. "I have panic attacks. I need my Xanax." He looked as if he were about to hyperventilate.

Em turned to Suzi. "Go get a plastic bag from Kimo. Anything. A Ziplock, whatever. Bring it back and sit with Wally. Make him breathe into it. And find his Xanax." Suzi hustled off. Em turned to Wally. "You stay here. Try to relax."

She heard guests calling out to one another across the grounds. There was no way they could cover all fifteen acres in the dark. She hoped Fernando hadn't wandered very far.

She followed the artificial stream that flowed through the house. Just past the front entrance, it passed beneath a low cement bridge that arched over the driveway. Beneath the water, brilliant orange and white koi glittered in the torchlight.

She heard the rush of the faux waterfall. When she took another step, something furry brushed the side of her foot. Em yelped and jumped back. It was one thing to step on a frog in the dark but there was nothing small and furry on island other than a stray cat. Or a rat.

She strained to see. Something long and slim trailed out across the grass near her foot. *No snakes in Hawaii,* she kept reminding herself. At least there weren't supposed to be. She nudged whatever it was with her toe.

Then Em bent over and poked the thing. When it didn't move, she picked it up between her thumb and forefinger.

Matted aqua feathers. A sopping wet boa. A shiver ran down her spine.

"Fernando?" she called in a stage whisper. Then she called out again but there was no answer.

She scanned the darkness and tried calling a few more times. Surely his white Elvis garb would stand out against the shadows, but there was no sign of him. She ran back to the house hoping to find a flashlight around somewhere. She stepped inside the expansive open-air entry. No one was around. She was crossing the bridge when she glanced down, her gaze drawn to something in the water. Something large and white.

Helpless, she watched as Fernando's body floated beneath the bridge and came out on the other side. Flanked and nudged along by his precious koi, he was face up, headed for the pool beneath the waterfall.

She screamed for help and ran along the edge of the stream, following the body. Fernando's eyes were wide open, staring sightlessly at the starry sky. Koi nudged him along, some nibbling him with fat fish lips.

The water was three feet deep at most. Em took a deep breath, stepped into the shallow stream and grabbed his wrist. She tugged and pulled but couldn't get him out. All she could do was keep the body from floating on down to the small pool at the end of the stream.

She continued to yell for help and didn't stop until Uncle Louie and Wally finally came running out. Wally took one look at Fernando and fainted. Marlene nearly fell over Wally on her way out. When she saw Fernando she covered her mouth with both hands and went tearing back inside.

Louie stared down at Fernando's body for a second. Then, as he climbed into the stream beside Em to help pull the pianist out, she heard him mumble to himself, "Gotta be orange. Something the color of the koi. Orange juice, maybe? I'll call it Koi Pond Kicker."

16

Deja vu

By the time Em heard Roland had arrived at the estate, it was past ten-thirty p.m. No less than six KPD units, a fire truck and an EMT rescue vehicle lined the drive of Kauai's latest celebrity homeowner.

Kauai's latest *dead* celebrity homeowner.

Em was impressed. The uniformed officers had things in hand in minutes. Party guests had been assembled inside the house. Two officers were stationed to make sure no one left as guests waited to give their names, contact numbers, and answer preliminary questions. Wally was on a sofa, sobbing uncontrollably beside Marley Martin.

Roland had just looked Em's way when Wally suddenly passed out, again, collapsing onto the lap of the guitar player. The detective headed straight for her.

"Pretty interesting," he spoke without a greeting. "The crew of the Goddess on the second murder scene in less than three weeks. And what a surprise—*you* found the body."

Speechless, Em blamed her blush on anger.

"Nobody leaves," Roland told one of the uniformed officers as the policeman passed by. Then he turned to Em again. "Especially you."

"Especially me what?"

"Don't leave until I give you the okay."

As he looked her over, she refused to feel intimidated. Her black slacks and Goddess tank top were still damp. Louie was all wet, too.

"You have a bad habit of turning up at murder scenes. So does your uncle," Roland said.

"So do you. Do they know how it happened yet?"

"No. The crime scene's been trampled. The body was pulled from the stream and covered with a tablecloth before the EMTs arrived. Everyone walked all over the place to get a look." He gazed around the room. "I'll need a guest list."

"I have one in my supply box. Your friend, Leilani, has one, too. She helped compile it."

Em emphasized the words *your friend*. If Roland noticed, he ignored it as he slowly scanned the room. "Speaking of Leilani, where is she?"

"She left a little while before Fernando went missing. He walked her outside and then he went looking for Little Estelle Huntington. That's the last anyone saw of him alive, I think."

"Who told you that?"

"Wally saw him last."

"When Leilani left?"

"I think so. Wally said something about her coming back for her keys. She gave him the message that Fernando had gone to look for Little Estelle. Then Leilani left."

"Where's your bartender? Ms. Chin, is it?"

Em checked her watch. "Still tending bar at the Goddess." She knew very well that he knew Sophie's name.

"Was she here at all this evening?" he wanted to know.

Em's hackles went up and she shook her head. "No. She hasn't been here. I left her in charge at the Goddess. She'll be there until 2 a.m. I brought Louie along to bartend because whenever I leave him alone at the bar we lose money." She watched him closely. "You don't think Sophie had anything to do with *this*, do you?"

"It'll be easy enough to find out if she left the Goddess for any length of time."

He paused a minute. Looked over Em's wet clothes again. "The murderer usually finds the victim."

She could tell he enjoyed getting to her. Across the room Wally had revived himself and was sobbing on Marley Martin's shoulder again, clinging to the guitar player's shirt.

"Where's your uncle?" Sharpe asked.

"He's over there." Em indicated the bar out on the lanai. Louie was talking non-stop to anyone who would listen. "The officers told him to stop pouring drinks."

"*Mahalo* for that. A drunk witness is an unreliable witness."

"Good luck then. Everyone was feeling pretty happy before this happened."

The Hula Maidens were draped across chairs and sofas like

wilted flower arrangements. Flora Carillo was passed out on the floor. Lil was sobbing into the ruffled hem of her skirt, and Suzi Matamoto tried to console her.

Fernando's other guests were taking his death in stride, chatting, taking photos with their phones. When Kiki noticed Roland, she got up and hurried across the room toward them.

"Marlene Lockhart killed him. I know she did." Kiki squinted up at Roland and wagged a finger. "That woman wasn't even invited and she showed up. You need to drag her butt in for questioning the way you did poor Sophie."

"Calm down, Kiki," Roland glanced around the room. "Where is Marlene?"

Kiki followed his gaze. "Ha! Gone. She snuck out early. Everyone was told to stay put but she didn't. That should prove something. What are you going to do about it?"

"I'll make certain she's interviewed."

"I hope so." Kiki righted the lei crowning her head and walked back to the sofa to join the others.

Roland devoted his attention to Em again. "Was she here? Ms. Lockhart?"

Em nodded. "For a while. She came in late at Louie's invitation, not Fernando's. She ran outside to see what was wrong right after I found the body. She looked like she was going to be ill." Em glanced around. "I haven't seen her since. She must have left before the police got here. I don't necessarily like her, but I don't think she's a murderer." Em shrugged. "It was dark outside and Fernando wasn't familiar with the place. Maybe he tripped and hit his head on a rock and fell into the stream."

"Pretty hard for a big man to drown in three feet of water unless he was out cold first." Roland frowned. "Was your photographer here?"

"Trish is still here somewhere."

"I want to see her photos before anyone else does, this time." He slipped his notebook out of his back pocket. "Where was everyone when Fernando walked out with Leilani?"

"Either here in the main room, on the back lanai, or out looking for Little Estelle. I can't possibly know where everyone was."

"Tell me her last name again."

"Who?"

"The missing dancer."

"Little Estelle Huntington. She's Big Estelle Paulson's mother. She had too much to drink and took off on her Gad-About. They found her passed out on the lawn." She watched him scribble down a notation in his little notebook.

"Was she at the Goddess the night Harold was murdered?"

"Yes, of course. With the Maidens. But she's ninety-five, Detective. I doubt she killed Fernando, or Harold, for that matter."

He continued scribbling frantically.

"What are you writing now?"

"I'm making a note to call the water department and have them check to see if something crazy-making was added to the North Shore water."

"Very funny." Em was in no laughing mood. "Wally was the last one to see Fernando, I think."

"Wally?"

"Wally Williams." She pointed to the man with a bad case of helmet hair. "He's . . . he was Fernando's partner."

"As in business?"

"As in significant other."

He wrote Williams' name down. "What about your uncle? Where was he right before Fernando disappeared?"

He hit another nerve. "Look, my uncle had nothing to do with this."

"You sure?"

"Positive. He was behind the bar all evening. Ask anyone. Besides, my uncle had no reason on earth to murder Fernando."

"Just Harold."

Her cheeks were blazing again. She decided he must enjoy keeping her pissed off.

"If you aren't going to book us, let us pack up and leave," she said. "It's been a long night and you know where to find us."

Over on the sofa, Wally Williams had passed out again. An EMT was lifting his eyelid while another took his pulse.

Roland surprised her when he said, "Your crew can leave. Tell Kiki her ladies can go, too. I know where to find them."

"*Mahalo.*" Em tried not to sound frustrated by his lingering suspicion.

"Don't leave the island," he reminded her.

"Don't tempt me," she mumbled.

17

Hula Maidens Unite

The next morning, the *Closed* sign was out at the Goddess. Inside, breakfast was being served to a select few.

After Wally was released from the hospital and the police were through questioning him, Kiki drove in to pick him up. On the way back from Lihue, she had called an emergency meeting of the Maidens and brought him along. Propped up on a banquette near a window, Wally was suffering from a bad case of bed head. Kiki had administered a couple of Valiums and some Zoloft. Fernando's poor bereaved partner was feeling no pain.

The Maidens had pushed four tables together in front of him and gathered around. Little Estelle's Gad-About was parked at one end. She was chasing a bad hangover with a double *Huli Huli*. Big Estelle was at the other end of the table, talking on the phone to her brother in California.

"If she doesn't shape up, I'm sending her back on a one-way ticket!" Big Estelle made sure her mother heard every word.

"Hang up," Kiki snapped. "Time to start the meeting."

"I have no idea what on earth I'll do without Fernando." Wally had roused himself for a moment to daub his eyes with a cocktail napkin. "I can't go back there. At least not yet. I'm afraid every time I *look* at that stream I'll see him lying there."

"MyBob said you're welcome to stay with us," Lil offered. Her eyes were as pink as her hair and puffy from crying.

"He's staying with *us*," Kiki said. "Kimo will give him *lomilomi*."

"I'm sure I could make him some *lomilomi*," Lil said. "I just need a recipe."

"Not *lomi* salmon. Hawaiian massage. *Lomilomi*." Flora grunted. "You transplants. All the time Californicating the place all up."

"I'm from Iowaaaaa . . . " Lillian started wailing again.

Kiki clapped her hands. "Now look what you've done. Everybody shut up. We've got work to do." They were driving her crazy. Nothing new.

"Who would want to kill Fernando? He was the most gentle, loving creature on earth," Wally sniffed.

"And so *mahu*licious," Flora added.

Lil wiped her eyes, and her mascara smeared into rings. She looked like a startled raccoon. "What's *mahu*licious?"

Suzi translated. "It's like gaylicious."

"He was certainly that," Wally sighed.

"Gaylicious?" Lillian paled and her eyes exploded inside their mascara rings. "As in Fernando was *gay*?"

"Hel-lo!" Kiki's patience hit the wall. "Close your mouth, Lil, and shut up."

For once Lillian was too stunned to cry.

By now they all knew what Kiki had learned in town; Fernando hadn't just fallen into the stream. He'd been hit on the back of the head with a heavy object and was dead when he went into the water. Kiki looked around the circle of haggard faces. It was going to take a hell of a lot of makeup to help this bunch.

"First things first," she said. "We have a performance later today at the blessing for the new Shave Ice truck."

Suzi frowned. "Should we do it? I mean, after last night and all—"

"The show must go on." Kiki couldn't believe Suzi would think of canceling. It wasn't as if Fernando was a relative. "Besides, Fernando was a performer. He'd understand."

Wally moaned.

"What'll we wear?" Big Estelle asked.

"Well, it's only the Shave Ice truck. How about our practice *pa'u* skirts?"

"Makes me look fat," Flora said.

No one rushed to contradict her.

"Four yards of fabric gathered on four bands of elastic make all of us look fat," Big Estelle said. "Even Suzi, and she's skinny."

"What time?" Suzi wanted to know. "What about adornments?"

"Stick some white spider lilies in your hair and be there at three-thirty. The blessing starts at four. We get a complementary shave ice for dancing, and it's on the highway. We're sure to be seen there and might get another gig out of it."

Flora said, "Maybe somebody ought ta make a sign; we'll work for food."

Just then, Em walked up to the table carrying three large plates. "Breakfast burritos all around."

Kiki waved her away. "I never eat this early." She held up her Shark Attack. "By the way, does anyone want my celery stick?"

"The police think it was Louie, you know." Flora reached for a plate.

Em handed one over. "Are you serious?"

Flora shrugged as she dug in. "They think Louie killed Harold. That's what I heard at the Post Office this morning. Somebody's sister said that her cousin heard from his grandpa that Louie is the number-one suspect."

"That's ridiculous." Em had passed out all three breakfasts. Sophie was in the kitchen dishing up more.

"Well, maybe that means Sophie's off the hook." Relieved, Kiki smiled.

Everyone nodded except Little Estelle. Her head was down, her cheek resting flat against the tabletop. Her eyes were closed. A puddle of drool had pooled on the table near her gaping mouth.

Em went back to the kitchen for more food.

"Where is Louie?" Kiki called after Em.

"I'm right here." Louie strolled in looking refreshed and far more chipper than all of them put together. He held up his right hand, showed off a band-aid. "Letterman's in a foul mood, though. I almost lost a finger trying out the Koi Pond Kicker. I'm never at my sharpest in the morning. Neither is Letterman."

He planted his hands on his hips and studied the women. "What are you all doing here so early? Practicing already?"

"Putting our heads together," Kiki informed him. "Trying to figure out who could have killed Fernando. The police still haven't solved Harold's murder and now there's been another one and we were all there. We're all potential suspects." She looked around the table. "We need to get serious and solve this one ourselves, ladies."

There were nods of agreement and Big Estelle said, "Right on!"

Kiki turned to Louie. "So, where's The Defector? I'm surprised she's not here spying on us."

"Give it a rest, Kiki." Louie's smile never faltered. "You're just jealous because Marlene's a better dancer than you."

"That's not true. We just have different styles. Did you know

Roland said he's going to be paying your Marlene a little visit today?" She folded her arms, smug in the knowledge she had the detective's ear. "She ran off before he could question her last night. I *wonder* why?"

Wally wailed, "Why? Someone tell me why would anyone kill Freddy?"

Little Estelle raised her head, blinked and looked around. "Who's dead now? Who's Freddy?"

Wally held the napkin to his lips until he collected himself. "Fernando. His real name was Freddy Castro. He's from El Monte, California."

"Not Spain?" Lillian looked stunned.

Wally rolled his eyes. "Fernando was a legend, literally, in his own mind."

"Like one of Louie's drinks." Suzi Matamoto tried to talk around a mouth full of burrito.

"All of my legends are true," Louie told her before he turned his attention to Kiki again. "Why on earth would Marlene kill Fernando?"

"Who knows why that woman does anything?"

Just then, Em rejoined them.

Wally went on, "Poor Freddy. He died in his prime, like Elvis and Marilyn. His candle burned out long before his legend ever did."

They all hummed *Candle in the Wind* for a moment and then fell silent.

Kiki watched Em draw a triangle on a napkin.

"What are you doing?" Kiki asked.

"Trying to find a connection between Harold, Fernando and the Goddess. Harold and Fernando—easy. Harold was landscaping for Fernando and probably watching over the koi. Harold and the Goddess—a shared easement for the driveway, and Louie and Harold's connection through Irene. Fernando's connection to the Goddess—hiring us to cater the housewarming." She shrugged. "I can't come up with anything that makes sense. Surely nothing that adds up to murder anyway."

Sophie walked out of the kitchen with more burritos. She handed them out and went back for a plate for Em then returned and sat down beside her. Sophie pulled a folded sheet of lined paper out of her back pocket.

"I found this. Maybe it'll help." Sophie handed it to Em.

Kiki leaned over to take a look. "What is this?"

There were names and phone numbers in crooked handwriting.

Sophie shrugged. "Harold's client list, I think."

"What?" Em set down her fork and picked up the paper. "Where did you get this?"

Sophie mumbled something that sounded like, "Don't ask, don't tell," and then added, "I was thinking we could call everyone on that list and chat them up. Ask if they know anything about why anyone would want to kill Harold. Maybe he said something to one of them that might be helpful." She looked at Kiki, then the others and shrugged.

"I can't do it," Sophie told them. "I don't think Em or Louie should be asking around either, seeing as how this second murder has put all of us under suspicion again."

"But we were *all* at both murder scenes," Kiki reminded Sophie.

The girl nodded. "Yeah, but I'm the only one who was hauled in so far. Em and Louie had the smoke beef going with Harold." She shrugged.

Suzi had already polished off her burrito. "We could split up the list. I wouldn't mind calling a few people. I'm sure there are lots of folks on there that I already know."

Kiki recognized some of the names near the top. "I know the top three."

"MyBob could make some calls," Lil volunteered. "Say we need a gardener now that Harold is gone."

"Was Harold your gardener?" Kiki asked.

"No. MyBob could say that, though."

Kiki grabbed the list from Sophie and carefully tore it into thirds. She handed one to Suzi, one to Lil and kept one.

"That's settled. Now what else does anyone know?"

Em said, "While I was serving last night, Fernando told me Harold talked to him about the property and the planning department. And something about the fish. It didn't make much sense."

"Harold never made much sense. Have you seen those piles of trash he called sculptures in his yard?" Suzi asked.

"Weird. Downright weird," Big Estelle said. She glanced over at Little Estelle, who was sound asleep again.

"What exactly did he say?" Kiki asked. Time was wasting. She had a wedding to set up on a luxury property overlooking Secret

Beach.

Em leaned back in her chair. She hadn't touched her burrito. Kiki reached for Em's fork and downed a couple bites.

"Something about fish bones," Em said.

"I remember," Wally sat up straighter. "Harold said something about *koi punda* bones."

"*Koi punda?*" Flora's heavy brow was more wrinkled than a Sharpei's. "No kine fish named *koi punda*. Get *aku* and *ama'ama*, *aweoweo*—"

"Oh, and I suppose you know *all* the names of *all* the fish," Suzi turned on her.

"I know Hawaiian fish." Flora's drink was gone. She was back to sucking on her water bottle.

"Did you tell Roland about the fish bones? They might mean something, if that's really what you heard." Kiki noticed Em blushed as soon as she mentioned the fire dancer's name.

"No, I didn't. Maybe you should call him," Em said.

"I think maybe *you* ought to call him. By the way, when Wally and I left the station this morning, Roland told me to 'give Nancy Drew' his regards."

Em was definitely blushing now. Kiki liked stirring the pot as much as she liked fresh hot gossip.

"I must have a memorial for Freddy here on Kauai," Wally sniffed.

"We'll perform, of course," Kiki volunteered. "No charge."

"Where?" Suzi wanted to know. "Here at the Goddess?"

Wally whispered, "At Fernando's Hideaway."

"What'll happen to the house now?" Lil wondered.

"Fernando left everything to me." Wally shuddered and closed his eyes.

Kiki blinked and couldn't do anything but stare at him for a moment before she glanced over at Em, who was studying Wally. Apparently Em was thinking what Kiki was thinking.

"He left you *everything?*" Kiki asked.

Wally casually waved his hand around. "Everything. The cars, the yacht in San Francisco. The houses . . . "

"Houses?" Sophie's spiked hair was standing tall with bright purple highlights this morning. "As in how many?"

"Las Vegas, San Francisco, Aspen." Wally recited the names with as much passion as he'd make a grocery list. "And now, Kauai."

"Wow." Sophie voiced what all of them were thinking. *Wow.*

"Where were you when Fernando disappeared, Wally?" Kiki could care less about offending him. If Louie went to jail for murder, there went the Goddess.

"In the little boys' room."

Little Estelle raised her head. "What little boys?"

"No little boys, Mother," Big Estelle shouted to her mother. "He's talking about the bathroom."

"I don't have to go right now. Stop badgering me." Little Estelle sat up, put the Gad-About in reverse, backed away from the table and ricocheted off the stage before heading for the lanai.

Kiki turned to Lillian, thinking it was time to make the pitiful woman's day.

"Lil, would you mind driving Wally out to my place? I've got to head straight to Secret Beach and meet the tent people. Kimo will see that Wally gets settled in comfortably."

Lillian grabbed her purse. "I'd be happy to. Anything, anything at all for Fernando's dear friend."

"Great. Maybe you two should get going," Kiki urged. "Wally looks exhausted." His comb-over was listing to one side.

Wally gingerly touched the bags under his swollen eyes. "Well, it's no wonder."

"If you want, make yourself an ice pack," Kiki advised. "Kimo will help you find whatever you need."

Wally slid out from behind the banquette. He folded his hands at his waist and sighed. "Can he bring back Fernando?"

"Kimo's good, but not that good." Kiki reached under the table for her purse.

Wally exited the room. Lillian trailed behind. Suzi's cell phone rang. She fled to the lanai to talk real estate. Big Estelle was the only one who tried to pay for breakfast. Em waved her off.

"On the house. For last night."

"But we didn't even dance," Big Estelle reminded her. "I can't help but think if Mother hadn't gone missing, Fernando might still be alive."

"Oh, Big Estelle, get a grip," Kiki snapped. "Not everything is your mother's fault."

Big Estelle ignored her, thanked Em and left. Sophie collected the dirty plates and headed for the kitchen.

Kiki was glad when they were all finally gone. She wanted to talk to Em alone.

"You thinking what I'm thinking?"

Em nodded. "Wally certainly had a motive."

"You think Roland knows about the inheritance?"

Em shrugged. "If he doesn't now, he's sure to find out soon enough."

"Maybe you should call and tell him about the fishbone thing and how much Wally stands to gain."

"You think?"

"Personally, I think they're both great excuses for you to call Roland." Kiki slung her purse strap over her shoulder and winked at Em. "If I was twenty years younger and single, I'd use them myself."

18

The Show Goes On

After the way the Hula Maidens had stood up for her, Sophie decided she'd repay them by showing up to help at the Chill Out Shave Ice truck blessing.

By the time she drove into Hanalei from the Goddess, the official blessing, an *oli*, or chant, was over. Kahuna Puana Kimokane was already in line waiting to order his complementary shave ice.

Seeing the Maidens huddled all together arguing about whether the seam in their *pa'u* skirts should be worn to the side or in back, Sophie sighed.

They were nothing like the *halau* she had danced with before her life started going down the wrong track. Her *kumu* was well versed in the art of hula. He had been tested both spiritually and physically and proven worthy of passing on the art of the ancient dance. Hula, he said, was a way to perpetuate the culture, a visual way to tie Hawaii's past to its present.

Sophie let the maidens go on a minute longer and then, fed up with the bickering, she clapped her hands to get their attention.

"You have to get it together, ladies. Em only gave me a couple hours off. Besides, your crowd is thinning." She handed the group's boom box to Suzi, along with an extension cord. Without live music, the Maidens relied on CDs.

"Plug this into the outlet on the side of the wagon." Sophie pointed to the rusting white RV with a take-out window cut into its side. "Then come back and line up right here." She scanned an ominously gray sky and hoped it didn't rain until the dancing ended. If it did, they'd have to unplug the boom box and run for cover.

"Line up, ladies," Kiki snapped. She stepped in front of Sophie to start a front row.

Little Estelle pulled her Gad-About into position at the end of the line and practiced a couple of 360's. Once they were ready, Sophie gave them a thumbs up and punched *Play* on the boom box. Unfortunately for them, fortunately for the audience, they had only finished three numbers when it started to drizzle.

Sophie walked along beside Little Estelle as the woman rode the Gad-About over to an awning that partially covered a picnic table, where Little Estelle waited while Big Estelle and the others got in line for their shave ice cones. With Little Estelle safely out of the way, Sophie headed over to the line by the RV. She noticed Marlene Lockhart approaching. She didn't like the woman any more than Kiki did. Marlene didn't try to hide her contempt for the Goddess even though the place was Louie's pride and joy. The woman was definitely after Louie, and Sophie just didn't trust her.

Sophie neared the line and heard Kiki say, "So, Marlene. Fancy seeing you here. Did Roland interrogate you this morning? I'm surprised he didn't cart you off to Lihue like he did Sophie."

"Actually, he stopped by my place, where we had a very nice chat and a cup of coffee." Marlene patted her perfect hair. Today she was outfitted in a lemon-yellow sheath with lemon-yellow accessories.

"What excuse did you give Roland for running off last night? The rest of us had to stay until the police gave the okay to leave," Kiki informed her.

Marlene's eyes suddenly filled with tears. "I was so shocked to see Fernando like that—I was right there a second after Em found him. It reminded me of the day my fourth husband died." She lowered her voice to a hush. "He drowned, you know."

By now not only Sophie but everyone else standing in line was listening.

"*Fourth* husband?" Kiki's jaw fell open. "I thought you only had three."

"I was only married to number four for eight months," Marlene said softly. "So distressing."

"Probably just long enough to collect the insurance," Flora muttered.

Just then there was a strong gust of wind. A passing cloud opened up and dumped a heavy squall of rain. Except for two or three folks at the front of the line, everyone scattered.

"I'm heading back to the Goddess," Sophie told the Maidens. "Anybody need a ride back to Haena?"

Flora raised her hand. Big Estelle was running for the handicap-equipped van so she could collect Little Estelle and the Gad-About. Kiki stared after Marlene as the woman ran through the rain, headed for the parking lot holding her yellow purse over her head to protect her hair.

"Come on," Flora tugged on Sophie's arm. "Let's get outta here."

Sophie bid Kiki goodbye but as she walked away, Kiki was still focused on Marlene.

"Four husbands," Kiki muttered. The rain was smearing her make up. "I hate to think poor Louie might be number five."

19

Nancy Drew Gets Boned

The next day dawned sun-kissed and radiant. The sky was brilliant blue and cloudless. The aquamarine ocean beyond their front door was so crystal clear Em could see every grain of sand on the bottom.

She took advantage of the perfect morning to work out with a swim. Afterward she showered in Louie's outdoor shower. One of her favorite luxuries of living in the tropics was showering behind the tall bamboo wall he had built around a showerhead on an exterior lava rock wall. He'd filled the interior garden with ferns, flowers, and hanging orchids.

As she stood on the shore, towel-drying her hair and wondering why Roland Sharpe hadn't returned her calls, she watched the gentle lap of the waves against slabs of worn rock that lined the beach. Louie walked out of the house and brought her a tall iced tea.

"Louie." She hoped she got an answer that made sense. "What were you looking for the day you went into Harold's house?"

"Harold's house? When?"

"When Sophie had to bring you out and Leilani showed up. You said you were after something of yours."

"I did?"

"This is serious, Louie. *Think*." This was no laughing matter. He'd been at two murder scenes in three weeks.

Then again, so had she. So had most of the Hula Maidens.

"You can remember how to mix every drink in that Booze Bible of yours. Surely you can remember why you snuck into Harold's place."

"Sometimes my ship is out of port, I guess."

Em sighed and thought, *way out of port*. She downed the rest of the iced tea and polished off the mint sprig. Calling Harold's client list had proven to be a dead end so far. Kiki, MyBob, and Flora had nothing to report other than the fact that some of Harold's clients had found a stray marijuana plant or two hidden in their gardens.

"That hedge needs trimming," her uncle said.

Em followed his gaze. The thick, mock-orange hedge between the Goddess and Harold's house was leggy and out of shape. Harold had planted it and maintained both sides. Now it was up to them. Em found it easier to think while her hands were busy working on mindless projects.

"I'll trim it a bit," she volunteered. "Where are the clippers?"

Louie disappeared into his garage and came out with some rusted, long-handled garden shears. "You sure you want to do this?"

"Exercise," she said. Back in weight-conscious Orange County she had had a home gym and a personal trainer. Here she stayed in shape without trying. She rarely sat down and when she had any time off, she liked to walk, swim, or putter around Louie's yard.

"Don't get over-heated," he warned. "I'm heading in to watch *The View* with Letterman. He wants to see who that skinny blond chick *pounces* on today. Speaking of blonds, Marlene might come over later," he told her.

It didn't take long for Em to build up a sizeable pile of cuttings. She was working her way around the end of the hedge and onto Harold's side when the bolt that held the clippers together fell out.

"Oh, doody." She'd worked up a good sweat and hated to stop now.

She wiped her forehead with the back of her arm, pulled the front of her tank top away from her breasts and fanned it in and out. Harold's carport and open garage were just ten feet from the hedge. Amid his other clutter, it contained an array of yard tools.

Harold certainly wasn't going to mind if she borrowed his clippers to finish the job.

The garage doors were always wide open. Inside it was cool and shady. Stacks of mildewed cardboard boxes lined one wall. A workbench covered with piles of scrap metal, nuts and bolts, automotive products and paint cans lined the other.

There were four huge trash bags filled with recyclable aluminum cans. Harold's humongous sit-down lawnmower was on a trailer hooked up to his shiny blue pick-up. Most of his power tools, rakes, and a weed whacker were inside the trailer, but there were no clippers in sight.

Em looked around and spied a pair of long-handled hedge clippers shoved onto a shelf over his workbench. She stood on tiptoe and used a fruit picker to try and pull them down. The clippers teetered and came clattering off the shelf, barely missing her. Then suddenly, what appeared to be a two-foot long bundle of burlap came tumbling after them. Protruding from the ragged, stained fabric was what appeared to be the joint end of a bone. A very *large* bone.

Em stared at the bone for a second before she picked up the bundle and gingerly unwound the cloth. The worn burlap was a coffee bean bag stamped Kauai Koffee. She opened it all the way and pulled out a long arm—or maybe a leg—bone.

She didn't know if it was animal or human. One thing was certain, it was long and it wasn't fake. It appeared to be old and was stained with brown-red dirt. There were bits of sand embedded in the end. She turned it over and over in her hand.

Then she looked up and scanned the shelf again. There didn't appear to be anything else up there. As she measured the weight of the bone in her hand, her last conversation with Fernando came back to her.

"So, what are we talking about?" Wally wanted to know.

"The last words of Harold to me."

"Ah. The fish bones."

"This is why we break the ground tomorrow," Fernando had said. "Because Harold said the fish are upset. And so Fernando's mind is made up."

At best this bone was something Harold found at the dump while picking over parts for his sculptures. Or it may have come from Fernando's property. She glanced toward the Goddess. Or somewhere close by. She re-wrapped it quickly. Wherever the thing came from, it was definitely no fishbone.

She reached for her cell in her pocket. She'd saved Roland Sharpe's phone number and was set to call him, but suddenly stopped before hitting autodial.

Harold had something of mine and I wanted it back.

Louie was an "unofficial" suspect. So was she. Sophie had already been taken for questioning once. The last thing Em wanted was to be the one to hand Detective Sharp a piece of human remains which may or may not have something to do with her uncle.

Em stared at the thing in her hand. *What if this is what Uncle Louie was looking for?* There could be any number of logical explanations. She didn't dare show the thing to Roland until she found out whether or not her uncle had anything to do with it. Maybe it was a stolen artifact. Or, God forbid, it had something to do with Harold's murder.

If someone could just identify the thing, tell her how old it was—

The image of Professor Nelg and his turtle headed-penis popped into her mind.

He was an anthropologist. He knew old bones.

There was no way she could hike into the Kalalau with so much going on. Besides, Nelg promised that he and Namaste would stop by when they were back on the North Shore. With any luck, they could show up any day. Until then she'd hide the bone.

She grabbed an empty utility bucket, turned it upside down, stood on it and slipped Harold's clippers back onto the shelf. Evidence tampering came to mind as she picked up the burlap package and headed out of the carport. Her busted clippers were lying next to the hedge. As she stooped to pick them up, a flash of white caught her eye.

Across the parking lot, Roland Sharpe tucked his unmarked white police car into a slot near the entrance to the Goddess.

Hi there, Detective. Wanna take a peek at the hopefully very old and possibly human bone I found while I was in Harold's carport snooping around?

She quickly stashed the burlap sack under one of the bushes in the hedge, dusted off her hands and started across the lot.

Harold had mentioned "bones" to Fernando. Something had upset the old man.

This is why we must *break the ground tomorrow.*

Had Harold been in a hurry to dig something up? Or keep something hidden?

"Nice to see you, Detective, but you could have just called." Em tried to smooth her hair into place.

"The notion of torturing you in person was too tempting. This is the first chance I've had to get out here."

"Is that a bit of humor I detect?"

"What are you up to?" He glanced at the hedge and then his gaze traveled over to Harold's and back to her.

"I was trimming the hedge." She knew she must look flushed and hopefully not too nervous. "Lemonade, Detective? Or some iced tea?"

"I'll take a lemonade. Thanks."

Em walked him inside. Sophie was at the bar and watched Roland as Em grabbed a handful of napkins and ushered him to a table in the back corner.

"Are you keeping me away from your bartender or hiding me from potential customers?" he asked.

"Both."

He settled back in his chair. Studied her. "Why'd you want to see me?"

"Talk to you. I wanted to talk to you. Like I said, you could have just called." She swabbed off her forehead with a couple of napkins. Without thinking she balled them up and used a couple more to mop her cleavage.

His gaze followed her hand. "And miss this?"

She flushed, instantly dropped the napkins, and sat back.

"I didn't see you out by the hedge when I pulled in," he said.

"You're very observant."

"That's what they pay me for. Where were you?"

"I told you. I was trimming on the other side."

"Harold's side? Very convenient. Were you snooping around a little, too?"

She crossed her arms beneath her breasts, caught him stealing another glance. She refused to look away when he met her eyes again.

He lowered his voice and leaned closer. "Be very careful, Nancy Drew. I don't want to see you hauled off in the coroner's wagon."

"I'm a suspect, remember?" She almost smiled. "How do you know so much about Nancy Drew?"

"There's a lot you don't know about me."

She switched subjects. "Trish said you didn't see anything out of the ordinary in her housewarming photos."

"Nothing stood out. So why did you call?"

"Because that night at Fernando's I had a conversation with Wally and Fernando about Harold."

"You just now remembered it?"

"I called you two days ago."

"All you said was that you really needed to talk to me. It kinda sounded personal."

"You wish."

Sophie served the lemonade. Roland downed half a glass before he took out his notebook. "Okay. So what did you hear?"

"They were talking about *koi punda* and fish bones. Fernando said that was why he had to break ground right away. Something about the planning department."

"*Koi punda.*" He wrote it down.

"Do you know the word? Or what it means?"

"No."

"You speak Hawaiian?"

"Some."

She was impressed.

"My grandma was Hawaiian, actually. *Tutu* only spoke Hawaiian to me. Made me learn. His brow crinkled. "You sure they didn't say *amuku?*"

"What does that mean?"

"Well, nothing has just one translation, but it can mean to cut off."

She glanced toward Harold's side of the property for a second, picturing the bone. "Cut off?"

He nodded.

She mulled a minute. "I'm pretty sure it was *koi punda*. But I might have misheard. Or Fernando did."

He shrugged. "Anything else?"

"For some reason fish bones were the reason Fernando felt compelled to break ground right away."

Roland stared up at the ceiling covered in tattered tapa cloth and then studied the ceiling fan. Em looked up and noticed the blades were coated with a half inch of dust. She made a mental note to have Kimo dust them. At least Roland wasn't still staring at her cleavage.

"That's all you wanted to tell me?" he asked.

"That and that Wally had a motive," she added.

"He inherited everything." Roland folded his notebook shut.

"I guess that was easy enough to find out."

"Yep. He told me himself."

She dabbed at the wet rings on the table beneath her lemonade glass and shrugged. "That's all I've got."

"Wow. Next thing, you'll be after my job."

"I believe you really are trying to be funny, Detective Sharpe." She wondered what might have happened if they'd just been two people who had met on the beach, if she wasn't still hurting and he wasn't the detective on a murder case that, for the most part, centered on the Goddess and its staff.

She thought he was about to smile until the radio on his belt beeped. He listened to the call, then turned down the volume and stood up.

"Thanks again for the lemonade," he said.

"You're welcome."

"And Ms. Johnson?"

"Yes?"

"Try to stay outta trouble, okay?"

20

Em's Close Call

Try to stay outta of trouble.

Easier said than done. Worried somebody might notice the burlap bag stashed under the hedge, Em headed for the parking lot as soon as Roland's car was out of sight.

She swept up the cuttings lying around the base of the mock orange bushes. Once she had a fairly sizable pile near the bundled-up bone, she knelt down and stuck her arm beneath the thick bush.

Her fingers had barely grazed the rough sack when she heard a soft rustle behind her. Before she could look back over her shoulder, something slammed into her head and everything went black. The next thing she knew she was lying face down on the hot parking lot gravel like road kill and Sophie was kneeling beside her.

Her head was throbbing. Em winced when she touched a tender spot near her crown. Not only was her nose killing her, but it was dripping blood.

"What happened?" She looked around the empty lot.

Sophie took her hand and helped her sit up. Em closed her eyes but her head wouldn't stop spinning. When she finally opened her eyes, she gingerly touched her nose. It was definitely bleeding and hurt like hell. She pulled up the hem of her tank top and pressed it against her nose. "Whoa." Nausea hit her hard. She swallowed bile.

"Maybe you'd better lie down again," Sophie suggested.

"I'm okay," Em lied.

"I walked out on the lanai to tell you that Wally Williams called, and I saw you lying out here. What happened? Did you fall?"

"No, I didn't fall. That's for sure." She remembered being on her hands and knees, reaching for the coffee sack and wondered it if was still under the bush. How long had she been out? She didn't dare look for the bone with Sophie there, if Uncle Louie was somehow involved.

"Somebody knocked me out," Em said.

Sophie's eyes went wide. She furiously clicked her tongue stud.

"You sure? Did you see who it was?"

"No, but I didn't fall, and I certainly didn't knock myself on the head." Em's hands were shaking. There was definitely a lump on the side of her head now. Blood was slowly dripping onto her tank top. "Somebody hit me from behind and I blacked out and fell on my nose." She looked around. "Where's Uncle Louie?"

"He went to the post office about twenty minutes ago."

She checked out their parking spaces by the house. Sure enough, his pick-up was gone.

The murderer usually finds the victom. So said Detective Sharpe.

Had Sophie just found her?

What if Sophie snuck up on me first and hit me in the head? Em wondered. The girl had absolutely no reason to harm her.

If she meant to kill me, she certainly could have finished the job.

Unless a car had suddenly come down the highway or someone started to pull into the parking lot and scared Sophie—or whoever her assailant was—away.

Em stubbornly refused to believe either Sophie or Louie was capable of murder.

If the bone was still there then she had to get the burlap bag out from under the bush and safely hidden somewhere. Hindsight told her that maybe she should have told Roland about it earlier and damned the consequences.

She looked up at Sophie and winced. She didn't have to fake her pain.

"Would you please run and get me some ice?" she asked. "My head is killing me."

"Sure." Sophie jumped to her feet.

"I'll meet you in the office," Em told her.

"Okay. Will you be all right out here alone?"

"I'm just going to sit here a sec longer."

Sophie took off at a jog. Em waited a moment and then, when she was sure the coast was clear, grabbed the bag, slid it under an armful of cuttings and slowly got to her feet. She carried the cuttings and bag toward the back door of the Goddess. The lot was, thankfully, empty for once. She opened the rubbish can, quickly dumped in the cuttings and went through the back door with the burlap bundle tucked beneath her arm.

Once she was in the office, she opened one of the rusty drawers of a lateral file cabinet that contained nothing but stacks of receipts dating back to the '60's. She'd been meaning to help Louie clean them out, but now she was glad she hadn't had the time. She tossed the wrapped bone inside a half-second before Sophie came in with ice wrapped in a dishtowel, and a wet cloth.

Em closed the drawer with her foot and reached for the ice pack.

Not sure what to ice first, Em thanked Sophie and gently applied the towel to the bump on her head. The bridge of her nose was killing her, too.

"You look like you were in a car wreck." Sophie handed her the wet cloth to wipe her face with. "Much as I hate to admit it, maybe you should call Sharpe. Tell him what happened."

"I'm not exactly sure what happened." She waited for Sophie's response.

Sophie frowned. "I hope someone didn't try to kill you."

"Did you see anyone out there?"

"No. But I think we should call the police."

"And have Sharpe jump to the conclusion that it was either you or Uncle Louie?" Em was thinking of calling Roland herself. Now she wondered if Sophie had suggested it just to throw her off. Em decided her expression must have given her thoughts away, for the clicking going on in Sophie's mouth stopped abruptly.

"You don't think *I* hit you."

"Of course not," Em tried not to feel guilty. "Would I be sitting here with you if I did?"

"Louie's been gone for almost thirty minutes now."

"Right. So it wasn't him," Em said.

"Then who?"

"If I knew that, then I might have the answer to a whole lot of questions."

21

Leilani Cleans House

The next morning, Em saw Shark Lady's Mercedes parked in Harold's driveway and went over to see what was going on. She found Leilani on the lanai staring at her uncle's eyesore of a shack.

"Aloha," Em called out.

Leilani visibly started. "What are you doing here?"

"I came over to see if everything is all right."

"Why wouldn't it be?"

Em shrugged.

Leilani shook her head. "I'm sorry I'm so cranky. There's just so much to do. This place should have been torn down years ago, but the old man said he had no need to rebuild. He was born in this house and he swore he'd die here." She sighed. "Looks like he got his wish."

"Are you going to sell it?" Em knew the property was worth at least five million without the shack.

"If I do a little face lifting, replace some of the dry-rot here and there, rebuild the front steps, add a new lanai railing and have the whole place painted dark green with white trim—the colors of the old plantation cottages—I could call it a guest house. The price of the place would go up another half million or more." Leilani added, "As soon as the police give me a green light, I'll start repairs." She looked at her watch. "The contractor who works on my flips is due to meet me here in twenty minutes."

She came down off the lanai, ignoring Em as she paced the drive, then crossed the small yard that fronted the highway. After staring at one of Harold's odd rubbish sculptures for a second, she gave it a hard nudge with the toe of her beaded gold sandal. The pile of welded cans and wires, rusted hubcaps and bedsprings tipped over.

"I'll have this trash hauled out of here first thing. Then the For Sale sign is going up. With any luck at all, the place will sell fast. Maybe even before I start renovations."

Behind the shack, the rectangular green lawn rolled to the edge of the coral-lined beach. Except for the hedge and a few coconut palms, Harold's landscaping was minimal and made the property appear larger than it was. Trade winds rustled the palm fronds. The lure of the tropics was undeniable. Leilani was right. The place would sell in a heartbeat.

"Mind if I ask you something?" Em couldn't let the opportunity pass.

Leilani glanced at her watch again.

"As I said, I am expecting my contractor."

"This will just take a minute."

"What's up?" Leilani raised her sunglasses, squinted hard at Em. "Do you have two black eyes?"

"Unfortunately."

"What happened?"

There was a hesitation. Leilani waited.

"I tripped. Fell on my nose." Em changed the subject back. "I was just wondering if our uncles had any partnerships going."

"You must be kidding. They hated each other," Leilani said.

"I wouldn't say my uncle *hated* Harold."

"You wouldn't? Harold loved Irene forever and they lived right next door to him. I can see why your uncle would want to get rid of him."

"Irene's been dead for years."

Leilani pointed to the Goddess. "That place is a shrine to her."

"So?"

"So. It was an in-your-face snub to my uncle. Why would you think he had any business dealings with Louie Marshall?"

Em tried to evade Leilani's stare and shrugged. "I was just curious. I thought maybe that's why Louie was over here the other day. He said he was looking for something of his."

"Incriminating evidence, no doubt. He probably came over to clean up after killing my uncle."

"He did not. It's a little late for that anyway."

"Then maybe it was your bartender."

"Sorry. Nope. I won't buy that, either."

"Then you're more obtuse than I thought."

"Obtuse?"

"It means thick. Or slow-minded," Leilani said.

"I know what it means. I'm just surprised you do."

Leilani took a deep breath and gave Em an insincere smile. "I'm going to get a restraining order against all of you people. Legally keep you from snooping around over here."

"Why? Are you hiding something?" Em had had just about enough of Shark Lady.

Leilani slipped her cell phone out of her pocket.

"Go back to your side of the hedge or I'm calling Roland."

"You're tattling to Roland?" Em laughed.

"Are you jealous?"

"Yeah. Right. That's it. I'm *way* jealous." Em walked back across the parking lot without another word.

22

The Timely Return of Nelg

Much to Em's relief, two days later the anthropologist and his squeeze showed up out of the blue. They arrived at the bar looking exhausted, bedraggled, and hungry. Em had them stash their backpacks in the office and treated them to lunch—green salad and island fruit—before she asked Professor Nelson if he would speak with her in private.

Namaste was happy to sip pineapple juice and chat with Sophie. Thankfully, Louie was in Lihue picking up supplies at Costco with Kimo.

Once she and the professor entered the office, Em locked the doors.

Nelg smiled. "Why, Ms. Johnson, I had no idea." He reached for the zipper fly on his Eddie Bauer hiking shorts. "Always time for a quickie."

"Keep your pants on, please. This is a professional consultation," Em said.

"Oh." His smile faded. He sat down in a rattan chair near the desk and studied her closely. "Do you have two black eyes?"

She thought she'd used enough under-eye concealer, but obviously not.

"A minor accident. That's not what I wanted to discuss. I need your professional advice."

"Happy to help out."

She opened the lateral file drawer and pulled out the burlap sack. "I found this and was wondering if you can tell me what it is and perhaps how old it is." She unwrapped the bone and set it down on top of the burlap spread out on the center of Louie's desk.

Nelg adjusted his glasses, leaned over the desk and inspected the object.

"Old or new?" Em held her breath.

"Definitely old. Very old, actually." He picked it up, held it, weighed it in his hands. "You see the rust color? That's the color of the red dirt on Kauai. It's full of iron."

Em knew all about Kauai's red dirt. It stained clothing, shoes, whatever it came in contact with. "Red Dirt" tourist tee shirts were dyed with the stuff.

"Old bones take on the color of the soil they're buried in." Nelg sniffed it. "It still has a musty smell, so it wasn't unearthed that long ago. This is the femur of a very tall person. Hawaiian, most likely."

"You can tell just by looking at it?"

"Just a guess."

"This isn't from one of your mysterious Menehune, then."

"Definitely not." He turned it over, studied the ends. "Where did it come from?"

"I really don't know for sure."

"If it's from your property, you could be in for some heavy expenses. I can see why you'd want to keep the burial site a secret but—"

"It's not from here." At least she hoped not. "What do you mean, 'heavy expenses'?"

"There are very well-defined burial treatment plans for landowners who discover remains on their properties."

"Does this happen a lot then? Seems like I just read about some guy who was allowed to build a home over thirty graves." Em shivered. She couldn't imaging wanting to desecrate one grave let alone thirty, no matter how old they were.

"These islands were populated with hundreds of thousands of Polynesians and Hawaiians over the centuries and there is only so much land. There are countless gravesites yet to be discovered and, as more and more property is developed, more and more will be unearthed. Especially in sandier soil close to the beach."

"So, let's say I did find a gravesite . . . "

"So did you?"

"No. I found this in someone's storage area." She wasn't about to say whose until she was certain Uncle Louie was in the clear. She felt a little better knowing the bone was old, but that still didn't clear Louie, or Harold, for that matter. Even if they weren't guilty of hiding a body, they might have been trying to cover up the discovery of an ancient grave.

The very idea gave her the creeps. She thought she'd gotten to know her uncle fairly well these past few months—but what did she really know about him or his past?

Her thoughts drifted back to the professor, who was on a roll.

"Let's say there's construction going on. All work ceases once a gravesite is discovered. Buffer zones are set up so bulldozers don't corrupt the site. The State Historic Preservation Division is called in and so is the Kauai Police Department. An archeologist is brought in at the landowners' expense to evaluate the site. And let me add, you can't call in just *any* archeologist. The state has requirements for experience. Each island has its own Island Burial Council. Specialists in Hawaiian culture are supposed to handle the remains and any other artifacts found on site."

Nelg set the bone down carefully and sank into the chair again. "Those hamburgers sure smell great. I'd love to have one."

"Have you stopped eating raw?"

"I only started because Namaste's so into it."

"And you're into her."

"I can't *get* into her if I eat meat."

"I can sneak a burger and some fries back here for you." She felt sorry for the man. There were hollows beneath his eyes, and his skin was beginning to take on his girlfriend's orange hue.

"Namaste would smell the beef on my breath. She says all the toxins come out of our pores." He sighed. "The things we do for love, eh?"

Em nodded, thinking of how she might be putting herself in danger for Uncle Louie.

"So what are you going to do with the femur?" He nodded toward the bone.

She tried not to appear distressed. "Put it back where I found it, I guess."

"For your own protection, you probably should turn it over to the authorities. There's a very stiff fine for not reporting discoveries of historical significance."

The way folks were dropping dead lately, and after being bonked on the head, she was beginning to wonder if she would be safer leaving Kauai altogether—but she wasn't about to walk away and leave Uncle Louie on his own yet.

"It's not even a whole person," she said. "Maybe it's not even from a burial site." She re-wrapped the bone and replaced it in the back of the file cabinet.

"I'm talking legal protection," Nelg said. "This was someone's ancestor, you know, and now his femur is tucked in a file cabinet in the back room of a bar. Who knows where the rest of him is? Think about it. Would you want your great-great-great-grandfather to end up this way?"

"Not really."

But she didn't want her Uncle Louie to take the fall for something he didn't do, either. From what Nelg just said, grave robbing on Kauai could be a serious offense that carried a lot of weight in court. Harold had "something" of Louie's. Hopefully it wasn't the bone—but if Harold *had* been blackmailing Louie . . .

"I should get back to Namaste," Nelg said.

"I'd appreciate it if you'd keep this to yourself." Em realized she had no guarantee that he wouldn't talk about her dilemma to someone.

"Not to worry." He reached into his pocket and pulled out a business card. "We're going to explore the west side of the island now, but you can reach me on my cell if you need any more advice. I'd like to hear the outcome of this little mystery."

She looked at the card in her hand. "Thanks, Professor. And if you find yourself having a burger breakdown, come on back. It's on the house. Anytime."

Professor Nelson left the office to join Namaste, who was working on another fruit bowl.

Em stared at the file cabinet, wishing answers could somehow emanate from the femur hidden inside. She sat down in Louie's office chair, closed her eyes and tried to think.

Harold had hidden the bone in his garage. Louie had been looking for something at Harold's that he claimed was his, but that didn't necessarily mean he was looking for the femur. Harold was Fernando's gardener. Harold was killed shortly after he spoke to Fernando about fish bones. Fernando was killed on the night of his party. Wally inherited everything from Fernando—which gave him motive.

But Wally didn't seem the type who could murder anyone. And he seemed genuinely distraught over his partner's death.

Could the femur be from Fernando's property? Or somewhere else? Who else knew about it?

Frustrated, she tapped her toe against the floor. She was usually steps ahead of the television detectives, or at least the television crime show *writers*. Apparently, real life mysteries were a lot more complicated, especially when people's lives hung in the balance. People she knew and cared for—like her uncle and Sophie, and even Kiki and the crazy Hula Maidens.

She decided to wait until it was almost dark, slip over to Harold's and look around. Maybe she would find evidence of digging on the property. It was a place to start anyway.

If she didn't find anything, she'd have an opportunity to check out the grounds at Fernando's the night of the memorial. The place was huge, but at least she could start searching the areas closest to the house and the beach and the soft sand where the professor had said there were likely to be graves anyway. She wondered how far down she'd have to dig.

Feeling better now that she had a plan, Em was about to go back into the bar when her cell rang. She waved to Sophie to let her know that she would be there to help out in a minute.

"The Tiki Goddess." Em forgot she wasn't on the bar phone.

"So, you've elevated yourself to goddess stature?"

Her heart flew into her throat. It was either her heart or regurgitation. Her ex was on the other end of the line.

She propped her right elbow on her left hand and walked over to the window. Staring across the back of the parking lot at the sunlit turquoise water beyond soothed her. She took a deep breath and let it go.

"This better be good, Phillip."

"I've missed you, too, Em."

She refused to respond.

"I want the Porsche," he said.

"I sold it."

"You sold my Porsche?"

"No," she said, reveling in the whine in his voice. "I sold *my* Porsche. It was the only asset you left me with."

"I'm desperate, Em. You know how much it costs to live in Newport Beach? Couldn't you find it in your heart to loan me a little cash? I promise I'll pay you back."

"With what?"

"I'm trying to get my feet on the ground again. The economy sucks."

"Actually, it's much better and so am I. Which is why I'm

hanging up now."

"Wait!" he said. "Please, Em. I'm desperate."

"Everything's been settled for a long time, Phillip. It's over. We're divorced. D-I-V-O-R-C-E-D."

He'd made his own bed and now he'd have to sleep in it alone— that or ask one of his bimbos to help him out. It wasn't her fault that he'd mortgaged the Newport house on Linda Isle to the hilt and they'd lost it. The Deer Valley condo was gone, too. So was the boat.

"Damn it, Em. I never knew you could be so vindictive."

"Just like I never knew someone could be unfaithful with so many women at once."

"Someday you'll be sorry," he muttered.

Em was about to blow, so she closed her eyes, leaned her head on her hand and rubbed her temple. "Look, I've got to go, Phillip. Don't call and threaten me again."

With that she hung up. Looking around Louie's shabby office, it took a second for her to remember where she was. She realized that until the phone call, Phillip and Newport Beach seemed like faded memories from a long-ago nightmare.

She also realized how much she'd changed. She was no longer mourning the loss of her marriage or her money. She had a whole new life and friends, and right now they needed her. She was a woman on a quest. She was a woman with a bar to run and a femur hidden in a rusty file drawer, and her only living relative was a murder suspect. So was she, for that matter.

Compared to the humiliation and embarrassment Phillip had put her through, things were looking up.

23

Fernando's Big Send Off

The afternoon of Fernando's memorial, Sophie grabbed a plastic bin of tablecloths out of her trunk and made her way up the curved stone path to the entrance of the Hideaway. She nearly jumped out of her skin when she ran into a life-sized cut-out of the entertainer placed near the edge of the stream. Cardboard Fernando was standing front and center at the entry looking as if he'd come back from the grave in time to greet the arriving guests. Lei of all kinds— *plumeria, pikake, puakinikini,* orchid and *maile*— had been draped around his neck.

Beside the photo, the biggest, tackiest wreath Sophie had ever seen was on display. Not only was it festooned with boa feathers, but a plastic baby-grand piano was anchored in the center.

Beyond the memorial display, the interior of the home spread out like a posh five-star hotel lobby. All the sliding pocket doors were wide open, giving the impression there were no walls at all. She shifted the box higher and walked through the rooms looking for Em. Low white sofas banked by koa wood tables and piles of floor pillows were scattered around the living area. Sophie was so dazzled she had a hard time taking in all the art work and the architecture as she headed to the outdoor kitchen, where Em was setting up buffet tables.

"Here are the linens." She set the plastic bin down.

"Great. You can start spreading them out over the serving tables," Em said.

Sophie began unpacking tablecloths. "Was Fernando's shrine set up when you got here?"

Em nodded. She seemed even more distracted that usual. "Quite a jolt, huh? I thought for a minute Fernando had risen."

"Wally would be thrilled."

"On the other hand, Wally might be bummed. Have you seen him?"

"Not yet. What's up?"

"He's dressed entirely in red. Fire-engine-red pants and shirt. Not only that." Em reached for a stack of napkins in the bin. "He's sandwiched between two male hunks." She nodded in the direction of the bar. "Look."

Sophie looked. Sure enough, there was Wally flanked by two muscular males. If they weren't models, they had missed their calling. Their loins were swathed in scraps of fabric that resembled native tapa cloth.

"You can close your mouth now." Em laughed.

"What a waste."

"You can say that again."

"What a waste."

"Okay, enough ogling. Go ahead and set up the bar after you finish those tables. The guests will be arriving any minute."

Sophie had been at the bar slicing lime wedges for about ten minutes when Kiki rushed in toting a load of garment bags made of Aloha print fabric.

"Em told me that we could use a guest room for our dressing area." Kiki glanced around. "Please tell me there's just one room in this place that has walls. We need a private place to change."

"Maybe the bathroom?" Sophie suggested.

"I hope so." Kiki glanced around. "Where's Louie?"

"Em decided tonight should be all about Fernando. Said this was too solemn an occasion for Louie to steal the show with his storytelling. He's at home running the bar."

"She's probably right. But did she really leave him in charge of the Goddess?"

Sophie shrugged. "Yep, but Buzzy is supposed to be keeping an eye on things without letting Louie know."

"Great. The stoned and the senile are watching the shop. Did you see the urn?"

"What urn?" Sophie straightened. Looked around.

"The one with Fernando in it, of course. It's huge and it's Waterford crystal. It's on a table next to the wreath."

"It wasn't set up when I came in. I saw the wreath, though. Was the florist on crack?"

"*I* made that wreath." Kiki ruffled like a rooster at a cockfight.

"What's wrong with it?"

"I've just never seen anything quite like it." Sophie had to bite her cheek.

Kiki was all smiles again. "If you think that's something, you should see our new outfits and the adornments I designed for our hair." She waved her free hand around her head. "Aqua boas in honor of Fernando. Tall hoops of white ostrich feathers entwined with white freshwater pearls threaded on floral wire. And we all have new dresses. Flora has been sewing nonstop for three days."

"I can't wait." Sophie had to turn away. She grabbed a bottle of blue Curacao. Louie had spent an hour coaching her on how to mix a perfect Fernando's Hideaway.

"Where's Em?" Kiki looked around.

"Getting stuff out of the truck."

"Where's Kimo?"

"He's out at the grill."

"I'd better find a place where we can dress." Kiki started to leave but stopped and turned around. "By the way, Roland is dancing tonight."

"The detective? Great." *Not. That's all I need,* Sophie thought. *Detective Sharpe wandering around pretending not to be watching me.*

"Wally had me book Roland. He said he saw a photo of a fire dancer on the front of Honolulu Magazine the other day and just had to have one."

"He wanted the photo?" Sophie knew very well what Wally wanted. Riling Kiki was so easy.

"No. A fire dancer," Kiki snorted.

"I don't think the cop is *mahu.*"

"Oh, definitely not. But he does one hell of a fire dance. Just you wait." Kiki reached for an olive in a bowl on the bar and popped it into her mouth. "These are better marinated in Grey Goose." She leaned in closer. "By the way, have you noticed anything brewing between Em and Roland?"

Sophie frowned into the olive bin. "Like what?"

"Like . . . " Kiki fluttered her fake eyelashes, " . . . attraction. *Serious* attraction. Heat."

"Maybe." Sophie shrugged. One thing she didn't need was a cop hanging around the Goddess all the time. He'd been there more than she liked already.

"Maybe? Just *maybe?* I think definitely." Kiki's head bobbed up and down.

"We'll see," Sophie said.

"We will, won't we?" Kiki winked. "I think if something's going to happen between those two, it just might be tonight at the torch-lighting ceremony on the beach. I've arranged for some members of the canoe club to paddle Wally and the urn out to the edge of the reef. The canoe will be lit with torches at either end. The Maidens will be carrying coconut shells filled with burning lamp oil—reminiscent of the way the Hawaiians used *kukui* nut oil—"

"Em approved all this?"

"Why wouldn't she? Besides, she doesn't have to. I'm in charge of the entertainment and the choreography for the Hula Maidens—unless you can teach us a new dance. I don't see what's wrong with my plans for tonight."

"The Maidens carrying coconut halves filled with burning lamp oil? Harold's big finale comes to mind. Do you think Em and Louie need another disaster associated with the Goddess?"

"I brought a fire extinguisher, for heaven's sake. And Kimo will be standing by with a blanket for stop, drop, and roll."

"I don't know, Kiki. It sounds like a recipe for disaster."

"For someone so young, you worry too much." Kiki popped another olive and headed for the interior of the house.

"If you lived my life, you'd worry, too," Sophie muttered as she watched Kiki walk away. All she could do now was hope everything went off without a hitch.

24

Em's Disappearing Act

So far so good, Em thought.

An hour and a half into the party, and Fernando's memorial was running as smooth as warm Tahitian coconut pudding. Kimo was on top of food prep and service. Sophie was fast and efficient behind the bar. Em found it easier to oversee things without having to worry about Louie, too.

The Maidens were another story. Big Estelle arrived upset. She had tried to leave her mother at home but as she drove off, she glanced in her rear view mirror and saw Little Estelle chasing her down the street on the Gad-About yelling, "Senior abuse! Senior abuse!" at the top of her lungs.

When all the neighbors came pouring out of their homes and took Little Estelle's side, Big Estelle was forced to load her mother into their handicapped-equipped van and bring her along. Em made Big Estelle promise to keep Little Estelle from pulling another disappearing act.

Once the Maidens began to change into their new costumes, Kiki went into hyper-hysteria. It turned out Flora got confused and made all their new gowns a size smaller than ordered. No one could zip them up. Suzi swore that there weren't enough safety pins in the universe to hold hers together. Lil sat down and started bawling. Flora made Sophie refill her water bottle with Bombay. The dresses were green, so Kiki quickly decided they could strip ti leaves from the garden and use raffia—she carried a purse full of supplies—to tie them together and fashion capes that would hide the open zippers.

When Em last saw them, the Maidens were headed into the garden to gather ti leaves. Little Estelle was trailing behind on her Gad-About trying to drive and balance a hurricane glass filled with a blue cocktail between her knees.

Em had just picked up a tray of Chicken Katzu Bites and was about to carry it out to the serving table when she found herself face to face with Roland Sharpe.

"You've got two black eyes." His eyebrow did a hook, the forerunner to a frown.

"So I've been told." She stepped around him, heading for the table. He followed close behind. When Em stopped at the table and finally looked up, he wasn't smiling.

"What happened?"

Was the edge to his tone there to hide concern? She couldn't tell.

"I tripped and fell on my face," she said. It wasn't the right time to tell him about the bone. She didn't know when exactly the right time would be, but certainly not in a crowd. Not as long as there was still the slightest possibility that Louie was involved. She needed more information before handing the thing over to Roland.

When she felt his hand on her shoulder, she nearly dropped the serving tray.

"What?" She turned around and Roland let his hand fall away.

"Your uncle didn't hit you, did he?"

"Uncle Louie?" She couldn't stop chuckling. They'd reached the long buffet table. She set the tray down between one heaped with teriyaki Spam-and-pineapple skewers and another of coconut-crusted shrimp. "Louie doesn't even step on cockroaches. Somehow you've gotten the wrong impression of my uncle."

"He seems to show up wherever there's a murder."

"As I said before, so do you. By the way, are you here as a guest or are you on duty?"

"Actually, I'm working, but not for the KPD tonight."

"You're *dancing*?"

He nodded. "A last-minute request from Wally. Kiki didn't tell you? I thought it would be a good way to keep an eye on things."

"She's in the middle of a costume drama right now. I guess it slipped her mind." Em checked her watch. The ceremony at the beach was to start an hour before sunset. "How long will it take you to dress?"

His mouth actually lifted at one corner. "For fire dancing, I don't dress, I undress."

She would have thought dealing with Phillip's I-want-the-Porsche-back phone call would have put her off men entirely, but her attraction to Detective Sharpe totally surprised her. She almost found herself saying that she'd be happy to help him get ready.

"I'll call you if I need help." He was definitely smiling now.

Em shook her head. Was he reading her mind? "Just don't expect me to light your fire."

She watched Roland walk away, thinking it was no wonder he didn't smile much. That smile had practically rendered her speechless. Not only were his good looks distracting, but his presence here tonight would make it a lot harder for her to snoop around.

When it was almost time for the memorial to begin near the water's edge, Kimo changed into a fresh Aloha shirt. Kiki had his shirts custom made to fit over his "party ball," as she affectionately called his pot belly. For tonight's somber occasion he had donned a shirt with a black background. Unfortunately there was a row of smiling golden pineapples dancing a can-can across the front.

Kimo carried a conch shell into the center of the house, blew it, and announced to everyone that it was time to gather on the shoreline. A line instantly formed at the bar. No one wanted to walk the few hundred yards empty handed. Em wished Sophie could mix faster.

While everyone was at the beach, Em planned to slip away alone for a few minutes to check out the garden. She'd worked up a good-sized case of jitters waiting for the memorial ceremony to begin.

She was just draping a piece of net over the serving tables to keep flies off the *pupu* platters when Leilani Cabral came strolling over with the obligatory champagne flute in hand.

Em couldn't help but admire Leilani's perfectly coiffed hair, her trim figure, and her manicured nails. Em's own nails were hopeless. She had had weekly pedicures and manicures, not to mention acrylic nails, on the mainland, but they were impractical for her now with all the dishwashing, swimming and gardening she did.

"Hi Leilani," she said.

Leilani ignored her as she waggled her fingers at a couple in line at the bar and mouthed, "Nice to see you." Then she finally turned to Em. "So, we meet again."

"Wally is trying to get everyone down to the beach." Em couldn't manage feigning a warm welcome—or even a cool one for that matter. Leilani didn't seem to care or notice. She was looking around the room.

"Have you seen Roland? We were chatting earlier, but I seemed to have lost him." Leilani smiled over the rim of her glass.

Finders keepers, Em thought. "He's probably on the beach already. He's performing tonight."

"Oh, that's right. His little moonlighting gig. In that case I'd better go get a good spot. I'd hate to miss it." Leilani looked miffed. Didn't she like Roland showing his stuff?

"How about your husband? Is he here?" Em had never laid eyes on Judge Cabral over at Harold's or anywhere else.

"Warren had a banquet tonight at Kilohana. Actually, I have to leave early and join him." She started to walk away and then paused. "Aren't you going down to watch Roland?"

"I wouldn't miss it for the world." Nor had Em missed the challenge in the woman's voice.

Em found a place to set the tray and walked beside Leilani along a stone path that wound around a thick stand of bamboo and on down to the sand. There was something cold and calculating about Leilani Cabral that accounted for her success. She wasn't the kind of woman Em would choose to hang out with; Leilani was obviously into competition.

"Did you try the *pupus*?" Em struggled to find something to say to the woman that wouldn't sound as antagonistic as she felt.

"I'm stuffed. I had a maraschino cherry." Leilani smiled.

Em sighed.

"I wish it was shady down here," Leilani said. She looked over Em's standard black pants and the Goddess tank top she had worn to work the party. "I hate to sweat," the realtor added.

Em ignored the comment. Leilani was focused on Detective Sharpe, who was ready to begin.

"Ooh, look. Roland is lighting his knives." Shark Lady actually cooed.

"I can see that." Try as she might not to, Em couldn't help but fantasize as she stared across the open circle of sand that separated Roland from the crowd. There wasn't a woman present who wasn't staring at his perfectly sculpted, well-oiled, 6'3" body glistening in the glow of the setting sun and flickering firelight.

Primal drums began to pound out an erotic beat as Roland stepped into the center of the wide arc of onlookers and paused for dramatic effect. Behind him, the deep, blue-green waters of the Pacific stretched toward the brilliant ball of orange just above the horizon.

Flaming knives lit on both ends began to twirl. Hypnotically slow at first and then faster, the movement matched the tempo of the drums. Roland threw one knife high in the air, caught it as he tossed the second. He twirled one behind his back before he dropped to his knees and leaned back in the sand. Then, lowering himself onto his back, with both feet in the air, he rested the burning ends of one knife on the soles of his feet, straightened his knees and tossed it into the air.

Em glanced at Shark Lady. Beside her, Leilani was sweating.

Em checked her watch. She told the Maidens they could only dance for forty minutes after Roland finished. Any longer and the crowd would go into a hula-coma.

Roland's drummer would liven things up after the Maidens' performance while the canoe took to the water with Wally, paddled by his beefy escorts with Fernando riding along in his crystal urn. A portion of the entertainer's ashes would be spread on the Hawaiian waters, more would be left in Las Vegas, a bit more in San Francisco. Some would remain in the urn. "Because I need him with me," Wally explained.

There would be so much going on that Em was sure no one would miss her if she slipped away for a few minutes.

Just as Em turned to leave, Sophie walked up beside her.

"I'll be right back," Em said. "I'm headed to the *lua*. Nature calls."

"Anything you want me to do?" Sophie asked.

Em shook her head. "Just enjoy the show."

Sophie turned to watch Roland as Em hurried back up the path alone. Drum beats drifted along the beach. Soft clouds floated by on a velvet breeze and palm fronds rustled against one another. A bullfrog hidden somewhere in the distance croaked like it was birthing a cow.

Em veered toward the expansive garden once she was out of sight behind the bamboo and glanced at her watch. She'd give herself twenty-five minutes. That way she would return to the ceremony at the water's edge before the Maidens finished—if they didn't end up torching themselves with flaming coconut shells. With all that feathered headgear, they'd go up as fast as Roman candles.

As she walked alone across the breathtaking grounds of Fernando's Hideaway, the pungent scent of *plumeria* and night-blooming jasmine perfumed the air. The yard, a multimillion-dollar carpet of green, rolled on and on. The sound of the surf matched the rhythm of the guitar and ukulele music riding on the trade winds.

Em raised her head, inhaled. She closed her eyes and imagined the ancient Hawaiians living here long before all the cars, bars, and fast food restaurants; before the hotels, timeshares, condos, mansions and pristine landscaping. A tingle ran down her spine, and she opened her eyes. She had the feeling someone was nearby, but as she scanned the area, she found she was alone.

Maybe they're here with me, she thought. *Those ancient ones. Maybe they are watching me right now.* The night was so lovely, the setting so magical, it was easy for her imagination to make the most of the moment. Em warned herself to snap out of it.

Hopefully it wasn't the spirit of an ancient with a missing femur watching her. She remembered Nelg saying that there were probably countless gravesites to be discovered as more property was developed. Especially this close to the beach.

If Fernando hadn't ended up swimming with his koi, his improvements would already be underway. Em stopped walking when she realized she had reached the spot Fernando had proudly pointed out as the location of his new guest house and pool. It was very close to the property line that his compound shared with *Hale Pua*, House of Flowers, the estate next door.

She hurried across the grass toward a hedge of thick, low palms that marked the lot line. She paced back, *mauka*, toward the mountains, then stopped, turned, and headed *makai*, toward the beach.

Head down, she focused on the ground, searching for any sign that someone might have been digging recently. Harold's murder had occurred nearly three weeks ago. With daily trade showers, new grass and weeds may have already covered any sign of disturbed ground.

This is nuts. Em glanced at her watch and edged closer to the beach. The Maidens were probably in full dance mode by now. The dense stand of yellow bamboo near the edge of the lawn hid the crowd from sight and Em from them. Now and again she saw the flickering torchlight through the leaves.

She'd all but given up when she nearly tripped over a low garden stake poking up out of the sandy soil. She dropped down to one knee. Brushing the sand with her fingertips didn't turn up anything either, so she worked her fingers down into the loose dirt. When she hit something hard she gasped and recoiled, then steadied her nerves and took a deep breath. She tugged a bit and pulled out a piece of coral worn perfectly smooth.

After another minute, she brushed her hands together and was just getting to her feet when something hard slammed into the side of her head.

Not again. It was her last conscious thought as she sank to the ground.

25

All Tied Up And No Where to Go

Em's head pounded like a Tahitian drum. She couldn't move her arms or legs or open her mouth and quickly realized that she was blindfolded, lying on her side with her cheek resting on a cold slab of cement. Tape sealed her lips shut. Panic set in and she tried to scream but all that came out was a muffled, "Mphhh!"

The pounding intensified, but the fog in her mind slowly began to lift. She tried to sit up but her arms were bound behind her back, her ankles taped tightly together.

Think, Em. Think.

She lay still, cramped and uncomfortable against a hard cold floor. The last thing she recalled was walking the grounds of Fernando's garden searching for evidence of a disturbed gravesite. She had felt as if she were being watched and apparently she had been, but not by someone or something as fanciful as the spirit of an ancient Hawaiian. The presence had been very real and very sinister. Not to mention someone who packed a wallop.

When the incessant beat suddenly stopped, she realized it wasn't coming from inside her head. It actually was a drumbeat and not very far away. She had to be somewhere close to Fernando's, close enough to hear the drums, anyway. The memorial was still in progress.

She pictured Roland nearly naked, twirling flaming knives on the beach. Had he noticed she'd left? Would he wonder where she was when she didn't return?

She struggled and flailed around until she finally rolled over on to her back. She tried not to panic, not to let the tape across her mouth freak her out. She closed her eyes against the thick darkness and practiced deep breathing through her nose. Once she was calmer, she decided she had to occupy her mind or she would quickly lose it.

She began to list the names of all of Louie's cocktails on the

Goddess drink menu—in alphabetical order.

26

Sophie Sounds the Alarm

The return of the canoe signaled the end of the party. Some of the guests ambled down the beach to the driveway, where young valets stood ready to jog down the road and retrieve their cars. A few lingered, winding their way up the torch-lit path to the house to grab another plate of *pupus* and one last drink from Sophie.

Kimo was clearing the tables and packing up. He stopped by the bar on his second trip to his van and asked her, "You seen Em?"

Sophie looked around. "Nope. I think she must still be down at the beach. I haven't seen the detective lately, either."

"Aha. That's it, then." Kimo winked and headed outside, toting a couple gallons of unopened teriyaki sauce. Obviously even Kimo noticed there was something between Em and the detective.

By the time Sophie had boxed glasses, packed up bottles, sorted out what to leave behind, bottled up the cherries and olives, bagged the limes and lemons and boxed the napkins, the cleanup was nearly done.

Kimo had enlisted Kiki to help. Suzi and Trish were still around somewhere.

"Where's Em?" Kiki was the next to ask as Sophie walked outside loading her trunk.

"With the detective, I guess. I haven't seen her since the ceremony began."

"That's odd." Kiki frowned. "I don't remember seeing her in the crowd. I saw you there for a minute or two. Where did you go?"

"To the *lua*, and then I restocked the bar. Kimo thinks Em and Sharpe are somewhere getting it on." Sophie pressed her hands against her back and stretched, then took a deep breath.

"Does your back hurt?" Kiki's concern showed.

Sophie shook her head. "Just been doing a lot of lifting."

"It's not like Em to just disappear." Kiki stared off toward the beach. Torches were still glowing near the shoreline. "Almost everyone's left already. Whatever she's doing, even *that*, she should be back by now."

"Hey, she's worked hard. And the way her ex keeps calling and bugging her, she deserves some down time."

"Really? He's been calling her?"

"Yeah. He was driving her so nuts she got a new cell number."

"I had no idea."

"He's a jerk. You haven't noticed how stressed she's seemed lately?" Sophie headed for the house. Kiki walked beside her.

"I'm glad she's rid of him, then." Kiki sighed, smiled. "There aren't many like my Kimo."

Just then Kimo passed them, pushing the portable bar, sweating profusely, huffing like a pregnant woman in the last stage of labor.

"Need a hand with that, Kimo?" Sophie stepped over to help him wrestle the bar to his van.

"I'll have a valet help me load it." He nudged his chin over his shoulder toward the house. "Wally's looking for Em. Wants to write her a check."

"I'd better go find her," Kiki volunteered.

"Wally can give the check to Kimo," Sophie suggested.

Kiki looked as if she were about to object when Roland Sharpe came strolling out of the house dressed in slacks and a shirt, carrying his scrap of a costume and his fire knives. He wasn't smiling.

Sophie's palms started to sweat.

"Speak of the devil. Is Em inside?" Kiki asked. "Wally is looking for her."

Roland shrugged, his expression shuttered. "I haven't seen her since the show started."

Kiki's eyes widened. "We thought she was at the beach with you."

He shook his head. "She was at the beach when I started dancing but I saw her leave right away."

"She said would be back after she used the *lua*," Sophie said. "She wasn't with you?"

"No, she wasn't. Where did you go, by the way? You left, too." Roland pinned her with a stare.

Sophie took a deep breath. "I went back up to the bar to get ready for the rush after the show."

"Come to think of it, I didn't see Em in the crowd when we were dancing." Kiki thought a moment longer. "I *know* I didn't see her."

Sharpe's expression was no longer closed. He looked worried.

"If she's not here, then where is she?" Sophie watched the detective scan the driveway.

"Her truck is still here," he said.

"Then she's got to be around somewhere." Kiki headed inside at a jog. "I'll ask the other Maidens if they've seen her."

Sophie didn't like the way Sharpe was staring at her and forced herself not to fidget. The last thing she needed was another trip to the station in Lihue. Another round of questioning

"You say she went to the *lua* but didn't go back to the beach?"

She nodded. "She told me she'd be right back, but she wasn't, and then I left, too. I thought I just missed her somewhere and that she was back watching the show."

The detective shifted his gaze to the surrounding garden. The sound of the faux stream—water tumbling over rocks—seemed to swell. He walked away, paced along the edge of the stream in one direction and then the other. Then he scanned the grass and the garden.

Sophie trailed behind. When they reached the waterfall with the pool beneath it they saw only koi.

"You don't think she could be . . . in trouble, do you?" Sophie forced the words out.

Roland Sharpe's expression hardened. His eyes narrowed as he turned to her.

"She'd better not be."

27

Roland Carries a Torch

Kiki was out of breath by the time she ran up to Roland again.

"We can't find her anywhere," she said. "We haven't searched the entire garden, but we looked through the house. There's no sign of her."

Kiki noticed Roland didn't hesitate. He called in a missing person's report even though it had only been a couple of hours since anyone had seen Em. He told Kiki that given the circumstances, he wasn't willing to wait around before he put all available manpower on alert.

"Fifteen acres is too damn much property to search on foot in the dark," he grumbled. "I radioed in for someone to bring out the lifeguards' ATV's stored at the county lot in Hanalei, asap."

Fernando's Hideaway was a search-and-rescue nightmare that encompassed the garden, the beach, streams, ditches, and natural areas that hadn't been landscaped. A tangle of *hau* bush, wild plum trees and false *kamani* covered the old jungle areas near the base of the hills. The land beyond the inland boundary was all miles and miles of nature preserve.

While awaiting help, Kiki and the Hula Maidens ran from room to room calling Em's name. They looked under beds and inside closets. Lillian even went through the dressers and nearly fainted when she found Fernando's rhinestone-encrusted thong collection.

"We can't find her anywhere." Kiki reported back to Roland and watched as he shoved his fingers through his hair. It was the first time she'd ever seen him lose his cool.

"How long before the ATV arrives?" She wanted to know.

"It's on the way. Is anyone else missing?" He faced the driveway as more patrol cars arrived.

"Not that I know of." Kiki reached up and pulled off her pearl and feather headgear. "You can't possibly suspect Em now, Roland."

"She was at the last two murder scenes. Maybe the killer is afraid Em saw something."

Kiki sighed. "Or maybe our snooping around has led to this."

"What do you mean 'our snooping around'?"

Kiki looked everywhere but at Roland. "We had to do something to get Sophie and Louie off the hook. You guys weren't getting anywhere, so we decided to do a little detecting ourselves."

"We who?"

"The Hula Maidens. Sophie. Em."

"What did you do, Kiki?"

"We had just a couple of meetings . . . and we phoned everyone on Harold's client list."

"Exactly how did you get a hold of his client list?"

She didn't like the way his dark eyes bored holes into her. She hesitated, hating to tell him, but Em *was* missing. Kiki swallowed and shrugged.

"Somehow Sophie came up with it."

28

Still in the Dark

Em drifted in and out of consciousness. Her wrists and ankles ached. Trussed up like a turkey in a roasting pan, she needed to stretch her legs, not to mention pee.

Lying there in the dark and in pain, she had no concept of time. She heard voices call her name and they sounded close. Once, she even thought she heard footsteps. She tried drumming her heels against the cement to make noise, but that proved too painful and didn't produce a sound.

She was thirsty, but not hungry, and wondered if the few bites she'd sampled before the party might be her last meal. She imagined Roland reading the coroner's report. *The meager contents of the victim's stomach included ahi sushi and bar-b-qued ribs.*

She struggled like a beached whale every time she rolled over. The concrete, cold as a slab in the morgue, was killing her shoulders. She pictured Harold, smoldering face down in the *imu,* and then Fernando floating with the koi. She imagined Uncle Louie trying to come up with a cocktail to honor her memory, heard him mumbling to himself.

"Something the color of duct tape. Maybe Quervo Silver tequila. I've got it! The Tape Worm!"

Not only was she convinced she was losing it, but her bladder was about to burst, so she practiced doing Kegels. She was up to forty-five and almost enjoying it when she heard what sounded like a key turning a lock. She went completely still and broke out in a cold sweat.

She heard hurried footsteps somewhere in the dark seconds before someone grabbed her by her pony tail and jerked her to a sitting position. Her joints screamed in pain. Her captor remained behind her. Em felt long fingernails pick at the edges of tape across her mouth. Without warning, the duct tape was ripped off.

"What do you want?" She croaked. "Why are you doing this?"

No answer.

She tried to turn her head and earned another jerk on her ponytail to keep her facing forward. There was a rustle of clothing and then her captor let go of her hair with one hand and held a bottle of water to her lips. Em refused to drink. The bottle was shoved against her mouth again.

Em took a few sips and then turned her head away. Water spilled down the front of her Goddess tank top.

A long, taut silence ensued. Too long, considering Em still had to pee.

"I have to go to the bathroom."

There was no response other than the sound of duct tape ripping off the roll.

"Please don't—"

Her assailant slapped a fresh strip of tape across her mouth again.

Em made a mental note to herself. Whoever was holding her captive had long fingernails. Very long acrylic fingernails.

29

Maidens Unite

Em had been missing for two nights when Kiki gave up on the KPD and called an emergency meeting at the Goddess—attendance mandatory.

All the Maidens were there on time, as everyone was desperate to find Em. As far as they were concerned, she was their hero. She had single-handedly brought the Goddess back from the brink of bankruptcy. She was keeping Louie focused and the books balanced.

Since Em came to town, things had been looking up for all of them. Their dancing venue was secure but now—unless they found Em alive—they were facing disaster on what Kiki considered a global scale. If anything happened to Em, Louie would fall apart and Marlene, The Defector, would step in and take over.

Flora was already so drunk when she arrived that she barely made it through the front door. Kiki had Suzi and Trish prop her in the corner of a long bench seat.

Little Estelle rolled in on the Gad-About looking happier than she had in a long time. Big Estelle came dragging in behind her on crutches with her foot in a cast.

"What happened to you?" Kiki demanded.

"My mother ran over my foot. It was no accident, either."

"Prove it!" Little Estelle revved her engine.

Suzi fielded business calls even though Kiki shot her a dark glance each time her cell phone went off.

"I could fine you for that," Kiki threatened.

"I'll pay a fine. I've got three places in escrow right now and can't afford to lose a deal," Suzi countered. "Besides, you aren't the boss of me, Kiki. Get over yourself."

Lil had been too upset to drive, so MyBob had accompanied her. They squeezed onto the bench seat.

Trish had brought in photos from Fernando's memorial and spread them out on the table. No one saw anything that might lead them to Em. Trish also brought in clippings from the *Garden Island* newspaper, where the front page headline screamed NORTH SHORE BAR MANAGER MISSING.

Louie had offered a reward of an unspecified amount for Em's safe return. He also took out a half page ad reading "Have you seen this person?" Trish had provided a photo of Em. She looked confident and happy, smiling in the doorway between the office and the bar. Louie couldn't resist including a small headshot of himself with David Letterman perched on his shoulder. "From my pirate phase," he said.

Anyone with any information was to call Detective Roland Sharpe or the KPD.

Goddess patrons, locals and neighbors had set up a shrine of flowers and candles on one end of the lanai. Yellow ribbons were tied around everything that didn't move—chairs, lanai railings, tiki barstools.

Kiki clinked the side of her martini glass with one of her diamond rings as a call to order. Everyone fell silent immediately. She slowly got to her feet and looked them all squarely in the eye all but Flora, whose eyelids were at half-mast anyway. Kiki called out to Louie who was tending bar.

"Where's Sophie?"

"She phoned to say she'd be a late. She sounded pretty upset."

"You all know why we're here." Kiki picked up a newspaper clipping and waved it around. "Em is missing. She came to our aid without question and now something terrible may have happened to her. The police haven't found her and apparently have no clues, so it's up to us to go where no man dares venture."

"Big Estelle's bedroom!" Little Estelle shouted.

"*Mother!*"

Everyone burst into howls of laughter.

"Shut up. All of you. Please." Kiki waited for silence.

Louie came shuffling across the room carrying a cocktail shaker filled with a deep purple concoction. He filled Kiki's glass. "We've got to find her," he mumbled. "Got to."

"We will, Uncle Louie," Suzi assured him. "We'll bring her home."

Kiki took a sip and spit it back into the glass. "What *is* this?"

"Kauai Kooler." Louie shrugged. "Purple is the color of Kauai. You know, pink for Maui, yellow for Oahu, red for the Big Island."

"I know that," Kiki said. "I want to know what's *in* this?"

"It's grape juice, Cointreau, and brandy."

"It tastes like something they'd serve at a Jonestown reunion."

"That was Letterman's reaction, but I'm really partial to the color."

Kiki handed him back the glass. "So, where is Marlene? Was she at the memorial? Has anyone seen her?"

Louie's smile faded. "She's at a hula retreat on Maui."

"Aha! So she *says*. She could be anywhere." Kiki was convinced The Defector was behind Em's disappearance. "Did anyone see her the night of the memorial?"

"That's when she left town," Louie said. "I know what you're thinking. You'd like to pin Em's disappearance on her."

"Even though no one saw her, she could have been slinking around at the memorial."

He shook his head. "I told you, she had already left for the hula retreat."

"Have you actually talked to her? Do you know she's there for sure?"

He shook his head. "No, I haven't talked to her, but I know she's there. They're out of cell range. Up in Makawao. Meditating. Dancing. Pounding *poi* or something."

Kiki snorted. The fact that Marlene left the Maidens still irked her.

"When did she take off? Right *after* she kidnapped Em, probably."

"You know, Kiki, I'm tired of you slandering Marlene. Why on earth would she want to hurt Em?"

"You're blind, Louie. Because *she wants this place*. She almost had it in her hot little hands before Em came and got in her way. That's motive."

"Your brain cell count is way down, Kiki." He drank half of the Kauai Kooler she'd rejected.

"I'll worry about my brain cells. You just get me a Chardonnay. House."

Louie polished off the rest of the purple Kooler on his way back to the bar.

Just then Sophie came walking in. Her usually spiked hair was pancaked flat. Except for the row of silver rings through her left eyebrow, Kiki thought Sophie could pass for one of those starving sad-eyed waifs in a television infomercial begging viewers to "Send This Kid Money For Food."

"Sorry I'm late." Sophie sank into the only empty seat at the table. "My car wouldn't start and so I had to hitch a ride."

"I should have waited. You could have come with me," Trish said.

"No worries," Kiki said. "We haven't gotten very far yet, as usual." She eyeballed the Maidens. "Let's go around the table and everyone take a turn telling us where Em was the last time you saw her. And what she said. We'll start with Suzi."

Suzi shoved her cell phone into her purse and zipped it shut. A second later the muffled strains of *Tiny Bubbles* floated out of the bowels of the purse. Kiki gave her such a stink eye that Suzi ignored the call.

"Em was in the kitchen helping Kimo fill a tray for the buffet. I asked if she had any aspirin anywhere. Em stopped what she was doing and got one for me from a pill box in her purse. She warned me to be careful with the flaming coconut oil." Suzi's eyes teared up.

Kiki never cried. She thought crying was way over the top. Dismissing Suzi, Kiki turned to Trish.

"Go ahead. Your turn."

"I was moving around the house taking photos. Everything was almost exactly the same as the night of the housewarming—except that Fernando was in an urn instead of his Elvis outfit." She waited for Big Estelle to stop snickering. "Em told me to head down to the beach to take photos of everyone once they assembled." She thought for a second. "She was on the back lanai then, near the stairs overlooking the trail to the beach."

"Anything else?" Kiki waited.

"Em kept gazing out over the lawn and seemed kind of distant," Trish said.

"I thought she seemed troubled, too," Lil chimed in. "I told MyBob that night. I said, 'Bob, Em seems troubled.' Didn't I Bob?"

MyBob nodded. Kiki noticed MyBob nodded on cue.

"Big Estelle?" Kiki said. "Go ahead."

Big Estelle stared forlornly at the cast on her foot. "Do you think I'll be able to dance again?"

"You couldn't dance before. Maybe by some miracle, this'll

help," her mother said.

"Shut up, you two. I've about had it," Kiki warned. "I'm about to fine you both."

"Bat poop," Little Estelle mumbled.

"I heard that." They were definitely giving Kiki a migraine. She yelled across the bar. "If you don't have chardonnay, Louie, then bring me anything but that purple crap." She turned her attention back to the table full of women and MyBob.

"Go on," she prodded Big Estelle. "Where did you last see Em?"

"I was having low blood sugar so she stopped what she was doing to bring me a glass of oj. It was right before we all trooped down to the beach to perform. She told me to take better care of myself." Big Estelle glared at her mother. "Caregivers get the short end of the stick, you know."

"Em said that?" Trish frowned. "About caregivers?"

"I added that last part," Big Estelle confessed.

"Where *was* she?" Kiki wanted to know.

"Who?" Big Estelle blinked.

Little Estelle shouted, "Em, damn it! Where was Em when you last talked to her? Keep track of the conversation. Sometimes I think you are really losing it."

"She was in the hallway, near the bathroom." When Big Estelle burst into tears. Lil patted her on the shoulder.

"What about you, Lil?"

"My cape came apart. It completely exploded. There were ti leaves everywhere. Em stopped what she was doing to fasten it back together for me." Lil started snuffling again.

Kiki didn't know anyone could produce as much snot and tears as Lillian had over the last couple of weeks and wondered if maybe all the pink hair dye was affecting her sinuses. By now the woman should be dry as a lava bed.

"She . . . she was on the . . . on the stairs near the beach path. Everyone else was gone." Lil covered her face and started sobbing.

"So you might have been the very last one to see her," Kiki said.

"No, I was. I think." Sophie finally entered the discussion. "Everyone was down at the beach by then. Lil had just had her cape repaired. We were watching Sharpe start the fire dance when Em said she had to use the *lua*. She said she'd be right back."

Exactly what Kiki had heard Sophie tell Roland.

"I wish I'd gone with her." Sophie's voice was barely audible.

"Don't we all?" Kiki said. "Don't we all." She took a deep breath and inhaled half the glass of wine that Louie had finally handed her. "But we were dancing."

Trish was stacking her photos. "It doesn't sound like anybody knows any more than we do. The police have spoken to all the guests. They've searched every inch of Fernando's Hideaway, inside and out, as well as the empty house at *Hale Pua* and the Anderson's place on the other side."

In the corner, Flora was conscious for the moment. "Mebbe we should have a bake sale." Before her eyes drifted shut again, she muttered, "Bake cookies or make some *lau lau.*"

"The fundraising discussion was three months ago," Suzi said.

Flora groaned, shifted around on the bench seat, belched and closed her eyes.

"What's up with you, Sophie?" Kiki had been watching the girl since she sat down. Sophie had been staring at the table, drumming her nails against the resin table top. Her acrylics were deep purple today, almost the color of Louie's Kauai Kooler. There were gold lightning bolts painted on a couple of them. They matched the shock of purple dye in her hair.

Sophie looked up, met Kiki's eyes for half a second and dropped her gaze again.

"Spill it," Kiki said. "You're hiding something."

"You know how Em said she tripped and fell on her nose to explain her black eyes?"

Kiki nodded. Silent. Everyone sat up a bit straighter and leaned in so as not to miss a word.

"She didn't trip. Somebody knocked her out," Sophie confessed.

"What?!" Kiki was furious. "Why wasn't I told?"

"Someone *knocked her out?*" Lil cried.

Sophie nodded. "I found her in the parking lot, lying on the pavement by Harold's hedge. I asked if she passed out and she said someone knocked her out."

Louie came running over. "Why didn't she tell me?"

Sophie said, "She wasn't sure who did it, but she said she was definitely hit from behind."

"Why didn't she say something before now? Why didn't you?" Kiki demanded.

"She told me not to."

"We've got to call Roland." Kiki pointed at Suzi, who quickly fished her cell out of her purse. *Tiny Bubbles* were bubbling again. Suzi shut off the ring tone and speed-dialed the detective. The night Em went missing they all synchronized their cells with his number.

"What should I tell him?" Suzi put her hand over the phone.

"Tell him to get his sweet butt up here. I don't care what he's doing. Tell him to drop it and get up here asap."

30

It's All In The Details

Kiki was pacing the bar by the time Roland finally arrived twenty-five minutes later.

"Where have you been?" She stormed toward him, sloshing white wine out of a stem glass in her haste to give him what for.

"I was in Kilauea. Rental cars are jamming the road in both directions. What's with all the yellow ribbons strung around the lanai? Someone should take that makeshift memorial down, Kiki."

He sounded as mad as she felt. He lowered his voice. "We haven't found a body. Besides, Em might not even be in danger. Maybe she killed Harold and Fernando and took off."

Kiki snorted. "You don't believe that any more than I do."

"No. But all those candles out there are pissing me off."

The bar was still closed to the public. The Hula Maidens had started munching on some edamame that Trish brought for them. They silently sucked the slippery white soy beans out of the fuzzy pods and tossed the empty shells into a communal bowl in the middle of the table.

Louie waved and said aloha to Roland. His tongue was purple. He wandered over to the bar mumbling to himself. Kiki noticed Roland staring at Sophie. The girl looked pale and shaken.

"What's up?" Roland snagged an empty chair, flipped it around and straddled it.

"Do you practice that move at home?" Kiki asked.

He ignored her. "I hate to say it, but I actually hope you women have come up with something." He looked at the group gathered around the table.

"Tell him," Kiki urged Sophie.

Roland looked over at Sophie. It took her a second to make eye contact.

"You saw Em's black eyes?" She took a deep breath, waited until he nodded. "She didn't fall. Someone knocked her out."

"When?"

"Last week when she was out trimming the hedge. She got a phone call. I went out to get her and found her lying passed out cold, face down in the parking lot. She said someone snuck up on her and knocked her out."

"Why didn't she report the assault?"

"She said she didn't want to." Sophie's gaze slid over to the bar and back to Roland.

Louie whistled as he carried a stack of plates into the kitchen.

"You think she was protecting him?" Roland nodded in Louie's direction.

Kiki looked at Roland, then Sophie, then toward the kitchen door.

"Louie? No way," Suzie whispered. "No way would Louie hurt Em. Or anyone else."

The women all nodded in agreement.

"I wouldn't put it past his darling Marlene, though," Kiki mumbled.

A call came in over Roland's radio. He listened for a second then turned the volume down.

"Is that about Em? Did they find her?" Kiki voiced what they all wanted to know. There wasn't a sound in the room.

"No," he said. "Some pig hunter hung a boar's head and hide on a fence post along Kaumu'ali'i highway. It's freaking out the tourists."

"Again?" Suzi laughed but quickly sobered.

"Why would anyone kidnap Em?" Lil wondered aloud.

"Maybe she discovered something about Harold's murderer. Or Fernando's." Trish gathered the photographs back into a pile.

"So what about it?" Kiki stared at Roland. "Do you have anything yet?"

"We're looking into Fernando's partner. He inherited everything. And, as it turns out, there are plenty of fans who used to Tweet with Fernando and post on his facebook page. They *thought* they were chatting with Fernando, but he hired someone to write his blogs, and do his Tweeting. He's got more than a few psycho-cyber stalkers, and the location of his "hidden" Hawaiian estate was easy enough to track down. He could have been killed by some nut case."

"But what does that have to do with Harold?" Lil wanted to know.

"Or Em?" Trish added.

"Her husband has been hassling her," Sophie said.

Kiki fiddled with a loose fingernail. "First you tell me the news about the black eyes. Now the husband's calls. Why didn't I hear any of this before?"

"Or me?" Roland asked. "You should have called me."

Sophie shrugged with a look that said *as if.* "Em said not to tell anyone."

Roland slipped his notebook out of his back pocket. "Anybody know her husband's name and whereabouts?"

"Ex-husband," Kiki clarified.

Kiki watched Roland underline *ex* twice.

"Newport Beach." Louie was behind the bar but obviously had been listening closely. "Phillip Johnson. He's a C.P.A. in Newport Beach."

"Anyone know if he's on island?" Roland reached for his cell.

"I never thought of that," Kiki said. "He could be."

The Maidens were talking among themselves. None of them knew anything much about Phillip but they were all convinced he was a bastard, a schmuck, a creep, and definitely an idiot.

"Maybe he sent a hit man after her," Lil said. "That could happen, couldn't it, Bob?"

MyBob wiped sweat off his bald head with a napkin and nodded. "Sure. Hit man."

"Sounds possible." Kiki said. "She never talked about it, but I think it was a pretty messy divorce. Maybe Phillip came after her. Or maybe Bob's right. Maybe he hired someone to do his dirty work."

Roland called mainland information.

"What about Harold? And Fernando?" Lil wondered aloud. "Em's husband might be after her, but we still don't know who killed those two. Or why."

Big Estelle was no longer crying. "Maybe the killer was here to get rid of Em, and Harold interfered. Maybe the same thing happened at Fernando's. Someone might have been stalking Em, but then Fernando got in the way and got killed instead."

Little Estelle downed a shot of tequila and slammed the glass on the table. "Maybe the other two murders were just to point everyone in the wrong direction."

Lil piped up, "Maybe they were decoy murders!"

Roland said *mahalo* into his phone and then hung up. "Her husband is sitting in his Newport Beach office," he told them.

"That doesn't mean he didn't hire someone," Kiki reminded him.

"No, it doesn't."

Kiki deflated like an old party balloon. "I hate to think we missed finding her at Fernando's. I hate to think the worst."

"We went over every inch of the place. It rained pretty hard the night of the party. Washed off any scent the dogs would have picked up the next day."

"What about the house next door? *Hale Pua*. The empty house that's for sale. Did you get inside?" Trish asked.

Roland sat down again and nodded. "That's Leilani's listing. She left a banquet to bring the keys all the way back out to us late that night."

Suzi shook her head. "Boy, that's another overpriced piece of property, but I heard she managed to unload it on some of Fernando's friends."

At the end of the banquette, Flora Carillo made a choking sound and woke up with a start. "Wha'did I miss?" She blinked, looked around. "Where's my Gatorade bottle?"

"Maybe if we danced we'd feel a little better," Lil suggested.

"Maybe you're right," Kiki said. "How about we do *Papalina?*"

The song about a woman with rosy "cheeks" whose flower had been picked a long time ago was one of Kiki's favorites. She called it her theme song.

"I'll put on the music," Louie volunteered.

The women all scrambled to their feet. Those seated along the banquette slid toward either end. Flora planted her hands on the table and hoisted herself up. There was a stampede for the stage. Chair legs scraped the floor.

Big Estelle tripped on her cast and would have fallen on her face if Roland hadn't been there. As it was she fell across his lap.

"I forgot about my cast," she wailed. As Roland propped her back up she explained, "Mother ran over my foot. Maybe I should press charges."

"How about a Kauai Kooler?" Louie was at Roland's shoulder offering a martini glass full of purple liquid.

"Do *not* drink that," Kiki warned. "It should have a label with a skull on it."

She was about to have the women line up when a tall, thin man in cargo shorts and shirt and a hat worthy of Indiana Jones stepped into the open doorway.

"Have you found her yet? I might be able to help." He announced his offer to the room at large.

MyBob turned down the CD player. The Maidens began to climb off the stage. Roland crossed the room to greet the newcomer before Kiki could get there.

"I'm Detective Roland Sharpe of the KPD. Are you referring to Ms. Johnson?"

The man nodded. "I'm Professor Nelg Nelson, Professor of Anthropology at the University of North Carolina." The men shook hands. "I've been camping over at Polihale and was on my way back to the North Shore when I stopped for breakfast at the Tip Top and saw the newspaper headlines. I immediately called the police. They said you were here."

"You have pertinent information?" Roland's notebook was at the ready. The Maidens gathered around the men like flies on a *pupu* platter.

"Where's the orange girl?" Sophie Chin asked.

The professor shrugged. "I got hungry. There's only so much a man can sacrifice for sex."

"The orange girl?" Roland frowned at Sophie, who quickly explained, while Louie got the professor settled at the table and headed into the kitchen to make him a half-pound burger and fries.

Kiki waved Roland into a seat beside the professor. The Maidens hovered in a tight semi-circle.

Roland looked at the women.

"I suppose telling you all to disperse would be a waste of breath without a tactical team to back me up, wouldn't it?"

"Right," Kiki nodded. "No time for back up."

"Tell me what you know," Roland urged the professor.

Nelson explained his private conversation with Em and described how she'd locked the office doors before she pulled a femur out of the file cabinet.

"Femur?" Roland stared. "A *femur?*"

"Yes. It was obviously old. She wouldn't tell me where she'd found it. I figure it came from somewhere here on the property. I told her that she had to alert the Burial Council and that would lead to trouble."

"We have a Burial Council?" Kiki asked.

"Where is it? Can I drop Mother off?" Big Estelle looked happier than she had since she hobbled through the door.

"Maybe Kimo and the men found the bone while digging the new *imu*," MyBob suggested. "Maybe they asked Em to hide it."

Kiki shook her head. "No way. I would have heard about it. Kimo can't keep a secret."

"Enough." Roland held up his hand. "Sit. Everybody. If you are going to stay here, then shut up. Please." He turned back to the professor. "Do you know where she put it?"

The man shook his head. "Maybe it's still in the office."

Roland turned to Louie. "Do you mind if I search your office?"

"'Course not. I'll help," Louie volunteered.

Everyone else jumped to their feet.

Roland sighed and turned to Louie. "Can you keep them out here? That'll be help enough."

"Not a good idea," Sophie said. "How do we know you won't plant evidence?"

Roland spread his arms. "Do I look like I'm packing an extra femur?"

Sophie shrugged. "You think I'm guilty. You think Em and Louie are guilty. Do really want us to let you search their office alone? Without a warrant?"

"Is that what you think?"

Little Estelle rolled over and parked beside Roland. "Police brutality!" She shifted the Gad-About into park and started singing at the top of her lungs. "We shall not be moved. We shall not be mo—oo—ooved! Come one everyone! Join in! We shall not be—"

"Quiet! Don't make me fire a round into the ceiling," Roland yelled.

Kiki slapped her hand across Little Estelle's mouth.

Roland said, "I'll leave the door open. Louie. You and Kiki can observe."

As Roland followed Louie to the office, Kiki heard him mumble, "Bunch of wackos."

After Kiki and Louie wedged themselves in the open doorway, the other Maidens, along with MyBob, Sophie, and a couple of tourists who had ignored the CLOSED sign gathered behind them.

The female tourist whispered, "What are they doing in there?"

"Looking for an old bone," Kiki explained.

The husband, a farmer in a hefty-weight "Beefy T" shirt, suspenders and jeans, chuckled and grabbed his crotch. "Hell," he said. "If it's an old bone they're looking for, I got one."

His wife hit him on the shoulder. "Shut your pie hole, Orville."

Inside the office Roland headed straight to the lateral files. Two of the four were so rusty the handles were hanging off. He found the burlap sack in the bottom drawer behind piles of yellowed receipts brittle with age. As they watched, he lifted it out carefully with both hands and set it in the center of the big wooden desk.

"Is that it?" Louie called out.

"Send the professor in," Roland said.

Dr. Nelson was there in a second. "Looks like the burlap."

Roland opened the coffee sack to reveal the bone.

"You're going to have to call in the experts," the professor said.

Kiki figured that it was all right to barge in now that Roland had the evidence in hand. The others followed close behind. They crowded around the desk, staring down at the femur.

"Looks like Em was up to something." Louie sounded forlorn.

"Yeah. Or onto something," Kiki whispered. "I just hope it hasn't gotten her killed."

31

Dumped Again

Gatorade and water was all her captor had given her. Em was so sick of Gatorade she swore that if she lived through this that she'd never even look at another bottle.

She hadn't eaten in what seemed like forever. She'd lost all concept of time lying in the dark, unable to move. She'd given up trying to hold her bladder and now the stench of her own urine added to her misery.

After she mentally recalled Louie's entire drink menu, she tried to remember the names of all her teachers from elementary to high school and beyond. She was up to her freshman year at UCLA when she heard the slap of her captors' flip flops against the concrete floor.

Maybe this is it, she thought. *Maybe now she'll put me out of my misery.*

Long nails and small hands had definitely convinced her that her captor was female. She still had no idea if it was the same person who'd killed Harold and Fernando, but she figured there couldn't be that many killers running around the North Shore.

The footsteps stopped behind her. Her ponytail had doubled as a leverage device already, so Em steadied herself for the painful grip on her hair. This time her captor's moves were determined. There was no hesitation as her abductor sawed through the duct tape at her ankles.

Em's first instinct was to kick out, but then what? She didn't want to risk being sliced to ribbons. Even if she did unbalance her captor, she'd still be bound, gagged and blindfolded. And her captor would really be pissed.

Em held still, waiting for the right moment, determined to go down fighting. After much tugging, the blade finally sliced through the tape. Then came a vicious tug on her ponytail. Sure her hair was going to come out by the roots, Em struggled to her feet and swayed, barely able to stand.

She was forced to walk but hardly managed a shuffle. Thankfully, she didn't have to go very far before she was dragged down two low steps. She felt herself propped against the side of a car, yet she could tell they weren't outside yet and suspected they were in a garage.

There was not a hint of breeze. The sound of the ocean was still muffled. She heard a passing car not far away and then the jingle of keys beside her.

A hinge in need of oil whined. Her captor grasped her bound wrists and pulled her around. Her head was forced down. A hard shove between her shoulder blades nearly doubled her over. Her thighs hit something cold and metallic. She fought back, straightened, and hit her head on the lid of a car trunk.

This is it, Em thought. *The big finale.*

She wasn't going into the trunk without a fight, not after watching every episode of the Sopranos. All five seasons. Nothing good ever happened to anyone who landed in the trunk of a car.

Her captor grabbed her hair again. Jerked her head back. She felt a blade against her throat. Em held her breath and waited with her heart pounding in her ears.

The threat was very, very clear. Another hard shove between her shoulders and Em got the message. She leaned forward and was pushed headfirst into the trunk. Her shoulder smashed against the floor before she was roughly tucked into a fetal position. She held her breath, certain this was the end.

The trunk slammed shut. There was a jingle of keys and then the sound of a garage door grinding open before the door locked into position. The carpet beneath her cheek was mildewed. She tried to stretch her legs but it was impossible. It wasn't a new car, or a roomy one, she decided. Then she heard the driver's side door slam shut.

The engine didn't start on the first try. The starter whined and stopped then whined and stopped again before the engine caught hold with a clunk and a rattle. Then the car slowly moved in reverse. Gravel ground beneath the tires. When Em recognized the familiar sputter of the engine, she was too stunned to cry.

She was in Sophie's car.

I trusted you, Sophie.

She'd trusted Phillip, too. She was 0 for 2.

Why? She wondered. Had Sophie seen her hide the femur under

the hedge? Had Sophie hit her on the head that day in the parking lot? Had she been in on something with Harold? Or with Louie? Or both?

Not Louie. Please God, not Louie, too.

The car made a right turn and Em figured they were on the highway. She knew this far north, the road was only two winding narrow lanes divided by a sold white line. There was barely any shoulder on the *mauka* side and on the *makai* side there were sections without guardrails, where the drop was a hundred feet straight down into the ocean.

Em tried to stop shaking and took deep breaths through her nose. It was impossible to calm down with her heart racing. Another turn. This one to the right. Now they were on a bumpy, unpaved road and must have hit every pothole before the car suddenly stopped.

Not now. Please. Not now.

The driver's side door opened. Then the trunk lid went up. The warmth of sunlight touched her skin for the first time in days. Em went perfectly still. This was it. This was the day she was going to die. She could imagine the story in the *Garden Island.*

Thirty-four year old Tiki Goddess bartender and former wife of Phillip Johnson III, of Newport Beach, met with an untimely death on an unpaved back road on Kauai.

The worst part of it all was that she would never know why.

She was grabbed by her ankles. With her legs hanging over the edge of the trunk, she was forced into a sitting position. A second later, she was hauled to her feet.

Again, her captor made her walk, this time over uneven ground covered with roots and leaves. Around her, the dense tropical jungle gave off a rotting smell where wild mangos and *liliko'i* fell, left to ferment on the ground. She was pushed down onto the wet, muddy earth.

Her captor sawed at the tape around Em's wrists and stopped just short of completing the job. Em was given a final shove and then there were sounds of receding footsteps. Em struggled to pull the tape apart. It was loose, but holding.

The footsteps were a ways behind her just before she heard the car door slam. The engine started up again. The Honda—she was sure it was Sophie's car—turned around a few yards ahead of Em and then passed her without stopping on its way back. She lay there for a few seconds, waiting for the next shoe to fall.

She soon recognized the high-pitched chirp of a cardinal. A rooster crowed nearby. Another answered from a short distance away. She heard the surf pounding against the shore. Beneath her, the ground was spongy and damp. Full of insects. A centipede bite would pack a hell of a wallop—but that was the least of her worries now.

On the verge of hysteria, Em forced herself to calm down.

After everything, she was still alive. If she survived she would create a cocktail to commemorate her ordeal.

Something green—the color of the jungle. Crème de menthe. A little coconut syrup. Some vodka. Lots of vodka.

She rolled to her knees, tugged on the loosened tape at her wrists. Finally it gave way and she fought the tape at her mouth. Then she yanked it away from her eyes with a cry and discovered she was somewhere near the end of the highway on an unpaved, overgrown side trail surrounded by huge trees and dense undergrowth. She struggled along the rocky dirt trail just wide enough for a car, walking slowly toward the highway.

Jungle Juice. If she lived to see another day, she was going to mix up a batch called *Em's Jungle Juice,* inspired by her miraculous escape from the jungles of Kauai.

32

Sophie's Regret

After the Maidens' emergency meeting, Sophie caught a ride back to the Jungalow with Trish, in the photographer's pink-and-white VW bus.

"I'm going to change and then I've got to hustle up to a wedding reception at the Princeville St. Regis," Trish said.

Sophie gazed out the window, watched the dense green foliage flash by.

"You've had a lot of work lately. Do you ever get tired of it?" Sophie found it was easier to ask questions than answer them.

"I love it. I mean, I go to parties and receptions and weddings and take pictures and people pay me. Some folks have to work *real* jobs." Trish slowed for a van full of tourists ahead of them. "Bobble heads." She laughed. "Can't blame them for looking around. It's not every day you see fantastic scenery like this. Besides, they're our bread and butter."

"Yeah." Bobble heads. Sophie liked that.

Trish turned on the tape player. The mellow sounds of Carole King's *Tapestry* filled the bus.

Sophie wished she'd told Sharpe someone had hit Em on the head sooner. It was a crucial piece of the puzzle. Holding out this long only cast more suspicion on her. *Dumb move, Sophie.*

At least she'd tossed Em's husband's name into the calabash of suspects. She should have thought of that sooner. Even if Phillip Johnson was still in Newport Beach, he had been harassing Em for at least a month now. Em's cell phone records would prove it. Em had tried to brush off how upset she was after talking to him, but surely someone else must have noticed. Maybe Louie.

Trish seemed content to sing along with Carole at the top of her lungs. Sophie rested her elbow on the edge of the open window, and leaned her head on her palm thinking about the bone in Louie's office. Seeing it had been a real shock. If Louie knew anything about it, he was one heck of an actor. Maybe that's where Em had found it in the first place. Maybe Louie had hidden it in the drawer himself. Sophie wished Em had confided in her. Things might have played out a lot differently if she had.

Trish flipped on her turn signal as they neared her place. If you didn't know the driveway was there, it was easy to miss. She said as long as her friends knew where to find her, no one else needed to know where she lived. Huge red hibiscus bushes framed both sides, camouflaging an old newspaper box with the address on it.

The house was late 80's Haena style, sky blue and built on pilings twelve feet high to comply with the planning department's tsunami codes. A matchbox on stilts. Trish had enclosed the open area beneath the house, turned it into a one-room studio decorated with island motif cast-offs. She named it the Jungalow and only rented to friends of friends.

Nobody had to tell Sophie how lucky she was to have landed an affordable room on the North Shore. She wondered how much longer she'd be able to stay.

Trish turned onto the ground coral drive, parked the VW bus, grabbed her camera equipment.

"Hey, where's your car?" Trish pointed at the empty space on the drive.

"It's gone." Sophie stared at the empty parking space while Trish started digging in her purse for her cell phone.

"Do you know where it is? Did someone come get it to repair it? If not, we've got to call the police right away," Trish said.

"I have no idea where it went. We should look in the house though, make sure everything's okay, before we call the cops." The last thing Sophie wanted was to be on Sharpe's radar right now. "Maybe someone borrowed the car and left a note inside." She started to get out..

Trish grabbed her arm. "What if somebody is still in there? We're not going in without a cop. Besides, almost everyone you know was at the meeting this morning. Who would have taken it?"

"Do you really think someone stole the car and left an accomplice in the house to wait for us?"

Trish finally found her phone but paused before calling. She looked at Sophie. "I thought you said the car wouldn't start."

"It wouldn't. I hitchhiked to the Goddess."

"Then where is it?"

"I have no idea." Sophie said. "But whoever has it probably won't get very far."

33

Em Holds Court

Em was propped up in her hospital bed. Kiki, Flora and Suzi had just come barging through the door of Em's room—which was half the size of her closet on the mainland.

Tears unexpectedly filled her eyes. Em told herself she was feeling emotional because of the trauma she'd suffered. Surely it wasn't the sight of the three older women bearing armloads of flowers that started her crying the minute they rushed to her bedside. They wore their concern as openly as they wore fake flowers in their hair.

Kiki was flushed. Flora was without her Gatorade bottle. Tears were streaming down Suzi's moon-shaped cheeks. The realtor immediately went to work filling all the available containers in the room, including the bedpan, with water. Best of all, Kiki was toting a MacDonald's Happy Meal. The smell of french fries permeated the room instantly.

"Here," Kiki said, shoving a box festooned with Ronald MacDonald at Em. "High-cal comfort food". I should know. I was here for my second thigh tuck."

"Second?" Flora stared at Kiki. "Did you do one leg at a time?"

"No. Both legs twice." Kiki tapped her temple. "Think, Flora. *Think* about it."

The tray on Em's bedside table was full of empty chocolate pudding cups. It was the only palatable food in the place.

"Hey, hel-lo. I'm starving." Em waved, reminding them she was still there.

Suzi festooned the room with flowers and then stood at the foot of the bed. Flora shoved the empty pudding containers aside and started rooting through the Happy Meal box. She pulled out the hamburger and then the fries and set them on the tray.

"Mind if I keep this?" She held up a miniature plastic Shrek.

"Please do." Em was alive and feeling generous. "Sure."

"Da shake," Flora held out her hand.

Kiki had forgotten she was holding a second Golden Arches sack. She handed the bag to Flora. Em's mouth watered the minute Flora slipped the chocolate shake out of the bag, impaled a straw in it and set it beside the food on the tray.

"There you go," Flora said. "Chow down."

"We thought you were dead." Suzi sniffed and wiped her eyes with the back of her hand.

"*I* didn't," Kiki said. "I knew she was all right."

"Thanks, Kiki," Em popped a couple of the skinny fries in her mouth. Pure joy. She smiled. "How did you get here, anyway?"

A police officer stationed outside the door was there to keep Em secluded until Detective Sharpe showed up. Apparently Roland wanted to talk to her before anyone else. The police hadn't counted on the Maidens.

"Same way we found out you was here," Flora said. "My ex-sister-in-law, Bunny, has a cousin with an uncle on the KPD. He heard it on the scanner and it got around on the coconut wireless. She called me on my cell and . . ."

Kiki picked up the thread. "We were in Walmart next door. We carpool in once a week to save gas—"

"And money," Suzi added. "We can only fit so much stuff in the car when there are three of us together. What with Flora's ass taking up the whole back seat, we can't buy that much."

Kiki shushed her so she could go on. "When we heard the news we started screaming and jumping up and down. Nearly gave the Walmart greeter a coronary. We left our carts full of stuff and were running for the exit when Suzi suggested we get you some grub. So we got your Happy Meal and the flowers."

Em unwrapped the burger. Savored the smell. No matter what happened in life, no matter where you ended up in the world, a Mac hamburger and fries always smelled like a Mac hamburger and fries; comfort food in a sack.

"We didn't know what to expect," Kiki said. "Whether or not you were even conscious. We called the other girls. They'll be here as soon as they can."

Suzi finally smiled. "We thought we'd dance for you. Cheer you up."

Sooner than later Big Estelle would hobble in on her crutches and Little Estelle would roll in on the Gad-About. Trish would be snapping photos. Em tried to picture all of them wedged into the room and wondered if Sophie would dare to show up acting innocent as always.

Then what? She desperately needed to talk to Roland.

"Is Sophie coming?" Em tried to hide her anxiety.

"We don't know if she's coming or not. Her car broke down," Kiki said.

Em stared at her hamburger.

"I think we should dance *Aloha Kauai*," Suzi suggested.

"Dumb idea. What does that have to do with being in the hospital?" Flora groused.

"What do *you* suggest?" Suzi shot back.

"A song about flowers. You bring sick people flowers—"

"Hey, I'm not sick," Em reminded them around a mouthful of fries. "I was kidnapped."

They ignored her. She sucked on the shake to wash down the heavenly grease.

"I don't have any flower songs recorded." Kiki produced a new iPod and a small speaker from her huge black-leather purse. She was setting it up on the bedside table when the uniformed officer knocked on the door and stuck his head into the room.

"Detective Sharpe is on the way up. You folks gotta go."

"Uh oh." Flora quickly reached for Em's tray.

Em clamped onto it. "Hey, Sharpe's not a doctor. Leave my Happy Meal alone."

Kiki grabbed her iPod. "Let's go, girls. We'll make a surprise appearance at the Long Term Care Ward and sneak back in here later."

"Yeah," Flora agreed. "They love us there. Nobody ever walks out."

Suzi sighed. "Most of them are strapped into their chairs."

Kiki kissed Em on the cheek and headed for the door. Suzi and Flora hustled after her.

To Em, it seemed the door had just closed behind them when her uncle walked in trailed by Roland Sharpe. Poor Louie looked as if he'd aged overnight. He rushed to her bedside, took her hand, and looked her over with tears in his eyes.

"Are you all right?"

She tried to smile but even that hurt. The skin around her mouth and lips was raw and red from duct tape. There were abrasions on her wrists and ankles.

"I'm fine." She had no way to explain that it was her heart that had been battered again.

"I don't know what I'd do if something happened to you, kid."

"Thanks, Uncle Louie, but you were getting along fine before I got here."

"Was I?" His forehead crinkled. "No one else thought so. Except Marlene, but the girls don't like her very much."

Roland walked over to stand beside Louie. He stared at Em, assessing her condition as carefully as he might read a map. Em wished she'd asked Kiki for a hairbrush.

"Thanks for bringing Louie," she said softly.

"I was heading back from Hanalei when the call came in that you were at Emergency. It was on the way to stop and pick him up. I had a few questions for him anyway, but he was pretty upset about you. Thought I'd wait until he could see you for himself. I hope you can help, if you're up to it."

"Do we need a lawyer?"

"Not if he's innocent."

She looked at Louie and then tuned her gaze back to Roland. "What's this about?"

"About the femur I found in the file drawer at the bar," Sharpe said.

"Oh. That."

"Yeah. That."

"How'd you find it?" She wondered who had been snooping through the drawers.

"The professor came into the Goddess and told me all about it." Roland turned to Louie. "You were coming back from Harold's house when I drove up today. Why were you over there again?"

Louie slowly pulled a folded piece of notebook paper out of his pocket and handed it to Roland. The detective read it without comment and handed it to Em.

IOU $1500 dollar. Need for one television set.

It was signed by Harold Otanami and dated two months ago.

"I was looking for the money," Louie said. "I was looking for it the day I went over and Sophie came after me. I knew Em would be upset if she found out I'd loaned Harold fifteen hundred dollars. He said he was going to pay me back within a week but he didn't. The morning that he told me he finally had the money, he ended up dead. I hated to think my money burned up with him." Louie stared at the floor tiles and shook his head.

"I thought you two didn't get along. Why would you loan him money?" Roland asked what Em was wondering.

"Irene would have wanted me to." Louie shrugged. "I loan a lot of people money. Not so much now that Em's here, though, because she goes crazy when the nightly receipts and the cash drawer balance don't match up. But people fall on hard times, you know? They usually pay me back."

"Usually?" she said.

"Do you keep any record of these loans?" Roland wanted to know.

Louie reached into the baggy pockets of his linen pants and pulled out a handful of creased, folded papers. He handed them to Roland, who glanced at them and handed them to Em.

IOU $300. I need for light bill. Charlie D.

IOU $50 I need gas. Buzzy

IOU $150. Get one car insurance. Flora

Em sighed. Uncle Louie was using the Goddess cash drawer to bankroll the community.

Roland shook his head. "You charge these folks interest, Louie?"

"That wouldn't be right. People are working two and three jobs now just to make ends meet. Paradise doesn't come cheap." Louie held out his hand for the receipts. Em sighed again and handed them back.

"You should have told us what you were after at Harold's a long time ago. What makes you think the money is in the house and not his bank account? If you had given this to Leilani, I'm sure she'd have covered it," Roland told him.

Louie shrugged. "Harold had a little gambling problem. Besides, I was afraid if I told Em about the loans, she might get upset and go back to the mainland."

"I'm not going anywhere anytime soon," she assured him. At least now she knew why Louie was always broke; he wasn't inept, he was too generous.

"Now that you've seen that your niece is okay, would you mind leaving us alone, Mr. Marshall?" Roland asked. "I've got a few questions for her before she's released."

"Kiki, Suzi and Flora are entertaining at the long term care ward." Em said. "Maybe you can find them."

"What would I want with them? I see those nuts all the time. I'll wait down the hall, where there are real pretty nurses at the nurses' station." He gave her a quick kiss on the forehead and was about to leave the room when Roland stopped him.

"Mr. Marshall?"

"Call me Louie. Everybody does."

"Louie, when I was looking for you earlier, your door was wide open so I went inside. I hate to give you bad news, but I think there's something wrong with your parrot."

"Something happened to David Letterman?"

Roland nodded. "I'm pretty sure he's dead. He was lying on the bottom of his cage."

Em bit her lips to keep from laughing. Louie dismissed the news with a wave.

"That's nothing," he assured Roland. "Just the usual hangover."

Once her uncle was out of earshot, Em indicated the foot of her bed to the detective.

"You're welcome to sit."

Roland leaned against metal footboard instead with notebook in hand. "Okay. How about we start at the beginning?"

She polished off the last fry. The sugar rush from the chocolate was making her giddy.

"I was born in Pasadena in 19—"

He cut her off. "Start with what happened at the memorial. When you were abducted."

"I was walking the grounds."

"Alone?"

"Yes."

"Why didn't you stay at the memorial ceremony?"

"It's not a crime to take a walk."

"It's a crime to hide evidence."

"Evidence?" She tried to suck the last bit of chocolate shake out of the waxy super-sized cup.

"Not everyone keeps a femur hidden in a file cabinet."

She nearly choked. "I can explain that. Besides, that's not evidence. That thing is very old. Ancient probably."

"So Professor Nelson told me."

"What else did he tell you?"

He ignored her question. "When you found out it was old, why hide the femur? Why not turn it over to the Burial Council and tell them where you found it?"

"I didn't find it. It came to me."

"By itself."

"Sort of. It fell off a shelf in Harold's garage."

He stared at his notebook. "Was that before or after someone hit you in the head?"

"How do you know someone hit me on the head?" The bruises beneath her eyes had all but faded to a yellow tinge she hoped complemented the reddened, chafed skin around her mouth.

"Sophie told me," he said.

"Sophie told you?"

"What's wrong?"

She sighed. Her legs were aching. She wanted to get up, walk around and stretch, but not with him here and particularly not with her butt hanging out of a hospital gown. Most of all she wanted to wish this whole thing away.

"When did Sophie tell you about me being hit in the head?"

"Kiki called me earlier today. Said Sophie had some information pertaining to your disappearance and ordered me out to the Goddess. Sophie told us you were hit over the head and fell on your face in the parking lot. And about the femur."

"Did she say anything else?"

"Just that she was there that day. Didn't you suspect her?"

Em looked down at her hands. It was impossible to ignore the bandages on her wrists. She thought about it for an instant that day, but she wouldn't believe Sophie could hurt her. *Stupid, Em. Really dumb.*

"Not at the time," she said. "I never saw who hit me that day, but that's when I found the bone in Harold's garage."

"Why were you in his garage?"

"I went in to borrow some hedge clippers."

"Was anyone else there?"

"No."

"You were trespassing."

"Like I said, I needed hedge clippers. Ours broke. Besides, Louie kept saying Harold *had* something of his. I'll admit, I was poking around, very innocently mind you, when the bone fell on my head."

"So let's get back to your abduction. You were walking the

grounds of Fernando's estate, by yourself, while everyone else was watching the ceremony at the beach. Why?"

She shrugged. He made it sound like a scene out of some gothic novel. She wasn't exactly parading around alone in the dark in a long white nightgown carrying a candle.

"Louie kept insisting Harold had something of his. When I found the bone I was worried that was what Louie was searching for. Louie seemed so desperate to find whatever it was. I thought maybe he might have . . . well . . ."

"Killed someone?"

"Maybe. Maybe he did it a long time ago. Maybe Harold found out somehow. He could have discovered the grave or something. I don't believe it now but . . ."

"You thought maybe Harold was blackmailing Louie."

"I thought the bone might be evidence. Or maybe they were in cahoots together. Maybe they killed someone years ago. I looked around Harold's yard one evening, searched for signs of disturbed ground, but I didn't find anything. I didn't find anything at Louie's either. So I decided to search Fernando's garden, where Harold had worked."

"The bone you found could be hundreds of years old."

"I didn't know that for certain, not at first. I tried connecting Harold and Fernando—because Harold told him something about bones. Fernando thought he was talking about fish bones, but maybe not. I thought maybe Harold was afraid Fernando's contractor would find the grave so I was in the garden looking for evidence of recent digging."

"Did you find anything, Nancy?"

She pursed her lips. Shook her head.

"Nothing. I was ready to rejoin everyone at the beach when I was knocked out. I came to bound and gagged and locked up somewhere."

"Did you see anything? Hear anything? Recognize the kidnapper's voice?"

"No one ever spoke to me. I was blindfolded. My wrists were duct taped behind me. My ankles were taped together. A strip of tape was across my mouth."

He stared at her lips for a second. Made some notes.

"When I came to, I heard drums. Later I heard people calling my name. I couldn't have been very far from Fernando's."

"Do you think you were inside his house somewhere? Maybe under the house?"

She shook her head. "I would have heard more. The music from the memorial entertainment was close enough to hear."

"You sure you weren't kept in a van or the trunk of a car?"

"No. That was later. I was hidden somewhere with a cement floor."

He stopped writing. "Later when?"

"Sometime this morning I was forced into a car trunk and driven out to the end of the road and dumped in the jungle. The tape was partially cut and eventually I freed myself. I pulled the tape off my mouth and took off the blindfold. Somehow I made my way out to the highway. I was weak and dizzy and barely knew what I was doing."

Her pants had smelled of urine. Her hair was matted. Her wrists and ankles were raw and bleeding.

"The way I looked, none of the tourists would give me a lift. Finally a local guy in a truck pulled over when he saw me wandering down the highway. He'd seen me around the Goddess and knew I was missing. By then I could barely speak. He called the paramedics."

"So you never got a look at your captor? Never heard his voice?"

"No, but I know who it was." Em sighed.

He set his notebook on his lap and stared at her. "You know who abducted you? When were you going to get around to telling me?"

"You said to start at the beginning."

"I think you've been hanging around Kiki and her crew too long. So who was it?"

"Sophie." She hated the disgusting I-told-you-so look on his face.

"You're sure?"

She began to tick off the clues. "It was someone with long acrylic nails. Sophie has them. It was someone strong enough drag me around. Sophie's young and strong but still wasn't able to pick me up. A man would have just picked me up, right? I was forced to walk. Most of all, I would know the sound of Sophie's car anywhere. I know I was in her trunk this morning. It had to be Sophie."

Em watched Roland walk out of the hospital room when her doctor came in. The doctor went to have her release papers readied and, until they gave her the green light, Em couldn't do much of anything but contemplate how she'd muster the energy to get up. Then Sharpe walked in again.

"I thought you were gone," she said.

"You can't get rid of me that easily. What's the verdict?"

"He said I can go home."

"You still look pretty bad."

"Thanks so much. You really know how to make a girl feel better."

"I just got a call about a stolen car. Turns out it was Sophie's. It was found in an overgrown lot near the end of the road at Haena, probably not far from where you were dumped. I asked the criminologists to go over it with a fine tooth comb and sent a plainclothes detective out to trail Sophie while we get an arrest warrant."

"But if her car was really stolen, then . . . "

"Yeah. Right. We'll see."

"I can leave as soon as the paperwork is finished."

"That should give me some time to get the information on Sophie's car. I'll go check it out myself over at the impound lot and pick up an arrest warrant. You stay put. I'll take you home after I get back."

Em studied the blanket across her lap and pictured the house on the beach, the broad, covered lanai. Home. It sounded so good. She looked up at Roland. "What about Louie?"

"I'll send him home with Kiki," he said.

"What about Sophie?"

"Like I said, I'll have someone trail her until I get the arrest warrant. I want to bring her in myself." His tone was cold and hard but at least he hadn't said *I told you so.*

She put her hands over her eyes for a moment, gently rubbed them. "I still can't believe she did this."

"I could kick myself for letting your soft spot for Ms. Chin keep me from listening to my gut." An awkward silence fell. He glanced at his watch. "I'll find Louie and the others and tell them I'm driving you to the North Shore."

"Would you please thank them and say I'll see them back at the Goddess?"

"Sure." He nodded. "No problem."

"Are you going to tell them what I suspect?"

"Not one of them can keep her mouth shut. As soon as word is out on the coconut wireless, Sophie will be on the run. If one of your friends finds her first she'll be lynched."

"You're probably right."

"I know I am."

"Thank you, Roland."

"For what? I'm just glad you weren't killed. I'd have to live with the guilt for the rest of my life."

"Thanks for not telling me how stupid I've been."

He shrugged and almost smiled. "Hey, it's going around."

Kiki left the others as they made their way downstairs to wait for her at the car. She spotted Roland in the hallway outside Em's room and went after him before he could take the stairs and ditch her.

"What are you going to do about Marlene?" she demanded.

"Marlene Lockhart?"

"Is there *another* Marlene running around kidnapping people?"

"Marlene didn't kidnap anyone."

"She kidnapped Em right before she ran off—supposedly to Maui. No one has seen or heard from her since."

"Kiki, listen very carefully. She had a 5:45 flight to Maui but she didn't make it."

"Aha! I knew it!"

"Because her car broke down just outside of Hanamaulu."

"So she says. Did anyone see her?"

"I've got a call in to the tow truck driver for the exact time he picked her up. She did make the next flight out."

"So she had time to kidnap Em."

"Not if the tow truck driver's time log gives her an alibi. There's no way she could be in two places at once. She couldn't have kidnapped Em, hidden her somewhere, and then made that second flight."

"But—"

"She hasn't been on any return flights, so she wasn't here on island to turn Em loose this morning, either."

"Maybe Marlene assumed a different identity. She could have somebody working with her. An accomplice! Someone from her new *halau*. She's enlisted someone to help her take over the bar."

"Let it go, Kiki."

"You thought it was Sophie and you were wrong. What if you're wrong about Marlene, too?"

Roland opened his mouth as if about to say something and then closed it again.

"What?" Kiki crossed her arms. "What aren't you telling me?"

"Nothing," he said.

"Give, Roland." She hated secrets unless she was the one keeping them. Especially juicy ones.

"You'll know soon enough." He started to walk away.

She called after him. "If you don't tell me Roland, you'll never dance on this island again!"

She got even madder when she heard him laugh.

34

Sophie's Luck Runs Out

Behind the Goddess bar, Sophie readied pitchers of Mai Tai mixer. Louie hadn't had time to concoct a drink in Em's honor so he decided on a favorite, the mai tai. Two for one, of course.

So far so good. At least that's what Sophie kept telling herself. So far so good. Anyone and everyone connected to the Goddess, including patrons and neighbors, was in on throwing a welcome home a party for Em that night. An hour ago, Louie got a call from the detective. Em had finally been released from Wilcox Hospital. She was on the way home.

Earlier, on his own way home from the hospital with Kiki, Suzi and Flora, Louie had called and asked her to come in to work. The Maidens put their heads together and, along with Kimo, came up with a menu for a last minute celebratory party. Kimo was grilling ribs to serve with Kilauea corn on the cob and coleslaw. And rice, of course.

The lanai in front looked like a circus wagon had exploded all over it. All afternoon people dropped off tributes: ribbons, handmade signs and votive candles along with huge arrangements of tropical flowers. Fifteen minutes ago someone called from the Hanalei Gourmet to say Roland's car had driven by. Em was due to walk in at any minute.

The Maidens were arguing over what song to perform first. Louie got into the fray, voting for the Tiki Goddess theme song. Kiki told him that was about Irene, not Em. Besides, it was always reserved for the big finale. They needed a welcome home song.

Puana Kimokane volunteered to chant.

True to form, everyone was still arguing when Em arrived. Sophie didn't miss the protective way Sharpe hovered behind Em as she walked in the door.

Em was white as a sheet. Her mouth and the skin around it were raw and chafed. Her limp hair needed a good shampoo and conditioning. Her usually bright eyes were lackluster. There was a sadness lurking there. Sophie's heart ached seeing her that way.

"Welcome home!" Kiki shouted. She slipped the first of what would quickly become a thick pile of lei around Em's neck as people pressed forward to greet her. Trish snapped photos of the happy reunion.

"Mai Tais all around," Louie yelled.

Puana began to chant and eventually the sound of his voice quieted the crowd. When Sophie finally caught Em's eye, Em didn't smile.

A chill went up Sophie's spine when Em looked away. People were still crowding around her, draping lei around her neck. The Maidens had descended and were clucking over Em.

When Puana finally ended his chant, Em's voice was soft yet it carried across the silence. She asked of no one in particular, "Will you please take me to the house?"

The Maiden's quickly closed ranks and whisked Em out the door. The minute she was gone people started talking again and lined up three deep at the bar waiting for a free round. Sophie started pouring sticky pineapple and guava juice mixer into tall hurricane glasses.

When she looked up, Detective Sharpe was beside her behind the bar. It irked her how cops never waited in line.

"What can I get you?" She ignored the crush on the other side of the bar. Having Sharpe so close definitely creeped her out.

"You have the right to remain silent," he began.

Within thirty seconds, you could hear a pin drop in the bar again.

"What's going on?" She tried to keep her hands from shaking as she set down a jar of mango nectar.

"Anything you say can and will be held against you."

"What did I do?"

He continued reading her the Miranda rights. At the end he said, "Do you understand?"

"Yes, but . . . "

"Then let's go. You can walk out peacefully or I can cuff you."

"I want to know why."

"Try kidnapping and assault for starters. I'm sure there's more."

"Do you have an arrest warrant?"

He pulled one out of his back pocket. "The ink is still wet."

"But . . . "

"But nothing. Let's go."

Louie was there now. Hovering. Confused.

"What's happening, Roland?"

"Ms. Chin is under arrest for kidnapping and assaulting your niece."

"Why would I kidnap Em?" Sophie asked.

"We have it on good evidence." Roland nudged her forward. "Lots of it."

"You can't possibly . . . "

"Your car was found three hours ago. The duct tape you used to tie Ms. Johnson, along with scissors and strands of long, blond hair were found in the trunk. I'm sure further analysis will prove them to be Em's."

"But my car was stolen!"

"Tell that to the judge."

In that very moment, Sophie's world came crashing down around her.

He took hold of her arm, pulled cuffs out of his back pocket.

"All right, I'll go," she said. Her heart was pounding so hard she was surprised they couldn't all hear it. "But please, don't cuff me here."

He kept a tight grip on her elbow as he walked her around the bar. The crowd parted. She felt all eyes on her. For a minute she thought she'd pass out before she got a grip on herself. At least she was able to hold her head high. She didn't look right or left. Didn't make eye contact with anyone.

When they reached the car, Roland cuffed her before he opened the back door. He put his hand on the back of her head as she sank into the back seat.

Before he closed the car door, Sophie looked him square in the eye, refusing to be intimidated.

"I didn't do it. I swear to you I didn't."

"Yeah," he nodded. "That's what they all say."

35

Em's Arsenal

The Maidens got Em comfortably settled on Louie's rattan sofa. Lil was in the kitchen boiling water for hibiscus tea. Em couldn't believe she was still crying. Her misplaced faith in Sophie's innocence had shaken her confidence. The betrayal hurt.

"Hey," Suzi handed Em a fresh Kleenex and drew everyone's attention. "Has anyone noticed how quiet it is over at the Goddess all of a sudden?"

"I wonder what's going on?" Kiki jumped up, ready to find out.

"Roland is probably arresting Sophie." Em wiped her eyes. Blew her nose. She told them how she reluctantly admitted that Sophie had kidnapped her and about what the police had found in the Honda.

"The evidence was convincing enough to press charges."

"Oh, great!" Kiki shot to her feet. "Now we won't have anyone to finish teaching us our dance for the Slug Festival."

"Kiki!" Trish admonished. "Sophie kidnapped Em! Try to think about something besides hula for once in your life."

"Hula *is* my life," Kiki shot back. "Besides, how could she have kidnapped Em and dumped her out when Sophie was at our meeting this morning?"

"She got there late, remember?" Trish reminded her. "*After* telling us she had to hitchhike to the Goddess. When she pretended her car was stolen she was covering for dumping Em."

"Have a drink and sit down." Flora passed Kiki the Gatorade bottle. Kiki took a swig and sat. She didn't look happy and kept mumbling something about Marlene.

"I didn't want to believe it either," Em admitted. "In fact, I still can't believe Sophie did it, but I was definitely in her car and when I felt those acrylic nails against my face . . . "

In a hula-worthy move the Maidens all raised their arms and

flipped their hands up, palms in, showing off their fake nails.

"Kiki makes us wear press-ons. But I only wear them for shows." Lil walked in carrying a cup of tea for Em and a wooden bowl full of rice crackers. "Hope Louie won't mind that I raided his pantry." She set the calabash in the center of the coffee table.

"Acrylics and press-ons make your fingers look longer." Kiki grabbed a handful of rice crackers. "I'm so damn pissed off right now. It just can't be Sophie."

"She stuffed me into her car trunk and dumped me out near the end of the road," Em said.

"But her car was stolen." Kiki countered.

"Very convenient, don't you think? She's young and strong. She's been arrested before. Who else could it be?" Em really didn't want to argue with them anymore tonight.

She was sick of wearing her trust like a welcome mat for hurt and betrayal. She felt terrible about implicating Sophie until she reminded herself that she was lucky to be alive.

"But what about Marlene? If she got rid of you, then Louie would have no next of kin. No one to inherit the Goddess."

Em sighed. "Roland is fairly certain she was in a tow truck when I was kidnapped."

"What does 'fairly certain' mean?"

"It means the truck driver has a very casual attitude about logging in pick up and delivery times."

"But why would Sophie do it?" Kiki still wasn't convinced.

"That's something Roland is determined to find out."

Flora started digging in her huge *lauhala* purse. Woven in the shape of a rectangular box with handles, it was the size of a small television and held everything but the kitchen sink. Em thought Flora was looking for another Gatorade bottle until she pulled out a small, serrated garden sickle. From tip to handle it was about a foot long.

"Keep this with you." She handed Em the sickle.

"You think she's going to be weeding any time soon?" Suzi rolled her eyes.

When Flora shook her head, her jowls jiggled. "No. It's for protection. That t'ing is sharp. You never know." Flora shrugged. "Mebbe you don't feel safe for a while. Carry that. No worries."

Em stared at the sickle in her hand. There were Chinese characters carved into the handle.

"*Mahalo*, Flora." She set it on the coffee table.

"The Estelles sent this over," Trish handed her a small canister.

Em turned it over. "Pepper spray?"

"They carry half-a-dozen of them in the van. Little Estelle's afraid crazed fans might recognize her from her Rockette years and rush the vehicle."

"If any of them are still alive, I doubt any of her fans have the strength to rush anything," Kiki noted.

"It's a lovely gesture, though." Em set the pepper spray beside the sickle. "I'll thank them tomorrow."

"I don't have anything deadly." Lil opened her purse and stared inside.

"Surprise, surprise," Kiki mumbled.

"But you can have this." She withdrew a foot-long needle.

"A *lei* needle?" Suzi shook her head. "How is she supposed to protect herself with a *lei* needle?"

"Well, you never know . . . " Lil started to tear up.

Em reached over and squeezed her hand and took the needle. "Thanks, Lillian. I appreciate the gesture."

Suzi reached into her vinyl designer knock off. Out came a fifteen-inch hunting knife in a worn sheath. She slipped it out of the sheath and held it up to the light.

"Good gravy!" Em reared back. "Where did that come from?"

"It was my brother's pig-sticking knife. Once when he was hunting he almost sliced off the end of his thumb with it." Suzi sheathed the knife and tossed it on the coffee table.

"I really don't think I'll need these." Em turned toward the window facing the Goddess. "At least I hope I won't."

"Keep them handy for a while anyway," Suzi patted her knee, "just until you've got your confidence back."

Last but not least, Kiki opened the huge leather bag she toted everywhere. When she pulled out a .9 millimeter Glock, everyone reared back.

"That thing looks big enough to blow a hole through a tank," Suzi said. "Why didn't you just bring an Uzi?"

"Because I couldn't find it." Kiki set the automatic on the table beside the rest of the arsenal.

"Where did you get that thing?" Trish picked up her camera.

"It's Kimo's from when he was the bouncer at the Nawiliwili Tavern. I took it out of his workshop after Em was kidnapped. I was thinking we might all be in danger."

"Is it loaded?" Suzi eyed the piece as if it might go off on its own.

"I couldn't find any bullets. It'll sure give somebody second thoughts, though."

Trish took a photo of the weapons pile. "For your scrapbook," she winked at Em.

"What scrapbook?"

"The one I started the night you went missing. Clippings from the *Garden Island*. Photos of the search at Fernando's. The ad for Louie's reward. The memorial shrine on the Goddess lanai. This and that. I've documented all of it."

Em looked at the faces of the women gathered around her. Most folks thought the group was borderline certifiable, but she knew without a doubt that she could count on them anytime, anywhere. Her eyes unexpectedly filled with tears again.

The heavily scented pile of *lei* around her neck had begun to weigh her down and make her sweat. Em tried to lift them over her head but Trish had to help. The photographer carried the pile of flowers into the kitchen. The house was filled with their cloying scents.

"I'll just put these in the fridge," Trish called out. "You might want to wear them tomorrow."

Em didn't feel like celebrating anymore. She knew she should be happy to be alive, but the sickly sweet smell of the flowers, not to mention the sight of the weapons pile, served as reminders of what she'd been through and Sophie's betrayal.

"I hope you all don't mind, but I'd really like to get some sleep," she said.

Kiki stood but wasn't happy. "I still think you're wrong about Sophie."

"I wish I was," Em said. The rest of the Maidens began to collect their purses and prepared to leave.

"Would you like me to stay until Louie closes up the bar?" Trish asked.

Em hoped Louie didn't hand out more free liquor or hard money loans than they could afford.

"I'll be fine." To prove it, she got up to walk them out to the edge of the lanai. It was a balmy night, the sky crowded with stars. Everyone had to hug and air-kiss cheeks and say aloha.

The chatting continued until the women started toward their

cars over in the parking lot, all but Kiki, who headed for the Goddess, where aromatic smoke still rolled off the grill.

Em let herself into the house and walked over to Letterman's cage.

"What's up, Dave?"

The big bird stared at her without blinking. *If only my life was easy as the Macaw's*, she thought. He spent as much time outside enjoying a perch in the shade of a big avocado tree as he did in his cage. He was well fed and enjoyed a constant flow of free drinks. Louie even let the bird watch his favorite television shows.

"Anything you need, David?" Em smiled.

Letterman began side-stepping back and forth on his perch and bobbing his head up and down.

"What do you want big boy?" She cooed.

He shrieked, "Survivor! Survivor!"

She couldn't believe it. The bird was trying to cheer her. Letterman was right. She was a survivor. It was time she threw off her sadness, her doubts, and celebrated life.

"Why, thank you, Dave. Thank you so much for reminding me, you pretty big boy. You good boy."

The bird grew more and more agitated. He opened and closed his beak and paced side to side on his perch and then screamed, "Survivor Island! CBS! CBS!"

So much for moral support. Em sighed, found the remote and turned on the television. Sure enough, *Survivor* was just starting.

36

Kiki and Suzi Talk Story

The next morning, Kiki and Suzi were stretched out on chaise lounges on Kiki's huge lanai finishing up a breakfast of macadamia nut waffles with coconut syrup. Though the only ocean view was sandwiched between two houses across the street, it still added value to the price of the house.

Kimo was busy building Kiki and the girls a hula platform in the back yard. With Marlene still on the loose, Kiki wasn't entirely convinced they'd always have the Goddess.

Suzi polished off her pancakes in record time. She pulled a bottle of nail polish out of her purse and shook it, then propped her foot on the end of the chaise and applied a coat of Tamarind Tangerine to her toes.

"Pretty sorry news, eh?" Suzi said.

"What news?" The very idea that she'd missed something always gave Kiki an instant headache.

"You know. About Sophie. And Em."

"Old news now, but I still can't believe it."

"Me either." Suzi capped the bottle of polish, leaned back into the overstuffed chaise and burped. "Good breakfast."

"Kimo's the best."

"Yeah." Suzi sighed. She was between husbands at the moment but was convinced that number four was out there somewhere.

"I still don't get why Sophie would kidnap Em. Or why she would kill Harold. Or Fernando, for that matter." Kiki finished off her coffee, set the cup on a small table beside her.

"We really know nothing about her. Maybe she's a psycho like the guy in Halloween. Psychos can't help themselves."

"Yeah, right. But not Sophie. Now, take Marlene. I can see her being a psycho. But Roland insists she left for Maui and couldn't have kidnapped Em."

"You've gotta get over the fact Marlene left us, Kiki. Besides, she's not the only one who has gone on to another group. We're better off without her."

"Left us? She's lucky we didn't vote her out. Besides, I've got more than one reason to hate her. She's trying to steal my business."

"Speaking of business, Shark Lady sure has a lot of For Sale signs up around here," Suzi noted. "I don't get one-quarter that many listings up here in Haolewood. Did you see there's a Sold sign on the place next to Fernando's?"

"Shark Lady strikes again," Kiki said. "I heard she sold it to friends of his."

"I don't like her. Never did." Suzi said. "Not even when we were small-time kids. Maybe now it's just professional jealousy, but she does work hard. Gotta give her that."

Just then Flora's gold Camry came hurtling down the road. She stopped in front of Kiki's driveway. They watched Flora park, grab her woven bag and climb out. When she wiped her brow with the back of her hand, the move set off a seismic ripple of underarm flab.

She shaded her eyes, leaned back and spotted them on the upstairs lanai.

"Hey, I'm comin' up," Flora called out.

"Come. Get breakfast," Kiki yelled back.

Flora started up the steps. Like Trish's house, Kiki's was elevated on pilings. By the time Flora joined them on the lanai, she was wheezing and her face was bright red.

"You got Medicare, eh?" Kiki asked.

Flora flipped her off.

"I'll get you some pancakes," Suzi volunteered. She started to get off the chaise.

"No need." Flora waved her back down. "I'm not hungry. But I been t'inking."

Kiki waited. Flora thinking wasn't necessarily a good thing.

Flora reached through the fabric of her muumuu to adjust her bra. "Em heard Fernando say that Harold told him something about *koi punda*. Everybody t'inks he was talkin' about fish, but *koi punda* is not a fish. Far as I know it means nu'ting."

Kiki and Suzi nodded. Flora was definitely on a roll.

"And that bone, the one in the drawer at the Goddess? One leg bone." Flora tapped her temple. "Last night I start t'inking. Finally, I get it. Mebbe Harold was talking about *kupuna*. Not *punda* or *koi punda*. *Kupuna*. Ancestors. Old Hawaiians. Old Hawaiian graves mebbe. With bones. Get it?"

"*Kupuna*." Kiki nodded. "*Kupuna* sounds like *punda*. Fernando could have heard wrong, for sure. Flora, maybe you're on to something."

"Yeah? I t'ink so, too." She folded her arms across her purse.

Suzi sat up in her chair. "Gravesites are nothing but trouble around here lately. Property owners have every right to build on their property—"

"Spoken like a realtor. What if someone wanted to build a house on top of your grandpa's grave?"

"Shush." Flora glared at Kiki. "You nevah let me finish."

"Go on, then." Kiki insisted. "Hurry it up and get to the point."

"Maybe Harold found a grave at Fernando's."

"While he was working on the yard," Kiki finished for her. "Maybe planting *pakalolo*."

Suzi picked up the thread, "And he knew Fernando's construction would have to be halted while the Burial Council met."

"Maybe forevah," Flora finished.

"Maybe Fernando had Harold killed so he wouldn't tell anyone," Kiki mused.

"Then who killed Fernando?" Suzi's face was scrunched so tight her eyes nearly disappeared.

"Who would want to kill them both?" Flora wondered. "And what's it to Sophie? Unless she knew Harold better than we t'ought."

"Maybe she was his drug connection," Suzi said. "She was arrested once on Oahu, remember?"

"So why kidnap Em and not kill her?" Kiki shivered. "If Sophie did kill the other two, why not Em? Unless maybe her conscience got to her at the last minute."

"Sophie said her car was stolen," Suzi reminded them. "Maybe it was. Maybe someone else used it to dump Em. Besides, you think Sophie is stupid enough to leave all that evidence in the car? The duct tape and stuff?"

"Maybe someone set her up." Kiki put her coffee cup down and got off the chaise. She slapped her fist into her palm. "That's it! Somebody set her up. The kid it sitting is jail and we've got to get her out."

"First we have to figure out who did it. We need proof." Suzi started piling dirty dishes on a bamboo serving tray. "And please, Kiki, don't say Marlene. Try thinking outside the box."

Flora was rooting in her purse. She found her Gatorade bottle, pulled it out and took a sip.

"What do we do next?" She asked them.

Kiki took the tray from Suzi and headed for the living room. "First, we talk to Roland about your *kupuna* theory. After that, we'll wait and see what brilliant idea comes to us next."

37

Roland Snoops Around

Kiki made a few calls, then loaded Suzi and Flora into her car and headed out to meet up with Roland at *Hale Pua*, House of Flowers, the estate next to Fernando's.

When they drove past Fernando's Hideaway they saw the place was still locked up tight. Wally Williams had been too afraid to stay there since the murder. The two huge estates, side by side, were both sitting empty.

Clouds were piling up against each other along the mountain ridges and rain was imminent. Hard rain. They could feel it coming.

Kiki pulled in and parked on the gravel drive at *Hale Pua* and spotted Roland on the lanai. The women piled out and began to walk the perimeter of the house.

"Hey Roland," she called out.

"Hey Kiki."

"I called the substation and they said you were here. We need to talk to you."

"What are you ladies doing out here?"

Kiki noticed he didn't look pleased to see them.

"We searched this place thoroughly but I wanted to double check to see if we missed something. Em is certain she was locked up close to Fernando's. She could hear us calling for her but didn't think she was inside Fernando's anywhere. She couldn't have been at the place on the other side of his either."

A local couple in their seventies lived on the opposite side of Fernando and were the original owners of the modest, wood-frame home. They had been there the night of the kidnapping, and a thorough search had been conducted. Em definitely hadn't been hidden there.

"You find anything here?"

"Some healthy *pakalolo* plants hidden between a couple of hibiscus bushes. Harold's supplementary income. I phoned in a report."

A light mist was falling, not just a passing trade shower but the prelude to something bigger. They all decided to take shelter on the lanai and had just made it before the rain started pouring.

"Has Sophie confessed?" Suzi asked.

He shook his head. "She's not talking."

"That's because she's innocent," Kiki told him.

"You got keys to this place?" Flora had her nose pressed to the window. "I'd wanna look around in there."

"Leilani must have keys," Suzi said.

"I gave them back," Roland said. "The night of the memorial we went over the place top to bottom."

"You checked the safe room?" Suzi asked.

Kiki and Roland both turned on the realtor and said together, "What safe room?"

"There's a safe room?" Roland pressed.

"The folks who built the place were paranoid types from New York."

Flora hiked her purse up her shoulder. "Whoa, they mus' have a lotta money if they need a room full of safes."

Suzi sighed. "It's a secret interior room. A place to hide from a home invasion or something."

"On Kauai?" Kiki snorted.

"How do you know about it?" Roland asked Suzi.

"If it's so secret—" Flora began.

Suzi shrugged. "Hard to keep a secret on Kauai, right? Everybody who works here knows about it. The contractor, the house cleaners, the window washers, the planning department, all the realtors who toured the place when it went up for sale."

"Everybody but the police, apparently." Kiki nudged Roland. She could see he wasn't amused.

"Leilani didn't mention it. She showed us everything else," he said.

"Why would she keep the safe room secret?" Suzi frowned, apparently mulling it over. "Unless maybe she forgot about it in all the excitement."

"No way anything ever slipped her mind—so what was she hiding?" Kiki wondered. "Maybe Em?"

The rain was coming down thick and steady now. They'd all seen worse.

Flora nudged Kiki. "Hey, tell him about our *kupuna* theory."

Roland turned to Flora. "You getting messages from the spirit world now?"

"You make fun, we won't tell you." She folded her arms beneath her heavy breasts.

Kiki tried to explain. "Flora thinks Harold might have been talking about *kupuna*, not *punda*. There's not even a 'd' in the Hawaiian language."

"If Harold found that bone at Fernando's—" Suzi began.

"And told Leilani—" Kiki cut her off.

Suzi finished, "There would be a lot of trouble. Big trouble that might have held up the sale. The owners might have even backed out if it seemed like too much hassle."

"Big humbug." Flora nodded.

"Major humbug." Roland stared through the rain at the hedge that bordered Fernando's and *Hale Pua*.

"Two properties side by side. Both Leilani's listings," Kiki reminded them.

"She sure couldn't risk Fernando suing her for nondisclosure when his contractor found a burial site and called in the state. Maybe Harold tried to warn her. Maybe the old coot even tried to blackmail her," Suzi said. "He was always out of money."

"Maybe Leilani was desperate to close these two deals," Suzi continued. "She stood to lose a lot in a non-disclosure case, that's for sure. I heard she let her E and O insurance lapse six months ago."

"What's E and O?" Roland reached for his notebook.

"Errors and omissions. She'd be up poop creek without it if this thing turned ugly."

"Yeah. I been there a time or two myself," Kiki laughed. "Without a paddle."

"How do you know? About the E and O thing?" Roland asked Suzi.

She smiled. "Everybody in real estate on Kauai knows everyone else's business. Besides, I have connections."

38

Just When She Thought It Was Over

As a tropical depression pounded Kauai, Em huddled on a comfy chair on Louie's front lanai, where she had amassed a stack of magazines and a couple of novels.

Water was running in buckets full off the roof. Pools formed all over the garden. Beyond the yard, the ocean reflected a steel gray sky. Not only had the power been out for an hour, but the Hanalei bridge was closed, cutting off the North Shore from the rest of the island. No one was getting in or out.

Em had never seen anything like it. If it rained any harder she was going to hunt up her snorkel and flippers. Back in L.A. this much rain would have sent the Malibu hills sliding into the Pacific.

She was lounging around reading, far from ready to go back to work. She tried to muster the energy, but she still felt as if she'd been hit by a truck. She reminded herself that it was only yesterday that Sophie had stuffed her into the trunk of the Honda. She deserved another day off.

Louie was over at the Goddess manning the bar. There were already quite a few cars in the lot. Tourists with no way to get back across the bridge stopped in to pass the time and usually wound up sipping drinks and "talking story" with the locals until the tide went out or the rain stopped and the bridge reopened.

Em hoped Louie could manage alone. No telling how much the cash drawer would be down tonight. Right now, she was too tired to care.

She glanced down at the romance novel with a half-naked pirate on the cover and imagined Roland Sharpe dressed as a swashbuckler in a puffy white shirt unbuttoned past his navel. She decided she wouldn't mind having her swash buckled by Roland and smiled. It was a far better fantasy than anything she dreamed whenever she closed her eyes. Last night she woke up in a sweat after having a nightmare about being bound, gagged and shut up in the dark on hard, cold cement.

Not only that, but Sophie's voice haunted her, too.

"I didn't do it, Em. I didn't kidnap you. Why would I?"

Sophie had used her one phone call from jail, not to call a lawyer, but to plead her innocence. The call had left Em shaken, doubting herself, doubting everything that had happened. Except for her own accusation and the tape and strands of blond hair found in Sophie's car, there was really no other hard evidence against her.

Sophie had sounded so sincere during the call that Em found herself wondering if she'd been wrong. She hated to send an innocent girl to jail. All she could do was hope that Roland would find more proof.

As she stared out at the falling rain, she heard a car pull into the gravel driveway next door. The house to the left of them was a vacation rental. Every couple of weeks a new family would move in.

Em thought that the bridge must finally be open when she heard someone walking around the front of her own lanai. A slim figure in a hooded plastic poncho carrying a small bundle appeared and walked up the side steps. For a second she thought it was Trish. The photographer often wore a plastic poncho to shield her camera from the rain.

"Hey, come on in," Em called out. She set her book aside. She started to get up and recognized Leilani Cabral the minute the woman stepped onto the lanai and pushed back the hood of her rain gear.

"Don't bother getting up." Leilani waved her back down.

Em was surprised to see the woman and thought how nice it was of her to call until she noticed the gun in Leilani's hand. She didn't miss the long, blood-red acrylic nails, either. Em's gaze flew to the woman's eyes. They were cold and calculating.

Before she could react, Leilani tossed a bundle onto Em's lap. "Put these on."

"No."

Leilani raised the gun with sure hands. Em willed her own not to shake.

"You wouldn't want your uncle to get hurt, would you? If he walks in before we're out of here he will be, I can assure you. So hurry."

Em stood up. "I'll change inside." She wanted to get to the newly acquired weapons stash that she had dumped into the bottom drawer of Louie's desk.

Leilani glanced over her shoulder. Em saw that there was no one outside the house. No one on the rain-soaked beach. A gust of wind blew a fine mist through the screens.

"You can change right here," Leilani said.

Em unzipped her shorts and shrugged out of them. She unwound the bundle, held up pair of black silk slacks. They were tight and a bit too short, but she got them on. She glanced at Leilani, wondering if she should bolt for the door and run into the living room—

"Don't even think about it," Leilani warned. "Now the blouse."

The top was patterned sleeveless silk with a Mandarin collar. Em slipped it on and buttoned the silk frogs up the front.

"Get some paper and a pen," Leilani demanded.

Em almost sprinted for the desk, then pretended to balk. "Why should I?"

"Do it —"

Em's mind raced. Paper and a pen. If she could just slip the pepper spray out of the bottom drawer. Leilani followed close behind, watching every move.

When Em opened the drawer, Leilani would see everything—the gun, the switchblade, the sickle, the pepper spray.

The only items in the top drawer were ball point pens and felt tipped markers. And Lil's *lei* needle. Em had dropped it into the pencil tray so it wouldn't get lost. She pictured herself whirling around, trying to stab Leilani with it. Death by *lei* needle? Impossible. Em picked up a pen.

"Write exactly what I tell you to," Leilani ordered.

"How did I guess that was coming?" Em poised her hand above the paper.

"Dear Uncle Louie. I'm sorry but I am too shook up to stay. I'm heading back to California." Leilani waved the gun at her. "Write that."

"Too shook up?" Em winced. "I'd never say shook up."

"What would you say?"

"Too stressed after what happened."

"Fine. Whatever." Leilani watched her write. "Now sign your name."

Em tried to think of a way to write in code. Leave out a few letters. Spell her own name wrong. Anything. But it was impossible to think with Leilani hovering over her with a gun in her hand. She read over Em's shoulder.

"Leave it on the floor, near the front door. Then roll up your clothes and bring them with you."

"The bridge is closed, you know. We can't get out of Hanalei." Em slowly put the pen back and then glanced at the front door. Leilani followed her gaze for a half second but it was long enough for Em to slip the *lei* needle out of the drawer. She quickly slid it though the fabric of the silk slacks along her thigh.

With any luck at all, she wouldn't be the one who ended up punctured.

"We aren't going that way." Leilani stepped in front of her and held out a plastic zip tie. "Wrap that around your wrist." She held the gun to Em's head while Em tried to get the plastic ties around her bandages.

"I need two hands," Em said.

"Use your teeth."

Em struggled, finally managed to bind her own hands. Leilani cinched the plastic strip tighter. Em thought about bringing her hands up and knocking Leilani backward, but she was too afraid of the gun barrel pressed against the back of her skull.

"Where are we going?" Em asked.

Leilani said quite pleasantly. "Anywhere I want to go."

39

When it Rains it Pours

After talking to Roland at *Hale Pua*, Kiki was so upset she called an emergency practice at her house in Haena to keep her mind occupied. Unfortunately, because of the rain, Big Estelle, her mother, and Lillian were now stuck on the north side of the bridge and couldn't go home.

"I'm sick of practicing," Flora announced. "No bettah anyway. Time for cocktails."

"I second that," Little Estelle mumbled.

"Is that all you can think about, Flora?" Lillian sniffed. "Really, you should have more self-discipline."

"Hey, it's five o'clock somewhere." Kiki headed for the refrigerator in the corner of her outdoor entertainment area. Kimo's latest project, the hula platform, was pronounced a success. So far, no one had tumbled off the edge.

Little Estelle was parked on her Gad-About while the rest of them sat in white plastic chairs lined up along the covered hula platform, watching it rain. Suzi filled them in on the conversation she and the others had with Roland at *Hale Pua* and their theory about Shark Lady's involvement in Em's abduction.

"Funny she forgot to show him the safe room," Kiki said.

"That woman never forgets anything," Suzi assured them. "Thank heavens Roland went to get the keys to search the place again."

"Hope he finds something that will clear Sophie," Lil said. "When and if he makes it over the bridge." Over the past hour, the rain had slowly let up and now the sun was struggling to show itself. "Hey, look at that. A rainbow." Lillian pointed toward the mountain behind Kiki's.

"Finally," Big Estelle grabbed her purse. "The bridge is bound to open soon. Let's go, Mother."

"I'm not finished with my drink," Little Estelle grumbled.

"Suck it up and get a move on. I want to be the first one up the hill. Thanks, Kiki." Big Estelle found her car keys and headed for the van. "I'm lowering the tail gate, Mother. Come on."

"I'm calling Roland," Kiki announced. "See what's up." She talked to him a few seconds and hung up. "He's stuck on the other side of the bridge at the substation but he says the river's going down fast. He left a message for Leilani but she hasn't called him back so he got a search warrant to enter *Hale Pua* without her."

Little Estelle handed Kiki her wine glass and revved the Gad-About while Big Estelle pulled their big white van closer. Everyone had assembled in the driveway. The rain had stopped but water was still dripping from the eaves of the house and leaves of the plants. The sun was fighting to break through.

"Nice with no cars on the highway, eh?" Suzi looked up and down the empty road. "Like the old days."

Big Estelle lowered the lift and Little Estelle rolled aboard. As the lift was rising back into place, a black Mercedes sped into view.

"Hey," Suzi yelled, pointing at the car. "There goes Leilani."

All heads turned as Shark Lady's car flew by.

"Did you see that?" Lil said. "That looked like Em in the passenger seat. I know I saw someone with blond hair in there."

"Probably a client," Big Estelle called out from the driver's seat.

"What if it was Em?" Kiki asked no one in particular.

"Why would Em be with her?" Suzi wondered. "Unless . . . "

"Only one way to find out." Kiki grabbed the van door handle. "Everybody get in. Hurry!"

They crowded onto the bench seats and grabbed their seat belts. Lillian kept yelling, "Click it or ticket!" Big Estelle managed a three-point turn and took off heading north.

"Step on it!" Little Estelle yelled from the back. "You drive like an old lady!"

"Shut up, Mother."

"I get car sick, you know," Lil warned as Big Estelle careened around a curve and everyone tilted to the left.

"Have a sip. " Flora tried to hand Lil the Gatorade bottle.

"She's already out of sight," Kiki said. "If she turns off anywhere we'll never find them."

They were flying along but the van was no match for the low-slung Mercedes, and it quickly disappeared around a curve. When they started to pass *Hale Pua*, Kiki yelled stop.

"Maybe she ducked in here."

Big Estelle backed up and turned into the drive. Everyone tilted right.

"There's no car here," Lil said.

Kiki opened the van door while they still were moving. "Pull up as close as you can get to the garage. I'll stand on the front bumper and look in the garage window. Maybe she has the opener and already slid inside."

"Just like Batman." Flora smiled and burped.

40

The Getaway Plan

Em was in the passenger seat of the Mercedes with her bound hands in her lap, staring straight ahead. Leilani Cabral was as cool as someone nicknamed Shark Lady should be, and her hands were steady on the wheel. Em wondered how anyone could stay so calm with a handgun clamped between her thighs.

"Isn't that kind of dangerous?" Em asked. "Keeping that gun down there?"

"Actually, it's kind of a turn on."

"You mind telling me why you're doing this?"

"Because everything was going perfectly well until you and your ridiculous friends started snooping around." Leilani checked the rear view mirror and sped up.

Em refused to show an ounce of fear even though she was scared out of her wits. She figured the best thing she could do was keep Leilani talking.

"Why did you kill Harold?" she asked.

Leilani smiled. "What makes you think I killed Harold?"

"Well, the fact that you've abducted me—for the second time— is a pretty big hint."

"Both properties at Lumahai were in escrow when Uncle Harold found some old gravesites while digging up his *pakalolo*. I helped that ingrate make a truckload of money over the last few years but he blew through it gambling and then he had the nerve to try and blackmail me. Thank God Fernando had no idea what my uncle was yammering about. I was so furious at Harold—"

"That you killed him."

"I hadn't planned to. We were arguing in the garage when he slapped me. *Him*. Slapped *me*. He turned around and I blew. I grabbed his machete and hit him with it. Then I waited until everyone next door went inside for the *luau* and used his wheelbarrow to wheel him over and dump him into the *imu*. I wanted it to look like your uncle was involved—after all, their feud over Irene was legendary. So was the beef over the smoke. Everyone knew your crew called him the Smoke Monster. I'd heard all about it from Harold. It was easy enough to toss in the murder weapon and dump in the body. I went back to the house, poured bleach all over the wheelbarrow and hosed it out. I propped it up where I found it before I split."

"But why kill Fernando? He'd already bought the house. He was bound to find out about the burial site soon enough."

"I wanted to delay construction for as long as I could. What better way than to get rid of Fernando? If that grave, or worse yet, multiple graves were found, one thing would lead to another and the *Hale Pua* escrow would be in jeopardy, too. Killing that peacock Fernando was easy. I told him one of his koi looked sick and when he bent over to check it out, I hit him in the back of the head with a rock and shoved him in the stream. Everyone started running around looking for that old woman on the scooter and things worked out better than I planned. I ducked out."

"So why kidnap me during the memorial?"

"Because Harold told me he had taken one of the bones for evidence. You and your crew were always snooping around his place. I saw you the day you were working on the hedge between the bar and Harold's. I figured you must have found it because I had looked everywhere for it but never found it. I was going to grab you that day after I knocked you out and toss you in my trunk, but that gal with the piercings started calling out to you and I was afraid she'd see me. I never did find that damn bone. Do you have it?"

"Actually now the police have it."

"I should have known," Leilani said under her breath.

"So why didn't you kill me?"

"While the police were busy hunting for you, they weren't focusing on Harold or Fernando's murders. I had to keep you alive. With no body, the search would be ongoing. Meanwhile, the *Hale Pua* escrow closed and, at the last minute, I got the idea to make it look like your little tattooed friend kidnapped you and murdered my uncle and Fernando. That took the heat off me entirely. Yesterday I took the wires off two of the spark plugs in your bartender's car and hid nearby. When it didn't start, she left home on foot. Then I took the car and used it to dump you."

"So far your plan is working fine. Sophie's in jail. Why kidnap me now?"

Leilani smiled. "I thought I'd be home free with both murders solved, but Roland is on to something. He called a couple of hours ago and wanted the keys to *Hale Pua*. He'll get in with or without them if he needs to. Once he finds the safe room where I kept you hidden, he'll want to know why I didn't tell him about it. I tried to clean it up, but there might be something left behind. You made a mess of the floor. I can't take a chance. Better to let everyone think I'm dead."

"Killing me will only cast doubt on Sophie's guilt, you know. Roland will ask why you never showed him the safe room and why you didn't take him the keys today. It'll all come out eventually."

"It won't matter because by then I'll be gone. I'm not killing *you*, I'm killing myself. Actually, I *am* killing you, but I'm going to make it look like I committed suicide. I'm switching you for me."

"In case you haven't noticed, I'm not Asian."

"Very funny. But you are wearing my clothes. We're almost the same height. I brought along a can of black spray paint to put on your hair. It won't fool anyone for long, but I'm hoping they won't find much of you anyway. I plan to make sure there is enough blood in the water to draw every shark within a five-hundred-mile radius. The police will find my car and my suicide note. Your friends will think you left the island to go home. By the time they realize what's left of *you* isn't *me*, I'll be long gone."

"Why me? Why do you really need to kill me when you could just leave your car and a note saying you committed suicide?"

"Because finding even one piece of you will keep everyone busy while I get further away."

Em was watching the road, gritting her teeth as they barreled around another curve. "You think you have it all figured out."

"It's a gift." Leilani assured her. "A lot of people owe my husband favors. I've got someone picking me up by boat at Tunnels. After I dump you, all I have to do is get there, and I'll be off island in no time"

"For such a smart woman that sounds like a stupid plan." Em sighed.

"You're tempting me to put on the brakes and pull over. Pistol whipping always looks like so much fun in the movies but unfortunately there's no time to try it. We're almost at the end of the road.

"Um, Leilani?"

"This might be the time to start begging for your life. I'm listening, but it's a waste of breath."

Em glanced into her side view mirror. "Better look behind you. Someone is following us."

Leilani looked in her rear view and saw the white panel van bearing down on them. She took the next curve and then smoothly accelerated. So did Em's heart rate. As she studied the van in the sideview mirror, she knew the Hula Maidens were closing in. All she had to do was keep Leilani talking.

"So, everyone is supposed to think you're dead until they realize the body parts they fished out of the ocean are mine," she said.

"You're not as stupid as you look." Leilani smiled, concentrating on the road, where pond-sized puddles had built up along the edges. Though the rain had stopped, huge water droplets still dripped off the trees and smeared the windshield. "Of course, if you were really smart, you wouldn't be sitting there right now."

"You know, I just might have a little plan of my own up my sleeve." Two could play at this game. Nothing wrong with buying time, Em thought.

"Oh, right," Leilani sniffed.

Em checked the mirror again. Leilani had lost the van around the last curve. Em prayed the Maidens had seen her and that they really were in pursuit and just not out on some joy ride or out picking flowers for hair adornments.

"There are officers watching Louie's house," Em lied.

"Oh, right. Would they be the officers who let me walk you out at gunpoint?"

"Roland knew it was you all along. We set you up."

"We who?"

"Roland and me."

Leilani turned to stare at Em. "You're lying. There is no Roland and you."

Em shrugged. "You hope. How about eyes on the road?"

From the look on her face, Leilani didn't appear to be completely sure of herself anymore.

With her gaze glued to the sideview mirror, Em pretended to stare out the window. The van was no longer in sight. They were nearing Ke'e Beach at the end of the road and because of the rain the lower parking area was deserted.

Suddenly the Estelles' van came roaring into view again and was gaining on the Mercedes. Em saw Big Estelle gripping the wheel, her eyes huge. Kiki was in the passenger seat beside her. Em could just imagine Kiki yelling instructions at Big Estelle. Flora, Lil and Suzi were lined up like bowling pins on the back seat. Em couldn't see her, but figured Little Estelle was tucked in the back perched on the Gad-About.

At the speed they were going someone could get hurt.

Em didn't know how she would live with herself if anything happened to any of them.

Leilani had almost reached the end of the road at Ke'e. There were only a handful of cars parked about fifty yards ahead of them.

Now or never, Em thought. She leaned right toward the door for momentum, then rocked left toward Leilani with all the strength she could muster. Her head butted Leilani's shoulder and connected with enough force that Leilani lost her grip on the wheel.

The Mercedes fishtailed. As Leilani stood on the brake, the wheels hit a patch of water and the car did a complete three-sixty before the hood connected with a tree and crumpled. Both airbags deployed.

Blinded by a white cloud, Em was deafened by the gunshot that followed a few seconds later. She was certain she was about to find herself floating above the car, looking down at her body wedged between the doughy air bag and the plush leather seat. When she realized she was still alive, still trapped behind the air bag, she tried biting it but nothing happened. A whoosh of hot, humid outside air hit her when the driver's side door flew open.

Em screamed for help. She'd worked her fingers down to the lei needle so she slid it out of the silk pants. After a few attempts, she finally punctured her air bag.

Seconds seemed like hours before the passenger door flew open and Kiki appeared.

"She's alive!" Kiki hollered. She grabbed Em's arm and tugged her out of the seat. Em stumbled but landed on her feet. Her ears were still ringing.

"We heard a gunshot!" Lil cried. Tears were coursing down her smooth, flat cheeks. "I thought you were dead."

"Leilani shot her air bag," Kiki called back. "Now she's getting away!"

Flora and Big Estelle were closing in on Em and Kiki. Flora stopped to hitch up her underpants and kept coming. Trish took off running down the road. She raised her camera and fired off a few automatic shots.

"She's got a gun!" Em yelled to Trish. "Let her go!"

"Come back, Trish!" Suzi hollered. "I called 911. Roland's already on the way."

The last they saw of Leilani, she was loping like a mountain goat toward the overgrown jungle area on the *makai* side of the road. She disappeared into a stand of overgrown plum trees draped with huge pothos vines.

Kiki dug a pair of scissors out of her purse and snipped the plastic zip tie off Em's wrists. There was blood seeping through the bandages. "Looks like your cuts have reopened."

Surrounded by the Maidens, Em stared at her bleeding wrists and blinked back tears.

She had to clear her throat before she could talk. "That was some driving, Big Estelle."

Big Estelle beamed.

"Heck, I'd have topped that in my day." Little Estelle revved the Gad-About engine. "I used to race T buckets."

"Oh, Mother. You never in your life—"

They stopped when Roland's unmarked car came screeching to a halt beside Leilani's Mercedes. Two KPD cruisers slid in behind. Sirens blared somewhere down the highway behind them. The officers started cordoning off the end of the road and turning back traffic.

Roland took one glance around the circle of babbling women and walked straight to Em. He reached for her and drew her toward him.

"Are you all right?" He looked mad enough to spit glass as he suddenly let go of her and stared off toward the water. The muscle along his jaw was working overtime.

"I'm fine. Really. I'm just sorry that Leilani got away." She pointed toward the spot where the woman had disappeared.

He took hold of her hands, stared at her bandages and frowned. "I radioed for a helicopter. We'll get her."

"She said some guy who owed her husband a favor is picking her up by boat at Tunnels."

The Maidens had fallen remarkably silent the minute Roland had taken hold of her hands.

"You had enough, Nancy Drew?" he asked.

"Yes." She nodded. "But I have one more favor to ask."

"Shoot."

"Take me to jail."

"Jail?" He frowned and let her go.

"I want to be there when you release Sophie. I need to apologize."

41

Free At Last

When Sophie walked out of the holding area at the Lihue jail, the first person she saw was Em Johnson. There were dark circles under Em's eyes, but she was smiling. Detective Sharpe was hovering at her side like a bodyguard. Em looked as bad as Sophie felt; her hair was a mess, her wrists bandaged, but when she saw Sophie, she rushed across the room.

"I'm so, so sorry," Em said, grabbing her hand.

It was the last thing Sophie expected. She glanced over at Sharpe and then turned to Em again. It was hard to stay cool with her heart pounding. "What made you change your mind?"

"It was Leilani. She abducted me. Twice."

"Shark Lady?" Sophie glanced up at the detective.

Roland confirmed with a nod and said, "I'll leave you two while I start on some paperwork. They'll be booking Leilani soon."

Em told him goodbye and watched him walk away.

"She's the one who kidnapped me the night of the memorial," Em said. "The one who stole your car. I'm so sorry."

Sophie had to give Em credit. She never once dropped her gaze as she apologized.

"I didn't want to believe it," Em went on, "But the morning I ended up in the trunk of your car—I was convinced you were the kidnapper. I recognized the sound of your Honda and you have those acrylic nails, but so does Leilani and . . . well, I just hope you can find it in your heart to forgive me, and I hope that you won't quit. We really need you at the Goddess." Em finally smiled and added, "The Maidens have been beside themselves."

Sophie shrugged. "I've got nowhere else to go. Besides, I'm guessing there's no one else willing to get the Maidens ready for the Slug Festival."

Em squeezed Sophie's hand. "Speaking of the Maidens, they're all out in the parking lot. When they start dancing, act surprised."

"They're going to dance in the parking lot?"

"To celebrate your release."

"Maybe we could slip out the back way?"

"They'd hunt you down."

They started across the lobby. Before Sophie could open the door, Leilani Cabral was escorted inside. Two uniformed officers flanked her like burly bookends. Her clothes were caked with mud from the knees down. Her hair was tangled and matted. Mascara encircled her eyes.

When she recognized Sophie and Em, she stopped dead in her tracks.

"I suppose you're both happy," Leilani snarled. One of the uniforms tried to nudge her along but she refused to budge. "I'll get out of this, you know. My husband is a judge. You have no idea how things work around here."

"I doubt you'll weasel out of two murder charges," Em said.

"Like I said, you're not from around here."

Each of the officers took an elbow and forced Leilani to start walking. Sophie watched as they hauled Shark Lady over to the booking desk.

"What if she's right?" Sophie wondered aloud.

"No way is she getting off," Em said.

"We'll see." Sophie had her hand on the door. "Right now, we still have to face the music."

"Literally," Em said.

Sophie pushed the door open, and a second later the lilting strains of *Blue Hawaii* came blaring out of a boom box across the parking lot.

42

Two Hot Surprises

Em's Jungle Juice was a hit.

David Letterman gave it his shriek of approval, so Louie made it the two-for-one drink at his "Shark Lady's Bon Voyage Bash."

From the minute the news broke that Leilani Cabral was denied bail and charged with double homicide and kidnapping, the Maidens had started planning the Bash. Kimo prepared two special dishes— Shark Poki and Lock Down Lemon Pie—along with the usual menu. Em listed the ingredients she wanted in her green cocktail, and Uncle Louie went to work blending just the right mix before he recorded the recipe in his Booze Bible.

The Hanalei School media class worked cheap so Louie ordered a banner for the occasion. A bulk box of blank DVD discs was all the class asked in return. The banner was so huge folks had to duck beneath it to get into the Goddess.

Tables inside and out were packed with locals and tourists alike. The tourists had no idea who Shark Lady was, where she was going, or why everybody was in such a great mood, but they ordered round after round of Jungle Juice and didn't care.

As Em negotiated between crowded tables, making her way across the room to join Sophie behind the bar, Kiki stepped out of the bathroom outfitted in a skin-tight, silver-lamé gown with a two-foot-deep mermaid flounce from her knees to the floor. She had a faux shark fin sprouting out of the top of her head.

Em knew her mouth was hanging open but for the life of her, she couldn't manage to close it.

"Do you *love* it?" Kiki executed a coquettish twirl.

"I can honestly say I've never seen anything like it," Em admitted.

"Isn't this fabric a trip? The expense of having these custom-made on Oahu was well worth it." Kiki ran her hand down the gown's shiny silver fabric. "Not only is it the perfect costume for tonight, but if we replace the fins with strands of shells, pearls, and some glitter, we'd look just like mermaids. You never know when you'll need a mermaid costume."

"Who knew you'd ever need to dress like a shark?" Em had a hard time keeping a straight face.

"Exactly my point. You just never know." Kiki glanced over at the bathroom door. "The girls are ready whenever you are."

Em checked the clock above the bar. "Do you know where Uncle Louie is?"

"I think he went next door to invite your new neighbor over."

"The guy is barely settled. I haven't even seen him yet."

"You know Louie. Besides, rumor is the guy is kinda famous."

"I heard he was a writer or something like that." Em had picked up bits and pieces of conversation. She was just thankful that the new owner of Harold's place hadn't torn it down to build a monstrosity. For now the man seemed content with the restored cottage.

Kiki looked smug as she adjusted the fin pinned atop her head.

"I heard that he writes for a television crime series," she said. "I figure he'll make a great resource when we get our license."

"What license?" Em scanned the crowd packed into the bar. If the entertainment didn't start soon there'd be another run on the bar.

"For our detective agency. I talked to Louie about it last week. He said he'd run it by you."

"What are you talking about?" Little Estelle came gliding into the main room on the Gad-About. As she passed the back row of tables, she barely missed Buzzy's right foot. She hit the break and hollered over the crowd, "The natives are getting restless back there in the dressing room. Flora has eaten so much *poki* it's putting a strain on her seams."

"Get the girls lined up, Little Estelle. We're about to go on." Kiki turned to Em again. "As I was saying, I suggested Louie apply for a detective agency license. It never hurts to have a backup plan. If this place ever goes belly up then we'll have something to fall back on."

"A detective agency?" Em wondered if she'd walked into an episode of *The Twilight Zone*. "I don't think so."

"We did a pretty good job of hunting down a mass murderer."

"I don't want to be that close to another murderer for as long as

I live."

"Speaking of evil, look at Marlene, sitting over there all smug, holding court." Kiki nodded at a table across the room, where Marlene Lockhart sipped green iced tea and waited for Louie to take a break. "She thinks she's so enlightened after her big trip to Maui to commune with *kumu*."

"You were wrong about her, Kiki. Admit it."

Kiki sniffed. "Time will tell. Mark my words that woman is up to something. Can you believe she actually asked me if she could dance a solo tonight?"

"What's wrong with that?"

"No way. She *defected*, Em. There are some things you just don't ever forgive or forget." Kiki huffed off to gather the troops.

Em made a mental note to have a little sit down with Kiki tomorrow after she cooled off. As long as Louie enjoyed Marlene's company, Kiki was going to have to back off and give the woman some space.

A minute or two later, with Kiki in the lead, the Maidens sashayed out of the bathroom in single file. Danny struck up a tune, and the school of great silver-lamé sharks took the stage.

Em finally got to the bar.

Sophie shook her head and sighed. "No wonder Kiki wouldn't let me see those outfits ahead of time. She said she wanted to surprise me. Now I know why." Her expression was less than enthusiastic about the costumes. "How about those fins?"

"Exactly. Fins."

"This is probably a new low for hula."

"But a new high for tacky."

"Louie says Tiki Bars are never too tacky."

"Right. But wait until you hear this," Em said. "Kiki thinks Louie should open a detective agency."

"Please. Tell me you're kidding."

"I told her no way. This Nancy Drew has retired for good."

"Speaking of detectives, have you heard from Sharpe lately?"

Em shook her head. "Not since the trial."

She couldn't take her eyes off of Roland during Leilani's trial. If he cared at all that his former high school flame was up for double homicide and kidnapping, he never once let it show. Leilani had remained as unemotional as a block of frozen fish sticks. Not so her husband. The now infamous Judge Warren Cabral had come unglued during the proceedings. The last anyone had seen of him, he'd been heavily sedated and was led shuffling and mumbling out of the courtroom.

"I thought Roland would have stopped by to see you before now." Sophie started mopping down the bar with a wet towel. Now that the Maidens were all on stage and the audience had been shocked into silence there was a lull in drink orders.

Em didn't tell Sophie, but she was surprisingly disappointed that Roland hadn't stopped by. She had started to think that maybe he was interested in her as more than just the victim in a kidnapping case, but so far, he hadn't even called.

No big surprise. She had pretty much decided she was totally off the mark when it came to reading men. Maybe Roland wasn't interested, but at least her attraction to him signaled all her systems were still "Go" after Phillip. Someday she just might find somebody to start the engines again.

Sophie leaned closer so that Em could hear her over the music.

"So are you planning to stay here now that things have settled down? Or will you go back to California?"

Em looked around the bar but didn't see Louie. Most days he seemed perfectly normal and capable of taking care of things on his own. Then there were times when he acted as if he was High Commander of the Space Cadets. Which, given the company he kept, was perfectly understandable.

She studied the jubilant crowd. Glasses filled with high-dollar green drinks she'd inspired lined tabletops covered with tropical fabric she'd chosen. The Maidens were dancing—or rather, trying. The regulars were happy. She had made a little headway here, after all. Slowly but surely. On Kauai time.

Business was booming thanks to all the press since the murders, her repeat kidnappings and the trial. CNN did a feature on the Goddess and one morning Em had seen John Walsh of *America's Most Wanted* in the parking lot shooting a piece about all the unsolved murders of Kauai.

It was hard to imagine missing anything.

"I'm not going anywhere anytime soon," she told Sophie.

"Okay, then I can put up with the Hula Maidens and their occasional shark frenzy as long as I have you for back up." Sophie was filling yet another hurricane glass with ice when she looked toward the front door and suddenly paused.

"Sweet. Check that out," Sophie said.

Em followed her gaze and saw a well-built six-footer in madras shorts and a yellow Polo shirt. He had dark blond hair and no nonsense tortoise shell glasses that didn't detract from his good looks. He appeared to be in his late thirties and, at the moment, he was following Uncle Louie across the room toward the bar.

"That must be the new neighbor," Em said.

"I hope he hasn't hung any curtains yet."

As soon as they reached the bar, Louie slapped the newcomer on the back a couple of times and said, "See, I told you she was a dish. Em, this is Nate Clark. Nate, this is my niece, Emily Johnson."

Then Louie introduced Sophie and said, "Nate's all moved into Harold's place so I invited him over to join the fun. Fix him up with a drink on the house, girls, while I go nuzzle up to Marlene."

Though he was in great shape, Nate Clark had the look of a guy who spent a good deal of time indoors. Sophie handed Em a drink that she'd just poured and went to take orders at the far end of the bar. Em had been rendered mute and could only stare.

"You uncle filled me in on what happened to you," Nate said.

Em handed over the Jungle Juice. Nate held it at arm's length and studied the glass before he took a tentative sip and then set the glass on the bar without comment.

"Uncle Louie is good at imparting too much information," she finally said.

"Everyone I've met here so far seems to have a real gift of gab."

"Me, not so much."

"Myself, I like to people watch. Everyone is a potential character."

"If characters are what you're looking for, you're in the right place. I heard that you write." Em hoped he could hear her over the music.

"I'm a staff writer for *CDP Hawaii*."

"*CDP Hawaii?*"

"Yeah. The new series, *Crime Doesn't Pay*. It's filmed on Oahu. It's a spin-off of *CDP Miami*."

The music suddenly grew louder, and Em had to lean across the bar to shout in his ear.

"That's one of David Letterman's favorite shows. He likes the Little Person who plays a cop."

"Letterman likes the show?" Nate smiled, genuinely pleased.

"Casting that guy was my idea."

Em hated to burst his bubble. "Letterman the parrot. Not Letterman of *The Late Show*."

"The parrot?"

"Yes. He's Louie's taste tester. I'm sure you'll meet him sooner or later."

Nate took another sip of his drink but just enough to be polite. He leaned on the bar.

"It really has been nice to meet you, but I was in the middle of working on a scene when Louie came over to get me. I told him I couldn't stay."

"No problem. I know how persuasive Louie can be." There was still a lull in orders so she started mopping up the bar with a dishrag.

"Really," Nate said. "I'll be back when it's quieter. I'm just not into crowds. I'd love to hear all about your experience—the kidnapping and all—if it's not too painful for you."

When he smiled, she couldn't help but smile back.

"Not at all. Stop by anytime. I'll introduce you to the feathered David Letterman." Em found herself staring at his even, white teeth. They would do a newscaster proud.

She watched Nate leave and found herself thinking, *So what if Roland never stops by again?* Somehow the thought didn't cheer her though.

On stage, Danny announced the Maidens would take a two-minute break because Lillian had lost her fin during one of their more complicated turns. Kiki refused to let them continue until it was found.

Uncle Louie came drifting back with a twinkle in his eye. The man liked nothing better than a party. He glanced at his watch and said, "Pour me a gin and tonic, kid."

"No Jungle Juice?" Em laughed.

"I'm not into green. Just thirsty." He took the tumbler she handed him. Thanked her and then smiled. "Would you mind running over to the house for me? I need my hat."

Years ago his precious Irene told him his Panama hat made him look sexy. It had become his trademark, but he usually didn't wear it at night.

"You need your hat? Right now?"

"I feel like singing The Tiki Goddess song wearing my hat, and I'd like you to go get it for me. Please, Em?"

She started to send Sophie, but any excuse to escape the heat and the din was too good to pass up.

"Okay. I'll be right back," she promised.

"*Mahalo*, Em. And don't hurry. If you can't find it, no big deal." He winked before she walked away.

She skirted the bathroom door, where the Maidens were assembled. Lil was drying her eyes, her fin once more anchored to her head. Suzi and Big Estelle were stapling Flora's side seams together. No one noticed when Em slipped through the office and out the back door.

Outside, the music sounded nearly as loud as inside. The thump of the bass and the drum reverberated on the night air and matched the rhythm of the surf. When she reached the house, Em realized the drumming wasn't coming from the Goddess at all, but from the beach in front of Louie's house. She paused at the foot of the lanai steps just before a ball of flame burst to life a few feet away from her. It was instantly followed by another.

The drums beat faster and the twin circles of fire began to rotate in perfect time. It was a moonless night, and the bright orange glow of the flaming fire knives reflected off the bronze-skinned man wielding them.

She glanced around, looking for Roland's drummers, but all she saw was a boom box resting on a wide tree stump. Recorded Tahitian drumbeats matched the tempo of the whirling fire knives.

Now she knew why Uncle Louie winked and told her not to hurry back—she'd been set up. Louie sent her out knowing she'd find Detective Sharpe alone on the beach waiting to dance just for her.

The soft trades caressed her skin as Em walked barefoot across the sand, drawn toward the twirling flames. More than ready to enjoy her own private show, she stared at Detective Roland Sharpe. He was oiled up, wearing nothing but a skimpy *malo* wrapped around his loins.

He might be a man of few words, but right now, Em thought he definitely didn't need to say a thing.

Tropical Libations from

Uncle Louie's Booze Bible

Great Balls of Fire

Dedicated to the memory of Harold Otanami, aka The Smoke Monster, who ended up facedown in the luau pit. Hot and smooth, one sip will forever immortalize this longtime neighbor of The Tiki Goddess Bar and call to mind those tropic nights when Harold sang his favorite Karaoke number, "Feel Like A Woman."

1 oz. Light Rum
½ oz. Dark Rum
¼ oz. Triple Sec
Dash of ginger
2 Drops Tabasco
Shake all together with ice. Strain into a martini glass. Preferably a clean one.

Huli Huli Boolie

Huli means "To turn." This one will keep your head spinning. Uncle Louie really gets the tourists rockin' with this one.

1 oz. Rum
1 oz. Vodka
½ oz. Bourbon
2 oz. Sweet and Sour
3 oz. Passion Fruit or ½ papaya
Blend all with ice. Pour into a tall glass, garnish with a pineapple slice and a cherry.

Tiger Shark Attack

Uncle Louie commemorated his near-miss off of Princeville when a six-foot tiger shark took a hunk out of his surfboard—now on display above the front door of The Tiki Goddess Bar.

¾ C. Spicy Hot V8 Juice
1 oz. Vodka
1 tsp. Worcestershire Sauce
2 dashes Tabasco
¼ tsp. prepared Wasabi
Squeeze of lime
Whisk the ingredients together until the wasabi dissolves. Pour over ice in a highball glass. Garnish with a celery stick and slice of red bell pepper cut in the shape of a shark fin.

About the Author

JILL MARIE LANDIS has written over twenty-five novels which have earned distinguished awards and slots on such national bestseller lists as the USA TODAY Top 50 and the New York *Times* Best Sellers Plus. She is a seven-time finalist for Romance Writers of America's RITA Award in both Single Title and Contemporary Romance as well as a Golden Heart and RITA Award winner. She's written historical and contemporary romance, inspirational historical romance, and she is now penning The Tiki Goddess Mystery Series, which begins with MAI TAI ONE ON. Visit her at http://thetikigoddess.com.

CPSIA information can be obtained
at www.ICGtesting.com
Printed in the USA
FSHW021944250219
55947FS